Death Stalks the Khmer

Patricia Harrington

AmErica House
Baltimore

ISBN: 1-58851-350-5
PUBLISHED BY AMERICA HOUSE BOOK PUBLISHERS
www.publishamerica.com
Baltimore

Printed in the United States of America

Dedicated with thanks and gratitude to Cheryl who started me on this journey. Special thanks also to Jean McCord, Bob Napier and Karla Stover who stayed with me during the learning years; Frank Lambirth for his tutelage; and Margot Rose, Sam Lee and Rong By for their wisdom and expertise.

Author's Foreword

This is a work of fiction. The SEAAA Agency, the town of Seabell and its police department, as well as all the characters in the book are fictitious. Any resemblance to actual persons, living or dead, is purely coincidental. The names, events, dialogue and opinions expressed are the products of the author's imagination and are not to be construed as real. The tragedy of the holocaust in Cambodia from 1975-1979 is a matter of history. During that period an estimated 1.7 million people died under the reign of Pol Pot and his Khmer Rouge. For ease of reading, the words in Khmer are phonetically spelled.

Is This the Way to Bliss?
Chapter 1

I could tell by Detective Jack Patrewski's expression that he considered me a nuisance. Or as my good friend C.J. would say, "A pure pain in the patootie." I almost walked out of the police station.

Patrewski swiveled in his chair, sliding close enough so that I could clearly see the fine network of red veins edging the whites of his eyes. His thin face had prominent cheekbones, probably an imprint from a Polish progenitor. The detective's lips were full, and his face, the color of fresh-turned earth in the spring, reflected his African-American ancestry.

He came to the point fast. "Mrs. O'Hern. Let's get something straight. I didn't ask for you, and I don't need your help."

"And I don't especially want to be here," I replied. "I came because Sovath Sovang from the Southeast Asian Assistance Agency asked me. Hahn Ly, the man who was killed, was a long time employee with the SEAAA agency. She said the police needed an American liaison with the Cambodian community. Maybe I'm not the best choice. But I'm willing to try." I stared at the detective with as much belligerence as I could muster.

The look didn't come easy. Early on, my mother had instilled in me that conformity was a virtue. Then married to John, I had made being pleasant at all times into an art form.

So here I was sitting across from a grumpy cop realizing that old habits don't die; they just come to life when least wanted.

C.J., who is fond of reading Joseph Campbell, says that my adventures since John died have been a way to "find my bliss." Maybe so. But looking around, I didn't think my bliss lay in the clutter of file folders and butterscotch candy wrappers strewn on a homicide detective's desk.

The phone rang and Patrewski brusquely answered it. As he listened, he sorted through the papers on his desk, found an unlit cigar and jammed it in the corner of his mouth. Finally, he muttered, "Okay." He hung up and jerked his head toward the door. "The captain wants to see us." He laid the cigar on the edge of a candy dish and said in a more conciliatory tone, "Will you come?"

When we walked in, Captain Gillworth's smile was as polished as the brass nameplate on his desk. Seated in front of him was a small Asian man who didn't turn around until the captain began introductions. "Mr. Nor Sang, this is Homicide Detective Patrewski, who will lead the investigation. Mrs. O'Hern is another public-spirited citizen who will be helping us."

Sang pushed his chair back slowly, and stood. He salaamed, hands together, thumbs almost touching his chin. Patrewski returned the greeting with a polite nod. Then Sang turned toward me and bowed, hands together again. On his right hand, he had two large moles that looked inflamed.

At five-foot seven, I was slightly taller than the Cambodian and larger in frame. The physical difference shifted dominance from Sang to me. I knew that culturally he would find that hard to accept. Raising my hands in the same respectful gesture of introduction, I said, "*Som joom reap sou.*" I am very honored to meet you. I was careful not to look at him directly.

He replied in Cambodian, but I only understood the "*Or koon,*" or thank you part. My skill at speaking Khmer was limited to a few polite phrases.

The captain smiled again, lots of white teeth flashing, "Good, good. Please take a seat."

Sang sat, his face creasing into an equally toothy smile. His eyes, though, held no warmth. Staring into them was like shining a light into a black pit: nothing reflecting back. Tingling began at the base of my spine and my stomach knotted. The *stirring* as I thought of it, was the first I had felt since John's death. Grandmother Kate had explained that the gift, as she called it, had been passed down from her side of the family and usually warned of nearby danger.

But I was out of practice paying attention to the signal. And as with a riffling breeze that comes and goes, my uneasiness left. I turned my attention back to the captain.

He said, "Mr. Sang, the police department and mayor want the Cambodian community to know that we will solve the Ly family homicides and bring the persons who did this to justice."

Sang inclined his head.

The captain glanced at the open file in front of him. "You have been sent by the Cambodian temple as a representative for your people. We're pleased to have you assist us contacting families and providing interpretation. Although you do understand, if we make any arrests, court-assigned translators will have to be used." He added, "We have legal procedures we must follow."

Sang responded with a gravity to match the lieutenant's. "Yes, I help many of my people who are uneducated and speak little English. They had bad experiences in Cambodia and do not trust government or police."

When he spoke, the visceral nudging began again. Though his statement was true enough on the surface, I sensed that his offer was probably self-serving. From my experience, most Cambodians who had

8

promoted themselves as leaders of Seabell's Khmer community had also corrupted their influence for personal gain.

Which would be understandable--if they were still living in Cambodia.

Phourim Nath, the youth worker at SEAAA, had told me that bribery and payoffs had been the way things were done in his former homeland. Phourim was my unofficial teacher on Cambodian or Khmer culture. He had explained how his family had once paid extra to get help for his sick grandmother at a free government clinic. The bribe had gone to a middleman who knew the clinic's admitting clerk who in turn demanded her own payoff. Spreading his hands apart, Phourim had said, "We pay or grandmother maybe die."

My distrust of Sang grew when he said with self-importance, "I am educated. The poor Cambodians cannot understand American culture. They need me to explain."

Captain Gillworth beamed. "Thank you, Mr. Sang. The Seabell Police Department appreciates your offer." He flashed another brilliant smile at me. He said, "Now, Mrs. O'Hern, I understand you're a consultant working with the agency where one of the victims was employed."

I gave him enough background to establish my credibility. "Yes. I've been doing staff training and program assessments with SEAAA for three years, and before that, I did volunteer work in the Cambodian community." Hoping to loosen up the captain, I smiled and added, "The name is Bridget, or Bridg, if you prefer."

He ignored my attempt to lighten up, and said formally, "I am sure we will have good results with both of you citizens available to Detective Patrewski."

Sang's expression didn't change, not even an eye blink. But, I sensed his reaction to the lieutenant's unintended slight. Sang had lost face. The captain had made the two of us equal in value to the police.

Quickly, I said, "Of course, because Mr. Sang is so respected and trusted, you will come to him first. Maybe after that I can help with small pieces of information."

"Of course," Gillworth echoed. He stood up and said, "Detective Patrewski is the lead investigator on the case, and he will be your contact. While his partner is recovering from surgery, I've assigned Detective Morales to work with him. Unfortunately, she couldn't be here this morning. She's finishing an important assignment for the mayor."

I peeked at Patrewski who didn't look impressed.

Gillworth came around his desk and shook hands with Sang and me. Showing us to the door, he said, "Thank you for your public spirit. The police and community working together can make a difference."

Patrewski led us back to his cubicle where the three of us passed out business cards. Sang started to leave, and then stopped. Glancing at the detective, he spoke as if embarrassed but compelled. "Detective Patrewski, my people have suffered much prejudice in America between the races." Sang paused, and his eyes flicked over the detective's face. "We hope you will catch the gang that killed the Lys."

Patrewski's expression remained as bland as the wall behind him. "Bullets don't care about color. And race doesn't matter when you're dead. We'll find the shooter."

Tilting his head in acknowledgment, Sang bowed. When he turned to leave, I saw a thin smile of satisfaction on his face.

After Sang left, Patrewski clenched his jaw muscles, obviously angry at Sang's parting words. Making a visible effort to relax, Patrewski picked up his cigar from the candy dish. He stuck the cigar in the corner of his mouth and chomped down, probably wishing it was Sang's neck.

To distract him, I asked, "What did he mean by gang?"

"There's some thinking the AZ gang was involved."

"That's a bad Asian gang, isn't it?" I asked.

"Yeah. What do you know about gangs?"

"I've worked with the youth council where Hahn Ly worked. If kids like you, they talk about what's going on in their lives."

Patrewski shifted the cigar to the other side of his mouth. I looked at the No Smoking sign on the wall. He shrugged. "I don't light up. I'm kicking the habit, but it's tough. The patches don't work. The candy's just a crutch."

I smiled sympathetically. "Did it appear like a gang killing to you? The news reported that the Lys were killed in their home."

"It's too soon to know. They were each shot in the head with a nine-millimeter. It's a handgun anybody could steal or buy."

"I don't remember any mention of a gang connection. Why did Sang think there was one?"

"Good question," he said. "I'd like to know the answer."

Patrewski leaned back in his chair and tapped his fingers on the armrests. His desk was a messy contrast to his clothes: a starched shirt in a color slightly paler than the candy wrappers' yellow, and a tie that looked like the Bill Blass one I bought for my son-in-law last Christmas. Patrewski seemed a man of interesting contradictions.

The detective squinted as if he were reviewing some internal document seen only by him. Then reaching into a stack of files, he pulled out a folder and flipped it open. He tossed over a black and white photo. "Ever see a crime scene before?"

I looked down and saw Hahn Ly and his wife lying on their backs on a rug. Their arms and legs were sprawled out from their bodies. The camera had caught them at an angle so that I could see a small hole in the center of each forehead. Dark patches and matter that must have been blood and brain tissue spattered the area around their heads. I glanced up. Patrewski's face gave no clue as to what he expected from me. Perhaps he thought the grisly scene would send me running out the door. I looked one more time at the picture. What a cruel end for them after surviving the Khmer Rouge times.

I handed the photo back. "I don't think I could ever get used to seeing human life needlessly wasted."

Patrewski stared at the folder in his hands. "Neither can I. That's why I'm a cop."

We sat back in our chairs and studied each other for a moment. I asked, "Why did you show me that photo? It's not normal police procedure, is it?"

He stuck the glossy into its folder. "No. But I've got a funny feeling-"

Which made two of us.

Smiling, I said, "Are you speaking from experience or a bad lunch?"

"Trust me. I know the difference. I've been at this too long."

Patrewski worked the cigar to the other side of his mouth and asked, ".What do you think of Sang?"

I thought through my answer before speaking. Phourim had impressed upon me over and over that nothing said in confidence remained a secret in the Khmer community. The Cambodian people had a communication system that predated cyberspace for velocity and speed and was just as invisible. He had cautioned, "Never say anything that can be twisted against you." I wondered if that held true even inside Seabell's police station.

I said, "If you're looking for a leader in the Cambodian community, then you might want to search for more than the first volunteer who shows up--including me. It's rare for one person to be able to speak for all the different Cambodian factions. And there are many. Political and otherwise."

I added, "If you want to get a quick fix on the culture, try reading Khmer fables. There's one similar to the story of Little Red Riding Hood and the big, bad wolf. Only in the fable the wolf's a tiger. The lesson's the same."

Patrewski blinked. Struck incredulous, I gathered.

Talking fairy tales to make an oblique point hadn't been the way to impress him. He probably wanted to throw me out, but couldn't because of his boss's orders. Yet, I thought I could help him. Patrewski might not have a color problem-- but as with Sang, many Cambodians would. With a black cop conducting the investigation, they would be polite but not forthcoming. And having only Sang as a liaison was no guarantee that the truth would come out.

Patrewski eyeballed me for a moment. "Do 'these fables' have one about choosing the lesser of two evils?" he asked.

Before I could answer, he stared over my shoulder and said, "I thought you were a no show."

I turned around in my chair, and Patrewski introduced me to Detective Morales who was standing in the cubicle's entrance.

Consuelo Morales appraised me from deep-set, dark eyes when we shook hands. And I assessed her, too. She was shorter and stockier than I with better curves in the right places, though her tailored jacket and neat slacks streamlined them. She also seemed intense--and young to be a detective, maybe thirty.

She said, "Sorry, about missing the meeting. How did it go?"

"Okay." He gestured toward me. "The captain has assigned Mrs. O'Hern to work with us in the Cambodian community."

She looked at me with renewed interest. "Do you speak Cambodian?" she asked.

"Just a few words."

"Oh. Did you know the Lys then?"

"Hahn Ly, but not his wife. I did some training with him at the agency."

"Do you live in Seabell?"

"No. Actually, near Chehalis."

Morales said, "Hmm." Apparently feeling I had nothing more to offer, she added, "Well ... it's nice to have met you."

She smiled briefly before turning to Patrewski. Patting the briefcase by her side, she said, "I had to pick up some papers for the mayor. As soon as I deliver them, I'll be back."

"Take your time," he said, straightening the files in front of him.

"I won't be more than forty minutes."

"That's okay."

12

Morales swiveled from Patrewski to me then back. "We can hook up as soon as I return," she said.

"Sure," he answered.

Morales waited, as if hoping he would pin down a time. When he didn't, she frowned and started to say something. Instead, she shot me a look.

I took the cue and stood up. Including both detectives with a glance, I said, "I have to be going. You have my card. Call me if I can help."

Leaving the police station, I thought that Patrewski's choices of the lesser evil to work with had broadened. Judging by his cool reception, he had three to pick from: Sang, his new partner, Morales, and me.

Doubts and Questions
Chapter 2

In the parking lot, I hopped in my '65 T-Bird. One time in a moment of indulgence, I had the car painted teal blue because the color matched my eyes. I loved driving it on the open road, feeling a free spirit. However, driving around city blocks dotted with Dairy Queens and Burger Kings didn't qualify as the open road. But then I had promised to see Sovath at the agency and give her a rundown on my interview with the police. That's where I was headed.

Sunshine had come out after a brief rain shower and the air was soft and fresh through my opened window. On the parking strips, cherry trees blossomed above red tulips spit-polished by the rain. I smiled. Even Detective Patrewski's sour attitude at the station couldn't rain on my one-car parade.

The SEAAA agency is in the town of Seabell, located between Seattle and Tacoma. It is one of several small communities on the I-5 corridor that had decided they didn't want King County controlling their destinies. They incorporated as cities and developed their own police and fire departments when they had enough tax base to support them.

Seabell was the most recent to vote in cityhood. Two years ago, the Lys' deaths would have been under King County Police Department's jurisdiction. Now, Seabell's Police Department was investigating the deaths that had occurred in a low-income apartment complex known as Little Phnom Penh.

Many of Seabell's police force were former Seattle and King County cops. I hoped that Patrewski had been with one of them and had worked the area where the Lys lived. He would need long time, trusted contacts.

After I arrived at SEAAA, I sat in Sovath's office while she finished talking to a caseworker. Before closing her door, she took one look into the open work area where the caseworkers had their desks. Then she walked gracefully to her desk and sat down. One of her friends had told me in awe that as a young girl Sovath had danced for King Sihanouk costumed in gold from head to toe for the presentation before the man many Cambodian people revered as a god-king.

Sovath, though, was far removed from that world as she sat across from me. Her desk was one step up from being Salvation Army cast-off. The rest of the furniture was a mismatched assortment including two blue-cushioned chairs that looked like they had spent their early lives in a bank lobby. Even though she was the agency's director, her office decor was pretty typical for a struggling nonprofit social service agency.

Sovath's heart-shaped face and soft rounded cheeks made her look younger than I guessed her to be, which was her late thirties. She had twin girls who were in high school, and they had been born after she arrived in America. The etched lines of sadness around her eyes, however, suggested her painful past.

Most Cambodians don't like to tell what happened to them during the Pol Pot years. They end up reliving their experiences for many sleepless nights afterwards. One time, though, Sovath told me about herself.

Her mother had been Chinese, her father a well-to-do Cambodian merchant in Phnom Phen. The Khmer Rouge had forced Sovath and her family, along with tens of thousands of others, out of the city to work in the labor camps and rice fields. Sovath's fair skin and soft, dancer's hands marked her as a member of the elitist class, and the solders singled her out for punishment. Her story stopped at this point. She never described what happened after that.

Sovath was the only one in her family to survive. Her old life of privilege was scattered like the remains of her mother and sisters in Cambodia's killing fields.

Bitterly, she had said, "Pol Pot called it the Year of Zero, the new beginning. He said the Khmer Rouge were *Angkar*, our brothers. But *Angkar* killed and destroyed. *Angkar* pulled out our traditions by the roots. Monks, teachers, artists, all were killed. Money was burned because it had no place in the new society. Pol Pot reduced us to clay so he could reshape us."

After Sovath told me that, I understood why she kept people distant, at least physically. I had never seen her shake hands nor hug anyone. In three years, I had rarely heard her laugh.

And here she was, dealing with death again.

Sovath carefully crossed her hands, palms down on the desk. "Bridg, what did the police say?"

"Not much. The homicide detective wasn't happy about having me pushed off on him But he didn't want Nor Sang either. The temple elders sent him. What do you know about Sang?"

She didn't answer right away, and I realized she wasn't sure who I was talking about. Phourim had said, "Americans have too many names and labels. It is very impolite to give so much attention to just one person. The family is the important one; always, the family is first." That's why people were simply known as Phourim's cousin, or grandmother or little sister. None of this formal Sovath Sovang meet Nor Sang.

Sovath arched her eyebrows and shook her head. "What does he look like?"

I described Sang, mentioning the moles on his hand. She said. "The *ahjar sar*! Oh, he is powerful. People are very afraid of him."

"*Ahjar sar*? What does that mean?"

"He is like a middle person between the monks and the families. He has the authority to make blessings and celebrate ceremonies in homes before weddings and funerals. These events can take many days. It is said that Sang also has the power to drive bad spirits away."

Sovath didn't look comfortable with the idea.

I asked, "Can he do the opposite?"

"What do you mean?"

"Can he bring bad spirits in or throw a monkey wrench into things?" I stopped and backed up at her puzzled expression. "I mean could he put a curse instead of a blessing on a marriage?"

"Please, do not talk like that," she said. She dropped her voice to a near whisper. "I think so. He may be *Krau Khmer* and can call the spirits to hurt you."

"Well, if the captain who heads up the Homicide Department has anything to say about it, Sang will be involved in the investigation. I think Captain Gillworth feels that politically speaking, he is killing one bird with two stones by using Sang and me."

My confusing metaphor didn't seem to bother Sovath; she was too deep in thought--and plainly worried. Maybe she was sorry that she had called me into the situation.

Sovath needed the support of her people to run the agency's education and training programs. I didn't want to jeopardize that relationship because I liked and respected her too much. She had a difficult balancing act, walking in American ways while honoring Cambodian customs. If I stumbled--committed a cultural blunder--it would reflect on her.

I said, "Sovath, I'll tell the police I can't help, that it was a mistake to ask me."

She reached across. Her curved fingertips touched my wrist and fluttered away. She folded her hands on the desk. "Bridg, I want you to help, if you can. I do not want Mr. Ly's death and his wife's to go unpunished. And I trust you. But you have been with us enough to know that you must be very, very careful."

Sovath's brown eyes looked at me until I averted my gaze, unaccustomed to her being so direct. She had made a plea and wrapped it in a warning.

We sat silently for a moment, then she said, "We are calling a staff meeting. Will you please stay?"

I hesitated.

She urged, "Please. It would be nice to know you are there Perhaps you will learn something helpful by observing."

"All right."

The staff was assembled in the community room that doubled for the elders' meal site. I sat near Sovath and Rick Howard, the agency's program manager, who stood at the front. Everybody seemed to be talking at once, reverting to native languages as anxiety levels rose. Rick had just told the dozen or so of the bilingual workers that the police were coming anytime to interview them about their murdered co-worker. The moment he finished, hands shot up like star bursts in a fireworks display.

Under the clamor, I heard Sovath tell Rick with a cutting edge, "You said it would be a good idea to do it this way. You handle it."

Rick stared over his half-glasses, surprised at her reaction. She ignored him, and he shook his head. Rick wore his usual attire of Levis, white long-sleeved shirt worn unbuttoned at the neck and shiny-backed vest. The first time I met him, I couldn't decide whether he wanted to be a yuppie or was into counter culture. What I discovered was that Rick was smart. He wrote the grants that funded the agency.

At the moment, though, the staff wanted more than smarts from him. They wanted reassurance.

Rick motioned for quiet and gradually the talking stopped. Adjusting his glasses, he said, "Look, everybody. Just answer their questions. Be honest, and then go about your business." He smiled nervously. "Don't be scared."

Babbling broke out again, but it stilled when Phourim asked shrilly, "Do the police think one of us is the bad person who killed?"

"I don't think so," Rick answered. Perhaps hearing his own ambivalence, he said more emphatically, "No. Of course not. The cops need to know about Ly and his wife in order to solve the murders. It's natural they would come to his work place."

Mindy Nguyen, one of the Vietnamese family workers, had begun to cry. She said, "I not talk to police without lawyer. I go home. My husband would be mad if I talk." She looked around fearfully as if expecting to see him.

18

Some of Mindy's co-workers edged closer to her. They stared at Sovath and Rick as if defying the two of them to stop Mindy if she got up and left.

Sovath stepped in front of Rick and began talking in a soft voice. Her staff leaned as one toward her. "We cannot hide. If we do, we will look as if we have a terrible secret. Our clients are watching SEAAA and us. There will be talk, bad talk that can grow and destroy the agency and our jobs because no one will come to us. So we must fight back not with fists or harsh words, but by being like children, open and innocent. And we must think of the Lys' family. How can we help the ones left? This is what our people must see." She paused and added, "In America, the police are not our tiger."

A few of the staff had nodded as Sovath talked. When she finished, the group stirred uneasily. Mindy, however, continued to cry into soggy tissues.

Ban Chhun, who taught Cambodian ESL classes, had been standing to one side of the room, arms folded across his chest and legs spread as if reviewing troops. Phourim had referred to him once in a mixture of fear and respect as the colonel.

Chhun's wispy goatee quivered with his intensity. "Tell the police to go after the gang kid. Ly's kid was bad. He cause trouble all the time."

Chhun's co-workers avoided looking at each other or else stared straight ahead. He had been too bold, confronting Sovath and voicing public disrespect about the dead man's son.

Rick glanced at his watch, then at Sovath whose face was closed tight. He said, "Don't start any rumors--stories that aren't true. If you don't know anything, say just that. Let's get the cops in and out fast. Go back to your desks. This will be over before you know it."

Sovath waited until the last person had straggled out of the room. Crisply, she said, "When the police come, Rick, don't say anything, bring them to me first. And stay with the staff now."

Rick flinched, but replied, "No problem."

Sovath turned to me. "Bridg, you talked to the detective this morning. Please stay. I want you to be here when they come. Will you?"

The old compulsion to please prompted me to say yes without thinking.

Back in her office, I said, "Sovath, why didn't you send Rick to be the liaison with the police? He's been with you longer, and the community knows him."

"That is exactly why I didn't want him to be the contact person. He is employed by the agency. I do not know what he will say, or if our clients will think he talks about them to the police. I am thinking of the agency's liability, its reputation."

I said, "Okay, but I don't think I can do much good. There have to be others who could help, even if you're doubtful about Sang."

"You don't understand," she said. "It cannot be someone from the Southeast Asian community. Any Cambodian working with the police would carry a cloud over him forever. He could never be accepted the same way again by my people. He would be shunned and his family, too. It is too high a price to pay."

"Sang doesn't seem bothered by the possibility."

Despite Sovath's usually controlled responses, which rarely fluctuated with emotion, she shivered. "It is different with him. He is feared. My people whisper that he has the 'evil eye'. Bridget, you are American. You understand the ways of your police--and I think you like us. Please do not be offended, but you are also old enough to be respected as an elder. My people honor age. So I ask you to help us."

I laughed, but more at my own reaction to being 'old enough.'

"You make me sound like an elder," I said. At forty-eight, I still felt on the sunny side of the hill that led to AARP membership. Since my depression after John's death had lifted, I was trying to smell roses. The task was turning out to be harder than I had anticipated.

Sovath smiled. "I know, but you have been like a teacher here to the staff, and they respect you. That is very important in my culture."

I sighed. "Okay. But tell me why you think someone with SEAAA might be involved in these killings. Do you suspect a specific person? You should tell the police."

In a low voice, she said, "I will answer the last, first. No. I will say nothing to police, and yes, it could be someone from SEAAA. But I will never, never say name unless I know for sure." She held her hand against her breast. "Here. Here in my heart, I must know with knowledge, that person is guilty."

Sovath rarely lapsed into idiomatic English. The words *a, an* and *the* do not exist in the Khmer language. That she had fallen back into this phrasing showed her distress. Trembling, she said, "I know what happens when accused falsely."

I had caused her to open an old wound. To give Sovath time to compose herself, I studied a picture of the Angkor Wat on a wall calendar.

20

She straightened in her chair and said more matter-of-factly, "Stories have been whispered that Ly had another woman he was seeing and that he was gambling and losing. He was known to spend all weekend at the gambling parties held in public housing. Much, much money is lost there. Perhaps the woman was on our staff, or Ly owed money to someone here at SEAAA. I do not know for sure, and you must promise not to tell the police I said this. Promise me, Bridget."

A rap on Sovath's office door saved me from having to crisscross my heart and give a two-fingered Girl Scout pledge. While I liked Sovath, caution outweighed commitment at this point. I didn't have enough insight into the situation to make such a promise. The police would need leads and Sovath might have one of them in her possession.

The door opened and Rick walked in, followed by Patrewski and Morales. She must have wrapped up her assignment for the mayor.

I couldn't help but smile at our little crowd that looked like a caucus meeting of the Rainbow Coalition. Captain Gillworth had outdone himself in fulfilling his EEO requirements. The Seabell Police Department had assigned a black and a Hispanic detective to investigate a Cambodian homicide and thrown in a Caucasian liaison. Gillworth had covered all bases, as well as part of his anatomy.

Sovath didn't shake hands with the police officers but touched her hands together in greeting after the introductions. Rick brought in extra chairs. After everyone was settled, Patrewski said politely to Sovath, "We want to make this easy for everybody. Detective Morales and I will split your employee list between us. We'll each need a private area to conduct interviews."

Sovath answered, "After your phone call, I made arrangements to have our client interview rooms ready for you."

Morales sat forward in her chair and asked Sovath, "Were you the one who hired Ly?"

Patrewski scowled when she asked the question. I didn't think he wanted his partner to jumpstart the meeting that way.

Neither did Rick. He sat with his chin jutting, mouth grim and bony knuckles gripping his knees. No soft yuppie cringed behind Rick's baleful glare at Morales. He appeared ready to throw himself across the desk between Sovath and the police.

Patrewski didn't look at Morales, but his body language said, "Back off."

Clearing his throat, he said, "Before we begin, Ms. Sovang, is there anything about cultural customs or taboos we need to know ?"

21

She hesitated. "I appreciate your thoughtfulness in asking. My husband was American, so I'm aware that the Indochinese cultures may seem difficult to understand. Each country has its own traditions and pride ... and at times Vietnam and Cambodia have been at war with each other."

I thought how true. The Vietnamese and Cambodian cultures were like rivers that poured into a sea. To outward appearance, where the fresh and salt waters met, the two seemed one and the same. In reality, they created turbulence below the surface.

Sovath answered tactfully. "Tensions--even here in America-- can exist between the two cultures who make up most of our clients. We have very few Lao here."

Morales said, "We'll respect the differences."

"Thank you," Sovath said, but directed her remark to Patrewski.

While Patrewski had seemed interested in the cultural overview, Morales had tapped her foot as if anxious to get on with the interviews. Apparently picking up on her impatience, Sovath said, "I'm sorry. I'm keeping you from your business." She handed two sets of papers to the detectives. "I've made copies of our staff list with their addresses and phone numbers for you. Do you wish to start with Rick and me?"

Patrewski said, "If you've nothing more you want to add." He waited, giving Sovath time to answer. When she shook her head, he said, "Detective Morales will go with Mr. Howard, and I'd like to meet with you."

Then he turned to me, "Are you finished here?" He said it in a way that was a toss up between a question and a request. Patrewski wanted me gone. My cheeks burned hot. I thought that the detective had pegged me as a tattler, running to Sovath after I left the police station.

Rather than justify my reason for being there, I followed grandmother's advice: "Never complain and never explain."

"Yes," I said, "for today."

I was about to leave the agency when Phourim intercepted me. He carried several file folders in his hand. "Bridget, please, could I speak with you?"

I followed him to his desk, which was one of six with visitor chairs in the open work area. When I sat down, he rolled his chair close to mine, shielding his words from the other workers by resting his cheek on his hand. He whispered, "I do not want to talk about clients. I am scared. Could I call you at home tonight?"

He opened a file, and we both pretended to study it. I noticed the client was 14-years old. Without looking at Phourim, I said, "Of course. You have my home number. But what's the matter?"

"I cannot talk here. Tonight, I will call. By nine o'clock, if okay?"

I assured him it was and left.

Outside, the soft mist had turned to pelting rain. As I hurried to my car, Phourim's worried face stayed with me. How different from what I had come to expect. In the time I'd been helping the agency, I'd seldom seen him without a smile splitting his broad face. Lit with good humor, his face reminded me of a cheerful jack-o-lantern carved by a happy child.

I broke away from thoughts of Phourim to check for my T-Bird. The parking lot fronted on a side street next to the warehouse-turned-offices that housed the SEAAA agency. I glanced across the street and saw a group of teens gathered at the corner, their loud laughter and voices carried easily. The kids slouched in clothes a size too big with sleeves hanging past fingertips and pants legs pooling over shoe tops. They wore the hoods of their sweatshirts pulled low over their faces like shrouds. Digging out car keys, I quickened my pace.

Once inside the T-Bird, I pushed the door lock down and started the motor. The exit from the lot was not more than fifty feet from where the kids loitered. When I pulled out, checking for oncoming traffic, I saw them watching me.

I turned left, accelerated, and looked back in my rear view mirror. Two kids had peeled off from the group and stood in the middle of the street. One in a red sweatshirt, stretched his arms up overhead and flashed hand signals. Panic set my heart pounding. Could they see me looking at them in the rear view mirror? I turned at the next corner though it was out of my way. Only after I'd put enough distance between SEAAA, and me did I double back to get onto the freeway ramp.

Working with the kids in the agency's programs the last few months had been fun. But these teens weren't raucous middle-schoolers. They were older and menacing. A gang.

If their goal was to intimidate me, they had succeeded.

Home and Friends
Chapter 3

My fear diminished in direct proportion to the miles I put between the gang kids and me. To be exact, it was eighty-five miles from SEAAA to Chehalis Exit 185, my turnoff to St. Mary's Corner and home. Whenever I gave friends instructions on how to get to my house, I could hear the surprise in their voices: St. Mary's Corner? Perhaps in the English countryside or an Agatha Christie novel, but not in an obscure part of Washington state.

Actually, the name came by way of French missionaries who founded a small settlement near the Cowlitz River in the 1800's. The Fathers built a mission on a gathering spot used by Indian tribes traveling between Canada and the Oregon Territory. The mission later built St. Mary's Convent and Girls Boarding School.

If the community once had the promise of becoming a thriving city like its neighbor, Olympia, it never came to fruition. Only the rebuilt mission church and the boarding school, now a conference center, remained. The locals still call the area St. Mary's Corner, but time and progress had bypassed it. After living in Seattle, however, the absence of mini-marts and stacked-and-packed apartment complexes suited me just fine.

I stopped at C. J.'s café to pick up the latest news and a bowl of his daily soup special. Since living alone, I'd practically stopped fixing meals that took more than a can opener or six minutes in the microwave.

When I walked in, C. J. was behind the counter. He smiled and nodded at an empty booth.

I had my choice of the café's six booths. Fortunately, C. J. wasn't in the restaurant business for money. When a cargo container fell from a ship, clipping him as he worked below, he spent five months in a hospital before he could walk again. Disability checks from the longshoring accident paid his basic expenses; the café gave him a reason to get up each morning.

I suspected that the café's regular customers came for the same reasons I did: good food and C. J.'s company. Somehow, when I talked to him about a problem, I walked away with new insights. C. J. didn't give solutions. He asked good questions, though. One of his best ones had jogged me out of a pity party I was holding for myself. He had said, "When are you going to turn the page and write a new chapter?"

I dropped my coat at the booth and then went behind the counter to pour my own coffee. "It's been a long day, C. J. Where's Callie?"

"She had to take her grandson to the doctor. I told her I'd handle the dinner crowd."

The "crowd" consisted of three men sitting at the counter eating meatloaf and watching Peter Jennings on a wall-mounted TV. I said, "C. J., you certainly have a way with words."

"It's because these lips have kissed the blarney stone," he countered.

"Blarney, indeed, Carl Patrick Johanson. Go ahead. Make your paying customers get their own soup."

He nodded affably.

I ladled a bowl of minestrone and carried it and the coffee to the booth.

C. J. limped over a few minutes later with his own mug. He sat and gave me a look. "Well?"

C. J. didn't get around much because it hurt to drive or sit for long periods. Fortunately, his small house behind the café made it easier for him to come and go as he pleased. I'd gotten into the habit of telling him about my work and proceeded to describe my visits earlier in the day. I hammed up the description of the rainbow gathering at SEAAA and finished by saying that I thought Patrewski had pulled out the photo of the dead couple expecting me to be so upset that I'd withdraw from helping.

Pointedly, C. J. didn't inquire about my reaction; instead he asked about the pictures in his academic manner. "What was your impression?"

"I think the couple were shot in their living room. I've seen the same carpet pattern when I visited other families in the apartment building. The couple were each shot in the forehead, probably facing their killer."

"Was there anything else?" C. J. asked from a keen interest to analyze, not from morbid curiosity. Still, answering objectively was an effort.

"Their arms were flung out to their sides. They weren't tied up."

"What is the significance of that?"

"They didn't look as if they had struggled. I didn't see bruises or scratch marks on their arms or faces, although the photo was black and white. Perhaps the two knew their assailant. Maybe the couple were too afraid to move."

I shook my head over the image. "Their mouths were closed, their eyes open. I thought they almost seemed serene. Shouldn't their faces have shown more trauma?"

"Did you ask your detective friend?"

"He's not a friend. Wary adversary would better describe him."

"Adversaries you respect can turn into allies. Sometimes friends."

26

"Not Patrewski. I'd say that he doesn't want to share his case with anybody, including his new partner Morales. In fact, I don't think he particularly likes women."

"A misogynist," C. J. said. He took a swallow of coffee and launched into one of his oblique stories that usually left me more confused than enlightened until I was long down the road.

"Did you know your name sake, St. Brigid, was supposedly an abbess in Ireland and also challenged a king to give her a piece of his land? She wanted to build a monastery on it. The king, being clever, said he'd give her as much land as her cloak could cover when she threw it on the ground. According to the legend, she drew the garment off her shoulders, laid it down, and the cloak grew, spreading across the ground as far as the eye could see. Finally, the king shouted, 'Make it stop! Take the land. It's yours.'"

C. J. chuckled at his story.

"What does that tale have to do with me? I don't have any magical powers."

"The dear saint's were mystical, not magical," he corrected. "I was just thinking: Only a fool plays with a determined woman."

I left C. J. sipping coffee, my place taken by a retired mailman ready to swap stories. Five minutes later, I was home.

When I walked in the front door, fifty pounds of Norwegian elkhound met me with tongue hanging in delight and curly tail wagging. After I petted her and apologized for being late, I fed her. As a puppy, Narvik had been named after a city in Norway, courtesy of our son who was studying eighth grade geography at the time.

After changing into sweats, I played back my answering machine to see if Phourim had called. He hadn't. What had him so frightened? He had an innocent joy of life about him that I didn't want to see lost. When we first met, he had been very pleased with himself, explaining how to remember his name. "You *pour in* your coffee, you think of me, *Pour-im.*" His infectious grin had made me laugh.

I hoped he had not changed his mind about calling.

In the living room, I started a fire and sat by it with a cup of Early Grey tea. Narvik slept by my feet, and I could feel myself relaxing. My house was my sanctuary, my security. In all the houses John and I had live in--no matter how upscale they became-- none had this feeling. When I had finally understood why, I turned a page on the past.

The phone rang at eight-thirty. When I answered, it was Phourim, his voice pitched, as always, an octave above middle-C.

"Bridg, I'm Phourim. It okay to talk with you?"

"Yes. I've been waiting for your call."

"Oh, good." He sounded relieved.

I had anticipated that Phourim would find the call difficult to make. Stating exactly what was bothering him would be as counter to his nature as swaggering into a room and shouting, "Look at me."

I tried to lead him gently. "Phourim, you are very troubled, I think. What is it?"

"It is the deaths," he whispered.

My pulse skipped. "You know something about them?"

"I'm afraid the police will find out."

"Be careful. Don't say anything more to me if you were involved in the murders. Get a lawyer," I urged.

"No, no. I not kill them." His indignation elevated his squeaky voice. "Hahn Ly know something bad about me. I'm afraid the police will find out and think I shoot him."

"Phourim, I want to help you. But if you tell me a secret and the police ask if I know anything, then I'd have to tell them."

"But I trust you," he said, sounding wounded.

"I want to keep your trust. That's why I'm telling you this."

The line could have gone dead for all either of us knew, because we didn't speak for a long while. Then Phourim said, "You know I am getting a bride from Cambodia."

"No. I didn't know."

"It costs much money. Money to her father for engagement, money to marry her, and much money to fly her to America."

I decided that the change in subject was Phourim's way of moving into safer waters with his shipload of confession. Now, he was only going to give me a peek into the cargo hold..

After listening to C. J. for three years, I felt somewhat prepared to carry on conversations the Asian way. No linear progression. Catching the point of their stories, whether C. J.'s or Phourim's, was like capturing fireflies. In talking with Phourim, I had no expectation of going in a straight line from point A to point B and the purpose of the discussion.

"That must be a burden to you."

"I work hard to get money."

"The agency does not pay you very much, either."

"I do other things." He paused, and I thought I heard him clear his throat. "You know about bear grass."

Many of the refugees went into the Cascade Mountains and picked the ornamental bear grass used by florists. The workers sold the grasses for cash to middlemen who made their profit by selling to wholesalers here and in the European markets. Few of the cash transactions were reported. Sovath had told me the undercounter activity had pretty much stopped because the law was cracking down and some arrests had been made.

"You know, Phourim, people have gotten into trouble over bear grass picking."

"I know. Hahn Ly knew, too. He make money."

"What do you mean? Bear grass picking?"

"No. He get money from people to not tell."

"He was blackmailing people ... forcing them to give money or he'd report them?" Phourim answered with a wisp of a yes. "I not tell police. If I get in trouble, I cannot get wife."

I sat on more than twin horns of a dilemma. Phourim hadn't actually said he'd made money bear grass picking or that Ly had been blackmailing my friend with the ready smile. I also didn't want Phourim to have his chances hurt bringing a bride from Cambodia.

"Phourim, the Cambodian community always seems to have one hand knowing what the other one is doing. You told me that 'Cambodians have more eyes than a pineapple.' There must be others who know about Ly's extorting money."

"I cannot say."

Or you're afraid to, I thought. I asked, "What is it you want of me?"

"You find way to tell police, but not say where you heard it."

His words brought a small measure of comfort. Phourim must not have been one of Ly's victims, if he wanted the police to know about his co-worker's blackmail activities. The feeling dissipated, however. Phourim had said that he'd done something bad. If it wasn't the illegal bear grass business, then what was it?

Phourim didn't linger on the phone. In fact, he almost bolted off it. Afterwards, I suspected he was still sitting by it, wondering if he had done the right thing.

I realized that Phourim had neatly shifted his burden onto me. Intuitively, he had known that once aware, I couldn't ignore what he had said and would act on it. Phourim's call had been a classic example of passive manipulation done with no malice intended toward me. He had strung a web that caught me because of our relationship and sense of responsibility. Culturally, he was carrying on in a way as natural and proper for him as paying a dowry for a bride. I either had to help or turn my back on him. All my instincts and training dictated that I help.

I stroked Narvik and wondered how Patrewski with his no-nonsense attitude would fare in the Cambodian community and what tolerance level he had for ethical fence straddling. Perhaps if I knew the answer, I'd have my reason for staying or climbing out of the web. The way Patrewski had politely responded to Sovath when she explained about the Southeast Asian cultures had surprised me. His interest seemed genuine.

Tomorrow, I'd call the detective and work my own passive manipulation on him for the answer.

After all, I prided myself on being a quick learner.

Paying Respects
Chapter 4

I stewed all night about phoning Detective Patrewski in the morning. I wanted him to go with me to the Lys' house the next day so that we could pay our respects to the bereaved family. News of the visit would spread quickly within the Cambodian community and Patrewski's simple act of courtesy would open more doors than all the "knock and talks" by a squad of police.

The odds were less than winning the state lottery that Patrewski would call me and ask me to go to the apartment. C. J.'s words about a "determined woman" stiffened my spine about calling the detective first. So after finishing a bowl of cornflakes for breakfast, I sat by the phone. Before dialing Patrewski's number, however, I called Sovath at her office as a precaution to confirm that my thinking was on the right track.

She usually came in to the office early to do paperwork before the staff arrived at nine. She answered on the third ring, and as part of preliminary pleasantries, I asked, "How did the interviews go?"

Sovath replied, "The police did not say. The staff would not talk to me afterwards. But I heard them whispering to each other. I would not be surprised if some called in sick today, maybe even quit."

"That's drastic. Particularly if a person has nothing to hide."

"It is not a matter of reason but of pride. Most feel like Chhun. He might resign because he has lost face. He felt that being questioned by the police made him look guilty. In Cambodia, the police would never have approached him. To have a policewoman interview Chhun, especially was a bad insult."

I asked, "If he left the agency, what would he live on?"

"He has a big family; many work. They put their money together. I think he has important contacts," she said, clearly tiptoeing to avoid saying what she really felt.

"Sovath, what you've told me seems like a contradiction. I understood that during the Pol Pot times, anyone high ranking, particularly an officer in Sihanouk's army, would have been among the first to be killed. How did he survive the Khmer Rouge?"

How was it that Chhun had his original family, I wondered. At least I guessed that was the case if he had grown children of working age. Most of the refugees I'd met had lost at least three or four family members in

31

Cambodia, or were on their second families because their first ones were dead.

Bitterness crept into her voice when she answered. "People who had money or influence got out and flew to Paris before the Khmer Rouge moved into Phnom Penh. Chhun and his family could have been one of those fortunate ones to leave before the bad times."

Not could but did. I concluded that Chhun's family had escaped intact; hers had not. But she had worded her response so cautiously. Was it because it hurt to compare what happened to her family to his? Or was she afraid of offending him--or worse?

I asked, "Would it be such a hardship if he quit SEAAA? Couldn't he be replaced?"

"Perhaps. But if he goes, it would give others the courage to follow." Her soft sigh drifted over the line.

Quick solutions to the developing situation at SEAAA seemed to be in short supply, so I changed the focus of the conversation. Lightly, I said, "Okay, Sovath. Now tell me about Detective Patrewski. When he interviewed you, did you lead him into a maze of dead ends?"

She rewarded my effort with a gentle laugh. Sovath and I had talked many times about the reaction of Southeast Asians when confronted with the straight-on, bulldozer approach of Americans. Nine times out of ten, the Asians left the encounter with serene complacency while the Americans were left in confused frustration.

"He was very kind, but he asked many questions." I sensed a smile in her voice. "He was persistent, like you."

Perhaps "persistent" meant that Sovath had given in and told the detective what she had shared with me earlier. She didn't say, though, and I didn't ask. Instead, I asked her opinion about my idea of calling on the Ly family. Would the gesture help in the investigation? While either he or Morales might attend the funeral, the bereavement ceremony in the home, was another matter.

"It could serve Detective Patrewski well. But if his only reason is to get something and his heart does not feel compassion, it will be known by my people."

Before we hung up, she said, "Mr. Nor Sang will be at the Lys' apartment. I understand he will represent the temple and officiate at the ceremony."

I barely noticed the slight check inside me when she mentioned Sang, I was too busy thinking about Patrewski's motive for going. What was my own? And realistically, just how much compassion did an overworked and cynical homicide detective have?

On the phone, sarcasm slid down Patrewski's voice like the raindrops on my windowpane. "You want me to do what?" he growled, which appeared to be the only way he talked on the telephone.

I repeated my request and added, "Going to the bereavement ceremony at the Lys' place is a way to gain acceptance, get answers. Tell me this. Did you have any luck with your interviews yesterday? Or were you stonewalled?"

He said something that sounded like, "Harrump." Undoubtedly chewing on one of his cigars interfered with Patrewski's ability to enunciate clearly.

"Look, Mrs. O'Hern---"

"Bridget, or Bridg is better," I corrected.

"Okay. I get your point about needing an in with the Cambodian community on this case. But why should you come along? I could use Nor Sang. The captain likes him," he added dryly.

"Two reasons. One, I can explain the Asian mindset from an American perspective, and secondly, I think Sang will already be there. Sovath believes he'll be conducting the ceremony at the apartment."

"You sure you know what to do at one of these things?"

"I've been to these ceremonies in homes before."

"Well ... maybe it'll work."

Hoping some warm, normal emotions pulsed in him that weren't visible, I said, "There's one other thing, Detective Patrewski."

"Ye-ah?" He dragged out the word as if bracing for the answer.

"Please understand, I'm trying to be helpful--about the customs. The usual bereavement custom is to call on the family and bring an envelope of money for the funeral expenses. An *ahjah sar*, probably Nor Sang, will pray and bless the gift and us with holy water. At any rate, food will be passed around, and we'll sit on the floor for maybe an hour while this is going on." I cleared my throat. "If you act impatient or look as if you don't care, Lys' family and relatives will be offended."

"Let me get this straight. You want me to give the victim's family money, spend investigation time but not ask questions, and get cramped legs sitting like a yogi."

Now that the thin ice with Patrewski had broken, plunging us into chilly waters, I paddled hard to make my point and not freeze up.

"I've worked closely with the Cambodian community for three years, and my instincts tell me it's the right thing to do. Quite frankly, the elders hear their kids tell bad stories about black gangs, and you're black. Most of the elders have had terrible experiences in their homeland with the police, and you're a cop even if you don't wear a uniform. They'll be frightened of you. So how are you going to reach these people, except by being human and understanding their loss?"

He chipped his words from a block of icy anger. "Look, don't tell me about suffering. I've seen it and lived it for twenty-seven years as a cop. It cuts all ways."

I held the receiver away from my ear, expecting him to slam down the phone, but instead silence filled the gap between us.

After what seemed an incredibly long time, Patrewski said, "When do you want to go?"

I exhaled the breath I'd been holding.

"This afternoon?"

"You're not some kind of cop wannabe?" Patrewski asked.

"No. But in my work I've found that if too much time passes after an event, truth filters through a muddy screen. It must work the same for you."

We arranged to meet at three that afternoon and drive together to the Lys' apartment. Some of my credibility would rub off on him if we arrived in one car. I just hoped I wouldn't live to regret it.

Before he rang off, Patrewski said, "By the way, call me Jack."

Patrewski was putting on his sports jacket when I walked into the Homicide Division. I looked around for Morales hoping she wasn't going to tag along. My standing in the Cambodian community couldn't stretch to cover her, too. Her brash and brassy ways would win no friends, or quick confessions. For all of Patrewski's gruffness with me, it sounded as if he'd been gentle in interviewing Sovath. That approach would go a long way in the Khmer Community.

"Is your partner gone? I asked.

He nodded. "She's at Seattle PD checking with the gang task force. Ready?"

"Sure. My car or yours? That is, if it's unmarked."

"It is. We'll go in mine," he said.

His tan jacket of worsted wool obviously had been tailored to fit his thin body, and if Patrewski was carrying--gun or cigars--they didn't create bulging outlines.

We rode down the elevator and went outside to the police parking lot. A weak sun shone, trying to warm the early spring day.

Before getting into his green Saturn, Patrewski took off his jacket, draping it on a hanger that he hooked above the rear door. When I entered the passenger side, I sat up tall and leaned back self-consciously, hoping the wrinkles in my linen suit would somehow iron themselves out by the time we arrived at the Lys'. I also promised myself to bring a clothes hanger and hang up my jacket the next time I drove into Seattle.

After our telephone conversation, I didn't know how to approach Patrewski since he was making this visit against his better judgment. Despite that, he needed some preparation, and I said, "I brought two envelopes with cash in them for the bereavement gifts. Do you want yours now?"

"I have mine with me."

While I had mentioned the custom of giving cash gifts over the telephone with Patrewski, still I was surprised that he had brought an envelope. I snuck a look, but didn't read any one-upmanship on his face.

"Great. It will help the family. Usually, older Cambodians don't have life insurance or money saved for burial expenses."

"You think most Americans do?"

"No. I wanted you to know that the refugees have reasons for their ways that don't seem strange once you understand them. The Cambodian community has been the target of a lot of hate talk."

He sighed, the kind that precedes a lecture. "It doesn't matter if this family is Cambodian, white, or blue with polka dots. There's been a homicide, and I want the guy who did it. If you can help me, I'll use you. If you can't, then it's goodbye in whatever language you want." Patrewski's words seared.

"I didn't mean you were prejudiced."

Making an obvious effort to be reasonable, he said, "That's how I heard it. Look ... O'Hern, I'll give you the benefit of the doubt. You mean well. We all have our biases, we can't help it. Anything different is a reason to be on guard. Anthropologists know that. It's a way of preserving the species or keeping the society intact. But if you're smart, you move beyond those prejudices."

"And if you care."

"Why do you?"

I wasn't ready to open up that box stuffed with old, painful conditioning that kept me on an emotional teeter-totter. Like Sovath, I didn't want to take out something I couldn't put back.

Patrewski waited for my answer and after a while, because I'd started the discussion, I gave him a simple explanation.

"You know the story about the Good Samaritan?"

"Yeah," he said, sending me an uneasy look.

"My reason is something like that. I happened to come along when someone needed the help."

Patrewski sounded skeptical. "You mean Sovath Sovang and the agency?"

"And the Cambodian people I've worked with. In fact a lot of people. I probably could even feel the same way about you--over time."

Somewhere deep in Patrewski's skinny frame, a rumbling laugh came out. When it subsided, he asked, "You trying to save the world?"

I shook my head. "Too big. I'm only picking up around my patch."

Wanting to get our conversation on neutral ground, I asked, "Were you an anthropology major?"

"No. My wife, Nicole, is an associate professor of cultural anthropology at the U of W. She can sound off more than you." He chuckled.

Surprised, I said, "Why didn't you ask her to help? She could have explained Southeast Asian customs better than I could."

He shrugged. "Maybe. But you have the personal contacts."

We drove the rest of the way without talking. I looked out the window thinking that it would be a very cold day in a very hot place, before I ever let down my guard again with Detective Patrewski. Or call him Jack.

Five minutes later we drove into the parking lot of the apartment building. They lived in a second floor apartment in a complex of seven buildings. Weather had faded them to a dull brown, and the paint on the window frames was cracked and flaking. Narrow strips of grass and bark-covered paths separated the buildings. At the edge of the asphalt parking lot, some teenage Asian kids played basketball under a hoop with a frayed net. A few of the youths had taken off their shirts, and their skin glistened in the sun's weak rays.

Though they barely glanced at each other, a kind of nonverbal communication seemed to pass between Patrewski and the kids. Each had labeled the other: make that one cop and one pack of potential troublemakers.

We rang the bell, and Dak, the Lys' teenage son, answered the door. Inside we took off our shoes, putting them with the pile of thongs and sneakers by the entrance. I didn't need to introduce Patrewski. He had met the family Monday after the shooting. I told Dak we were there to pay our respects, and the boy, adult responsibilities already maturing his face, nodded. Otherwise, he gave no sign of his feelings about having a policeman there.

Dak didn't look up at me when I talked to him, so I took his hand and then hugged him. After all, he was still a kid: "I'm truly sorry about your loss." I liked Dak. He had a bright imagination and real leadership ability, which he'd demonstrated in the youth forums started by Phourim.

I looked around the living room. Eight people sat on the floor around the edge of a rattan mat laid over wall-to-wall carpeting. The carpet's pattern was the same as the one in the police photo. The living room opened into a small dining area to the right, where I could see bowls of food on a table and fruit baskets wrapped in yellow and red cellophane.

Sang, as the *ahjah sar*, sat at the head of the group near the dining area. In front of him was a low, white cloth-covered table, perhaps a foot high and two feet in length. On it was a hammered aluminum bowl with an ornate stamped design, a pair of tongs with a rounded scoop at the end, and another filigreed platter. With his white shirt open at the throat and sleeves turned back at the cuff, Sang seemed dressed too casually for the occasion. Next to him was a Buddhist nun, easily identified by her shaved head and white robe.

Dak led us around the mat to his grandmother, who sat on the long side, close to a couch that had been shoved against the wall.

She couldn't have weighed more than ninety pounds. Wrinkles curved along the sides of her face like plowed rows in dry earth, and strands of gray hair escaped the bun tied low on her neck. She wore a long sarong and a white blouse that gaped over collar bones as frail as a bird's. Dak introduced us to her in Khmer, gesturing first toward me and then to Patrewski. The two of us bowed. Then Dak showed us where on the floor to sit. I sat with my legs curled to one side, but Patrewski surprised me. He sat cross-legged, apparently comfortable, contemplating his surroundings.

Dak spoke with a dignity befitting his status as the oldest male in the household and showed us how to present the gift envelope. We held it vertically pressed between our palms while bowing. Sang used the tongs like a priest sprinkling holy water, dipping them in the bowl of water and with a flick of his wrist, sprinkling the gifts and us while intoning prayers for our safekeeping and prosperity. When he had finished, a woman next to him carefully put the envelopes into a plastic bag.

Afterwards, Dak's younger sister, Lily, came into the room and served jasmine tea and Nabisco crackers. Conversations swirled around us in Khmer, punctuated by the sharp "ch" sound that I had struggled to learn, but could never manage to pronounce. While the others talked, Patrewski leaned over and quietly asked, "Is the grandmother Hahn's mother or his wife's?"

"I think she's the maternal grandmother."

"What's her name?"

"I don't know. They just call her grandmother."

Except for performing the blessings, Sang had not acknowledged Patrewski or me, which was fine with me. His expression didn't change until he talked to the other men in the room. Then Sang's face grew animated, and I sensed him basking in their deference. I wondered if Sang's indifference toward us was because of his duties as the celebrant or was a more subtle form of rejection.

While we sipped tea, Phourim came in with Chhun and Mindy. Several of the older women moved to the kitchen or busied themselves elsewhere, leaving space for the newcomers. After the trio had made their obligatory bows to the grandmother and the elders, they sat down on the edge of the mat. Dak didn't introduce the newcomers, which made it seem all the more unusual that Dak had gone against custom to introduce Patrewski and me to his grandmother.

After the gift and blessing ritual was repeated for the SEAAA guests, one of the women in the dining room handed Lily a bamboo tray with teacups on it. Dak had mentioned once that his sister was a couple of years younger, which would make her fourteen. She had a slight figure just beginning to bud with curves.

She was growing up but not to the point where she had learned to mask her feelings. Anger twisted her features. The older woman was speaking sharply in Khmer to Lily who hung her head but didn't move. The woman gave the girl a shove, rebuking her again in a loud voice. Slowly, Lily walked toward the three SEAAA members, carrying her tea tray. Mindy sat between Phourim and Ban, her eyes downcast. Lily bowed and served Phourim first, balancing the tray while giving him a cup. She moved next to Mindy, who looked at her and then away. Lily took a step, appeared to stumble, and the cups fell, with the tea spilling on Mindy.

A stream of harsh-sounding words came from the grandmother, who struggled to her feet in anger. Holding the tray like a shield in front of her, Lily stared at the floor. Two women rushed to Mindy, dabbing her clothes with paper towels. Chhun helped her up while the women cleaned up the mess. Mindy murmured in Khmer to him.

The grandmother hobbled to Lily and grabbed her arm, pushing the girl toward a hallway. Thinking that Mindy didn't need my help but Lily might, I slipped to the hallway's entrance where I heard the sharp sound of a slap, a hand hitting flesh. Fearing what was happening, I hurried down the hall even though I was way out of bounds for doing so. I called out with false cheerfulness. "Hi, does anybody need my help?"

I found the two in a bedroom barely big enough for the beds in it. Lily sat on one, crying silently. Her cheek had the marks of a handprint on it. The grandmother stood in front of her but turned when I walked in. She looked at me wildly, terror mixing with confusion on her sagging face. Her hand curled into a trembling fist against her breast.

Dak entered the room, brushing by me to reach his grandmother's side. He put his arm protectively around her shoulders, soothing her with soft words. He said, "Thank you, Bridget. I will take care of everything" Then he led the old woman away without speaking to his sister.

I knelt by Lily, "Will you be all right?"

She shrugged.

I sat down next to her. "Spilling the tea. It wasn't your fault."

The girl covered her face and pulled away from me.

I thought about the scene again. Lily, young, agile, walking on the smooth mat and tripping.

39

I asked her gently, "Do you feel embarrassed about what happened? No response.

"Did you feel it brought shame to your grandmother?"

A small nod.

"Were you sorry the tray things fell on Mindy?"

This time she shook head.

"Don't you like Mindy?"

"No!" she said, with an adolescent's petulance.

"Were you glad she got all wet?"

Her head bobbed up and down, and she leaned against me, making snuffling noises.

We sat together for a moment, close enough for comfort but not enough to crowd her. I looked up, and the woman who had sat next to the nun, appeared in the doorway, staring at me with disapproval. "I am the aunt."

I stood up to let her sit beside Lily. The aunt said, "I will take her home with me now. This house has too much sad in it."

Remembering the look in the grandmother's eyes when I walked into the bedroom, I asked, "Will the girl be safe when she returns?"

"It is not your concern." The woman spoke to Lily in Khmer. The two huddled together, shutting me out.

When I returned to the living room, Patrewski stood talking with Sang and Chhun. Except for the women chattering in the kitchen, all the others had left. Chhun smiled frequently as if he were telling a good story, sure of his listeners' interest. I caught Patrewski's eye to let him know I was ready to leave.

Before we could edge toward the door, however, the doorbell rang and Dak answered it. Three Asian youths stood in the doorway. They might have been the ones playing basketball when we arrived, but I couldn't tell.

Dak blocked the doorway, speaking to them in Khmer, motioning toward us as he talked. Apparently, he didn't want them to come in. The kids ignored him, however, and backing Dak into the living room, came inside.

The leader of the youths, who looked eighteen or nineteen, had a package under his arm and shoved it at Dak. "This is for you. From us," he said, including the two hanging behind him. He added, "Your people being dead and all."

He had spoken in English, and I thought afterward that it had been done for Patrewski's and my benefit.

40

The women, who had come in from the kitchen, froze, when they saw the two young men. The leader seemed to enjoy the attention--and the tension in the room.

Near me, Chhun and Sang shrank back, trying to make themselves smaller, less conspicuous. Evidently, Sang couldn't--or didn't want to--use his special powers to send the gang kids packing. Patrewski casually unbuttoned his jacket and rested his hand near his hip. He watched the leader intently.

Dak's face paled. He didn't look at the package in his hands, but drew himself up. He spoke in Khmer to the older youth.

When Dak had finished, the leader smiled insolently. He turned and said something to his two followers who laughed. The three moved toward the door. Before stepping outside, the older youth paused and pointed at Patrewski and me. "Make sure he opens the box. Dak will need what's inside."

After they left, Patrewski examined the package before letting Dak open it. The box wasn't tied with string or Scotch taped. The top cover had cutout notches on each side and fit loosely over the bottom. Dak gingerly lifted the lid and unwrapped the tissue paper inside. He pulled out a jade green satin athletic jacket. Embroidered across the jacket's back was a red and gold fire-breathing dragon.

Patrewski said, "The AZ's must want you pretty bad, kid. Now what are you going to do?"

"Excuse me," Patrewski said, leaning across to get a cigar out of the glove compartment. Clamping it firmly in the corner of his mouth, he started the engine. After we had driven for several blocks, he said, "Get it off your chest."

When we left the Lys' apartment, I had been frustrated and angry. My frustration increased while Patrewski took his time hanging up his jacket before sliding behind the wheel.

The day had been filled with rituals: Patrewski's habit with the jacket, Sang's ceremonial incantations in the apartment, and finally, the AZ gang leader's gift to Dak symbolizing that he "belonged to them."

What had happened between the gang kids and Dak had been wrong. Worse, Patrewski had done nothing about it.

I said, "Why didn't you stop those kids from threatening Dak?"

"What threat? You hear something I didn't?"

"They intimidated him! You said yourself the jacket sent the message, 'join the gang or else'."

"Yeah, he's in a tough situation."

"Well, you sure didn't help."

"Look, acting like a punk isn't a crime. They didn't break and enter. I could have chased them off, but it wouldn't have helped Dak in the long run."

"Why not, for heaven's sake?"

"Do you have kids?" Patrewski asked. "Any boys?" He said it in a way that made me feel I was on the wrong side of an interrogation table.

"I have a boy and a girl. Danny's twenty-five."

"He's a man now. Right?" Patrewski let the thought linger for a moment. "What was the turning point for him? When did he stop being a boy?"

His question threw me off-stride. Was Patrewski justifying his non-action by deflecting the focus to me? I didn't have to answer, but unbidden, the thought crept in: Do I know the answer? ... Shouldn't I know the answer? When had that important passage happened in Danny's life? I sighed. Patrewski had unerringly triggered one of the conditioned operatives governing my life. Guilt.

After a while, I said, "Maybe it was in high school, when his girl friend broke up with him and his best friend got her pregnant. Danny beat him up because the boy wouldn't marry her. Up to then, I think Danny had this rosy picture that he had his future under control. He lost his innocence then."

Patrewski chewed on his cigar, working it around in his mouth as if it helped him think. He said, "Dak is sixteen, maybe seventeen, old enough to be a soldier in Cambodia or have his own kid. He'll have to make a choice about going into the gang. Whichever way, he will be punching a ticket to manhood. Back in the apartment, the kid did okay. Maybe that's as good as it can get right now."

A sadness curled up in the pit of my stomach for this boy having to make choices he didn't ask for. "It's cruel."

"Life is."

"If he only had more time to grow up safe."

"The worst is, it's not just the kid. If he beats the gang--somehow stays out of it-- there's still his sister. "They could get to him by recruiting her."

"No! I'll talk to Sovath, tomorrow. Maybe she can help. If the kids went to different schools, moved out of that neighborhood, they'd have a chance."

Patrewski shrugged. "It's worth a try."

My mind raced, reviewing all that had happened. I recalled that Detective Morales had gone to talk with Seattle PD's gang specialist while we were at the Lys'.

I asked, "Do you think the gang killed Dak's parents to get to him? Would they want him that much? There have to be a hundred kids they could go after. Why him? None of this is reasonable."

"Not in your world, maybe."

"What does Morales hope to learn?"

Patrewski said, "The Asian gangs are hard to infiltrate, and they're mobile. A carload of teen gangsters will leave Minneapolis, drive straight through to Seattle, hit a home, and be gone in a weekend."

"From Minneapolis and back in a weekend? No. I can't believe that."

Patrewski looked irritated at being interrupted. "Believe it. Gang members drive up from Long Beach, too. Anyhow, the AZ's that want Dak are newer in Seattle. The OLBZ, Original or Oriental Local Boyz, depending on who you're talking to, have first claim on the area. Morales is checking out whether the Lys might have been the victims of a gang feud."

Wrapping my arms around me, I blew a straggling piece of hair off my forehead. "That's an ugly world."

Patrewski didn't acknowledge the comment, but took the cigar out of his mouth, holding it between two fingers of the hand on the steering wheel. "We've looked into the possibility of a home invasion, but according to the grandmother, no money or jewelry was taken. The Asian gangs threaten to kill anyone who talks to the police and rape the women to make their point. The girl and the grandmother could be keeping quiet because they're afraid. The apartment didn't look tossed, though the grandmother and Dak's sister swear they heard nothing."

"Surely the neighbors heard noises?" I said.

"They heard nothing, saw nothing. Like clam shells, they're shut tight."

"But the gun shots ... ."

Patrewski shrugged. "No one's talking. The neighbors are Cambodian. They're scared."

I nodded. The neighbors were afraid of the police and probably afraid that they might be the next victims. No wonder they said nothing.

I asked, "Who did the interpreting for the grandmother?"

"Dak. He made the 9-1-1 call after he discovered the bodies. He talked to the officers who responded to dispatch.

"Are you going to re-question the grandmother, using a different interpreter?"

"The prosecuting attorney's office will send over a state certified interpreter. When this case does go to trial, we don't want her testimony thrown out because the interpreter was biased or lousy."

"I'm glad it won't be Sang."

"Why?" Patrewski glanced at me.

"It's a gut feeling. I guess with the Cambodian community that works better than a rational approach.

To give Patrewski credit, he didn't nail me to the wall with that last remark.

Talking about the grandmother made me think of how angry she was with Lily. I turned toward Patrewski and said, "You know, Lily may have spilled the tea on purpose."

"Where'd that idea come from?" Patrewski exclaimed.

In the back of my mind, I had been thinking of Sovath's comment about Ly having a girl friend, possibly someone from the agency. The link led to Mindy and Lily's evident dislike of her. When Lily spilled the tea, making a scene, she had risked embarrassing herself in public as well as incurring her grandmother's wrath. Either one of those would have been too humiliating for a teenage girl to contemplate doing. But while Lily had cried; she didn't show remorse. I decided to tell Patrewski about the possible Ly and Mindy connection, chalking my theory to feminine instinct. I needn't mention Sovath as a source.

"Lilly doesn't like Mindy. In her room, the girl indicated that she had dumped the tray deliberately. Given the opportunity, she probably would do it again. Maybe Mindy had been involved with Lily's father, and the girl knew about the affair. Mindy could be a suspect."

"Go on," Patrewski said.

"Well, Mindy has a jealous husband or at least she's fearful of him. She said as much at the SEAAA meeting. Talk about bringing shame. She's Vietnamese and Ly was Cambodian. I wouldn't think they'd get together, but then Mindy's a beauty, and she speaks Khmer. I heard her talk to Chain in Cambodian after the tea incident. Maybe Ly was going to tell her husband about the affair and was blackmailing her so he'd stay quiet. So she got rid of him."

"That's a dumb idea--" Undoubtedly aware that his reply didn't add to police-citizen good will, Patrewski backtracked. "What I mean is, she'd have to be pretty stupid to buy that story. If Ly tells the husband, he gets mad as hell and shoots Ly for screwing around with his wife. Your idea makes Mindy's husband the more likely suspect."

"Could be, but I'd be willing to bet that Mindy's husband also would have punished her, if he knew of the affair. Mindy's fear of her husband might have pushed her into killing Ly." I mused, "What if the husband found out, but Mindy didn't know that he knew. Then they would both have motives."

Smiling sheepishly, I said, "Detecting isn't all that easy. Is it?"

Fortunately, Patrewski didn't answer.

When we arrived at the station, Patrewski pulled in beside my T-Bird and parked. He shifted around to face me.

He said, "Most cases are broken because an accomplice talks or the shooter brags. Sometimes the ex-wife or husband tips the cops. I'll work with you because you have an ear into a community that's pretty insulated from most outsiders. But my ground rules are this: you inform and I investigate."

I nodded, mentally crossing my fingers. "Did you find out anything about Ly from your interviews yesterday?"

"One thing," Patrewski said. "Illegal gambling goes on big time in the Asian neighborhoods. I asked if Ly was a gambler. People admitted that he was. Otherwise, I ran into enough stony faces to lay a foundation."

I wondered if Phourim had also stonewalled the detectives, or if they had come close to finding out the young man's secret. When Phourim wasn't smiling, his feelings dissembled, and he wore them for anyone to see. I didn't want to implicate Phourim, after all he had said that he had nothing to do with Ly's murder. Still... niggling doubts about whether I was doing the right thing, keeping quiet, made me decide to leave Patrewski with some thoughts. Whether they merited follow-up was up to him.

I said, "You know, if you're looking for possible connections, I'd check whether any of the SEAAA staff came from Ly's town or village in Cambodia. Find out if any of them belonged to the same associations or temple here. Ask Sang and watch his reaction. See if Ly had been involved in local Cambodian politics. Those would be good starting places." Opening the door, I said, "Thanks for going and for the ride."

I was putting on my seat belt when Patrewski strode over to the T-bird. I rolled down my window and he stuck in his face. "Remember what I told you. Don't snoop. Tell me what you hear. Two people are dead. This isn't an interactive video game where you flip a switch and walk away whenever you want."

Before leaving Seattle, I called my son, Danny, at the Public Defenders Office. He wasn't in so I left a message on his voice mail. I asked him to discreetly nose around to see what he could find out about Patrewski then call me. With 27 years in the cop business, the detective must have built up a reputation. Some background information at the beginning of a project always helped.

The CLOSED sign hung in the window when I reached C.J.'s. But I saw Callie's car and parked along side it. He was probably still in the café, too. The door wasn't locked, so I walked in and found him counting the day's till. "Ah," he said, "The weary traveler reports in."

I patted him on the shoulder and went behind the counter, said "hi" to Callie cleaning the grill, and poured the last of the coffee into a cup. I perched across from him. "Have a good day?"

"About as usual," he said. "Yours was more interesting, I dare say."

I took a sip and told him briefly about Dak and the gang, about Dak's grandmother, and the incident with Lily and Mindy. I said, "Let me ask you a hypothetical question."

He chuckled. "The best kind to ask because the answer will create 'no foul, no harm."

Shaking my head, I said, "You don't talk like someone who unloaded box cars for a living."

"They were cargo containers, dear Bridget, and don't stereotype."

47

I held up my fingers in a peace sign. "I've been thinking about the possible motives for the shootings. Do you think emotions carry equal weight regardless of the culture?"

"What does your detective say?"

"He's not mine, and he'd tell me to stop the dopey questions."

C. J. sat down and propped up his bad leg. The fjord-blue of his eyes deepened, a sure sign he anticipated a lively discussion. He said, "The emotions should be the same. The flash points might be different."

Talking with C. J. not only helped me sort ideas, but he also had more useful information stored in his head than the local library.

I said, "Sang, the temple's liaison with the police, says a gang probably shot the couple. I don't think so. Although, my opinion's really a gut feeling." I added, more for my benefit, "I seem to be having a lot of them."

Seeing C. J.'s face light up, ready to respond, I wagged a finger at him. "Don't interrupt. This is as much brain work as I want to do for the rest of the day." I went on. "Control. I think that's a flash point. Getting control, keeping it, or losing it. Jealousy, greed, envy, or hate, they all spring up because people want control over their lives. Control gives power."

C. J. beamed, and I groaned, knowing he had his opening now.

"What about karma? How does your control theory fit with a people who have a Buddhist tradition?"

"I don't know, except that I believe in the small day-in and day-out acts of life, human nature is the same everywhere. As a certain Seabell cop puts it, 'It doesn't matter if you're white, black or blue with polka dots. Under the skin, we operate alike.'"

That night, a panic attack awoke me, my heart pounding to escape my body, my breath labored, as if I were running out of air to breathe. A feeling of doom settled on me. Narvik came over to the side of the bed close to me. I slid to the floor and wrapped my arms around her solid warmth, laying my head next to hers.

I practiced biofeedback, blowing out my breath slowly and stroking Narvik to calm myself. I concentrated, looking for the cause of the attack. I traced it to the conversation with C. J. The talk about control. I reminded myself that I *was* in control now, making my own choices. John was dead, and I had moved on.

We had been married 23 years, when he announced, "I'm bored and you're boring. I'm getting a divorce." When the papers were final, he married Cindy, then died of a heart attack six months later. Afterwards, it took me three years to realize what I had lost. Me.

I had been so anxious to please John, wanting the perfect marriage that I hadn't recognized how I was changing. His ways were subtle. It was so gradual over the years. In social settings, he frowned with tight-lipped disapproval until I stopped giving opinions, or laughing too much or doing anything that might embarrass him. My friends slowly drifted away. Or I quit talking about them, anticipating John's shrug of disinterest. The silences were the worst. Days of them. Often, he brushed past me with cold indifference, and I didn't know why. What had I done? We would eat, sleep, play with the children, but he wouldn't talk or touch me. Pleading with him to tell me what was wrong, made things worse.

The cruelest part was that he wasn't always like that.

Over time, John's silences and disapproval wore me down like dripping water erodes the earth beneath it.

Letting this happen to me became my secret shame.

But I reminded myself that I knew better now and had moved on. I hugged Narvik, too tightly. She squirmed to get away. "Sorry, old girl." She slurped my cheek, and I gave a shaky laugh. The attack was lifting.

I knew the drill. Sleep was impossible, constructive activity needed. So we went into the kitchen with me flipping on every light along the way. I got out pad and pencil, plus hot cocoa, and fixed Narvik a midnight snack, too. I'd take charge and write a case statement for myself, just as I would do for an organization.

The police investigation will benefit from my helping because ... No. Reword it. Why do I choose to stay involved?

Narvik and I would stay up until the small beasties lurking in the night left us alone.

The next morning I devoted myself to some of the small acts I'd told C. J. about: pulling in the spheres of lives orbiting around me, making sure all was right with them.

After feeding Narvik, I called my daughter, Mary Rose, whose behavior was as predictable as the moon and the tides. I harbored a secret guilt about her--thinking that she had inherited a double dose of conformity genes from me. Although, I certainly don't enjoy dusting lampshades and baking bread like she does. So when Mary Rose hadn't made her weekly phone call, the morbid notion surfaced that she had finally rebelled, leaving Stephen and the babies to join an ashram. I smiled at the picture of Mary Rose giving up Esteé Lauder and Liz Claiborne. But just the same, I dialed her number in Seattle.

Over the phone, she explained that she had not called because Benjy and Sarah had the chicken pox. They were doing all right, but she had her hands full. I listened for any disapproval in her voice. Sometimes Mary Rose distanced herself from me for reasons I couldn't fathom nor do anything about. Of course, I could have chosen to stay out of the Ly investigation, which would have suited Mary Rose. She liked law and order, but not with her mother involved. I offered to relieve her one afternoon, but she declined. Only after much persuasion on my part, did she concede to let me baby-sit one evening so she and Stephen could have dinner out. After she hung up, I sagged by the phone, wiped out from negotiating with her.

Later, seated at my trestle desk in my office that used to be the sun porch, I made my other calls. I had my "go to business meeting suit" on because I planned to leave shortly for an appointment with the Hillaire Family Foundation. Dressing up also helped me to feel professional even though the dog's dish in the kitchen was just a few steps away. After all, consultants in organizational management did not wear garden clogs and old jeans while talking business.

I was reviewing my schedule when the phone rang. It was Patrewski, and he got to his point quickly.

"O'Hern. I'm going to the Cambodian temple at three this afternoon. Can you meet me there?"

Surprised that he wanted me along, I said, "Why?"

"I want a second pair of eyes and ears."

"But what about your partner, or how about Sovath or Rick? " I asked.

"Morales is following-up on the gambling angle, and the other two aren't exactly disinterested bystanders. I have as much chance of getting a straight answer from them as staying dry in a monsoon."

A feather-light shiver ran up my spine. "Who will you talk to at the temple?"

"The head monk, the Venerable One, and Nor Sang will interpret."

"Sang won't like my being there."

"Let me handle that part. We'll say the captain insisted. We'll be creating positive community relations." Patrewski sounded pleased at making his boss the subject of a lie.

I thought for a moment, flattered that he had asked and curious about what the monk would say. I also thought that Patrewski wouldn't take me if I'd be in harm's way. Brushing aside any doubts, I said, "How about after my one-thirty appointment in Seattle? I should be able to meet you by three, although it will be cutting it close," I said. "You are talking about the Seabell temple?"

"Yes," he answered, and double-checked the meeting time and how to get there. Before hanging up, Patrewski said, "By the way, did you actually see the grandmother slap Lily?"

"No. Remember, I thought she had done it because of the marks on Lily's face."

"Do you think it was a one-time occurrence from the strain of the murders?"

"I hope that's what it was. But I don't know."

"Don't mention the incident to Morales, at least not yet, or she'll have child protective services down on the family and the kids farmed out. I've talked to the police liaisons at Dak and Lily's schools--the kids' bus to different ones. The cops at the schools will keep an eye on the two. I'm checking with other contacts to find a high school where the AZs aren't active. I think we can get Dak transferred--if he wants it," Patrewski finished gruffly.

I didn't think the peppery detective wanted thanks for his efforts. Instead, I said, "Good. I hope Dak will."

"The girl, though," Patrewski said.

"What about her?"

"According to the liaison, she's starting to run with some wannabes."

"Gang wannabes? The AZs?"

"I don't know, yet."

"Then she needs to get away from her school, too."

"Yeah, maybe. I'm staying out of that one. With a teenage girl, things can get touchy. Morales will follow up. A woman who's friendly with the family might help, too."

Lily weighed on my mind long after Patrewski had rung off. I wondered not only about how sympathetic Morales would be with her, but also about Lily's safety. For now she would be all right with her aunt. Perhaps she could stay there permanently and have some kind of normal family life. But what about the despair I'd seen in the grandmother's eyes? Could that ever be fixed? Impatient to do something that produced action, I picked up the phone and called Sovath.

She was in and listened to my fear that the AZ gang might recruit Lily to get to Dak. I also mentioned my apprehension about the kids' grandmother. Sovath seemed neither surprised nor concerned.

"I do not know if I can help you, Bridg. Talk to Rick. He has lots of ideas." Thinking of Patrewski's remark, I asked, "Wouldn't that be a problem? A man getting involved in an adolescent girl's problem."

"He will get someone else to handle it. Maybe he will ask a female case worker that he knows from another agency."

Sovath was polite as always, but distracted. I asked, "Is something wrong?"

"Mindy is talking about suing the agency."

"Whatever for?"

"She feels that we have ruined her reputation and caused her emotional damage."

"Ridiculous."

"She said that she was hurt at the apartment by the Lys' daughter."

"I was there, Sovath. Lily spilled the tray. The tea wasn't even very hot."

"Mindy is not threatening that she was physically hurt. She wants to start whispers and rumors. To create an impression of innocence among our people. You should be aware how these things work."

I said, "Mindy's the one you wouldn't name, isn't she? The co-worker who had the affair with Ly."

Sovath didn't reply.

I knew that a lawsuit, even a frivolous one, would cost in time and emotion as well as dollars. Neither Sovath nor SEAAA had those kinds of resources.

I tried to reassure Sovath. "If Mindy sues because her reputation has been damaged, the details of her affair with Ly will come out in court. Then she really would have her reputation ruined in both the Vietnamese and Cambodian communities."

Sovath replied, "You may not think it is logical, but her attack will work. No one will say anything now. Clients will stay away, maybe some on my staff because they do not want to become part of something ugly. Mindy knows that, or her husband does." Sovath added anxiously, "You didn't tell the police what I had said in privacy?"

"I didn't repeat your suspicions. I came up with my own. Mindy wasn't comfortable at the ceremony, which could have meant anything. But Lily clearly disliked Mindy. Dropping the tea things on purpose proved that. Later in the bedroom, I had the sense that Lily was angry-- jealous--of Mindy. At least I read the signs that way. If the girl knew her father had been fooling around, then she probably knew who the woman was."

"But you told the police?" Sovath asked.

"Yes, Sovath. How else are they going to solve these murders if they get nothing but a stare and a shrug when they ask questions? The detectives need leads. I'm willing to bet that Mindy won't be the only one from the agency investigated." Then pushing the limits of our friendship, I added, "Maybe you really don't want the killings solved. Maybe protecting the agency is more important than finding the killers."

When I said that, Sovath began sobbing.

"I'm sorry, Sovath. I had no right to say that." And I didn't. Who was I to be making judgments after all she had been through?

"No ... no," she said so low that I had to strain to hear. "I think only of myself. You are right. I want to believe that the police in America are good and will try to find the people who have done this bad thing, but it is so hard to trust."

"They will try, especially Detective Patrewski," I said, surprised at my conviction.

"Thank you, Bridget."

I could sense Sovath straightening her slender shoulders, assuming a serenity that belied her fears.

I asked, "How is the family going to survive without the father's income?"

She said, "The grandmother is on SSI. While she might have lost it under the welfare changes, she now will get assistance from the state because she is the head of a household with underage kids."

"I hope Dak stays in school and doesn't quit to go to work and bring home money."

"The grandmother may engage Lily to get money."

"What do you mean?"

"Lily is fourteen going on fifteen. Her grandmother could get several thousand dollars in jewelry or money from an older man who wants to marry Lily. She would be promised to him and married by the time she's seventeen."

"But she's what, just a freshman in high school? There are laws against that."

"If she is married in the Cambodian tradition, who will know? No one in our community will talk to the outside about it," Sovath answered.

"Phourim told me that Lily's parents wouldn't let her participate in the agency's afterschool activities because they were co-ed. Now you're saying the grandmother might barter Lily for money?"

Sovath said, "It is the old way, but still done. There can be much pressure on a family to marry off the pretty, young girl while she is pure and her prospects good." Sovath added, "If someone ever tried to force me to marry my beautiful daughters to old men, I would..." With a shaky laugh, she said, "But my girls are too American. They will fall in love and pick their own husbands when they are ready."

The Past Is in Our Present
Chapter 8

I walked out of the Hillaire Family Foundation office with a contract in hand. Heather Hillaire had asked me to do an assessment on four community-based organizations. Her foundation had given them start-up funding three years ago. She wanted an independent report on whether the Foundation's investment was still paying off. The contract would give me enough work to keep the wolves away, which would please Narvik, though Norwegian Elkhounds were supposed to be kissing cousins to wolves.

My meeting had finished early, and I set out for the temple with time to spare. When I didn't find Patrewski's car, I parked on the street across from the temple so I could see him when he arrived. The temple was actually a house situated in a mixed-use block of older homes and small shops that included a bicycle repair hole-in-the-wall and a thrift/junk emporium with a sign in Cambodian and English. Scrolled white wrought iron fencing surrounded the temple's property, and the carved finials on the corner posts looked like large, lush pineapples.

While I waited, I saw a school bus stop at the corner, discharging kids who chattered and jostled each other playfully. A few minutes later, Rick drove up in his silver Saab and pulled into the temple's driveway, and I wondered if Patrewski had changed his mind, invited the program director after all. But then, not more than ten minutes later, the Saab's nose edged into traffic and sped away.

Rick was barely out of sight when Patrewski arrived from the opposite direction. I tapped my horn lightly to catch his attention, started the engine and followed his Saturn. We parked in what had been the large side yard of the house. Actually, the temple's property consisted of two houses, the one I saw from the street and one next to it on the south side. The houses were joined by a new addition at the rear of the property, making the temple's buildings into a wide u-shape. The adjoining side yards had been made into a parking lot in front and a fenced courtyard behind it. Three wings of the temple had windows looking out on the courtyard.

We got out of our cars, and Patrewski walked over. I swept a glance over his blue blazer, white shirt and taupe slacks, and then down at my own navy blue suit and white blouse. "We look like a set of book ends," I said.

He grunted and bared his teeth for what I took as a smile. "You ready?"

"Yes. I'm curious. What are you trying to find out?"

"Hahn Ly was on their elder committee, or whatever they call the group that runs the business side of the temple. Maybe this guy will tell me about Ly and his connections, his pals."

"You think the temple runs the thrift shop down the street?" I asked, jerking my head in the direction of the dumpy store. "I noticed it has a bilingual sign."

"Haven't looked into that, yet. But bills have to get paid, and I don't think a monk writes the mortgage check each month. This place has one, in fact two. Ly probably had clout here. I want to find out if the temple's financial condition leads us anywhere." Patrewski motioned impatiently. "Sang should be waiting inside. Let's go."

I touched his arm. "If we get alone with the monks and Sang's not around, be careful what you say. It's quite possible that the monk or others will understand more English than they may want us to know."

"I figured as much. All I want from you is to keep quiet and read their body language."

"I'm pretty good at that." I put my hand on my hip, and said, "Are you?"

Either he didn't "read" my response, or it didn't perturb him. Patrewski just nodded and started walking.

I had already planned to keep a low profile because it made sense. Explaining that now would sound like whining. I shook my head and followed him.

Near the temple's front steps, we passed two flagpoles. A Cambodian flag with its Angkar War emblem swayed on one, while on the other, the Stars and Stripes rippled in the breeze.

Sang met us inside, and we slipped off our shoes in the entrance that opened onto a long hallway. He wore black pants and a tight fitting gray rayon shirt with green and black markings on it. Apparently, Patrewski had explained that I would be coming because Sang didn't seem surprised. In fact, he showed no emotion.

As we looked around, he waited patiently, appearing to understand that we needed time to adjust, moving from one world to another: from honking cars and the strident beat of boom boxes to the hushed sounds of fountain waters, and wind chimes softly tinkling somewhere out of sight.

From where we stood, we looked into a sanctuary area that once must have been the living and dining rooms, with the dividing wall removed. Opaque rice paper screens in black-lacquered and mother-of-pearl frames covered the windows. The heavy fragrance of burning joss sticks hung in the air. A life-size Buddha statue dominated the room, his face beaming benevolence, his large belly promising ample providence. Prayer mats were laid in front of the gold-gilded figure, and on either side of it were low tables draped with red silk and satin coverings and intricately detailed brass vessels. Votive candles flickered on the tables.

It seemed impossible that the room existed in the middle of a rundown neighborhood. For a moment, my senses were overwhelmed

When we finally turned back to look at Sang, he bowed, and with a sweep of his arm, ushered us down the hallway

The smell of fresh paint became stronger as we walked to the rear of the building. Two barefoot monks in saffron-colored robes walked by us, averting their eyes. We passed a window that looked out the courtyard where water flowed over large flat rocks into a pool sheltered by bamboo and Mediterranean fan palm trees.

Patrewski asked Sang, "How many monks are here?"

"There are five. You are meeting the elder monk."

"How many people belong to this temple?"

"Oh, many come from all over," Sang said.

I spoke up. "By chance, does Rick from the SEAAA agency belong?"

Sang swung toward me and said, "I do not know who you talk about." His eyes bore into mine. Sovath's words echoed in my head, "He has the evil eye."

I broke contact first, fumbling in my purse to find tissues and blow my nose. Sang smirked when I looked up; then he smiled, mocking, as if he knew something I didn't. I drew back, and he continued walking with Patrewski.

The smell of paint and the heavy incense had caused my allergies to flare up and my nose to run. But truthfully, I was glad for the excuse to collect myself. I blew my nose and caught up with the men.

At the end of the passage, we turned a corner and found ourselves in the new wing. On each side of the corridor were three closed doors, and at the end was a metal one with a green fluorescent exit sign over it. We could have been guests in a motel looking for our room number. Sang stopped at the second door to our right. He rapped lightly while saying something in Khmer.

When we walked into the room, my attention flew past the monk seated at a table, to the opposite wall where Chhun leaned against a windowsill. He held a cigarette to his lips, pinched by thumb and forefinger underneath, exhaling smoke through his nostrils. A current of air from the open window stirred the vertical blinds behind him. With a cool smile, he said, "Good Afternoon. I am here to represent the temple committee."

59

Then he gestured us to chairs across from the monk. I glanced at Patrewski, but he gave no sign of surprise. We sat down.

Sang and Chhun placed their chairs at right angles to the table so that they faced both the monk and us. For a moment, I had the unsettling impression that we were the accused and they the judging tribunal. Either that or the two men were guardians of the man who sat placidly in front of us.

The monk could have been any age from forty to seventy. His shaved head and bare shoulder above his saffron-colored robe was as smooth and shiny as the water-washed rocks in the pool. His face was unlined and his expression serene.

Sang introduced the monk as the Venerable Tuch, and Patrewski explained we were honored to speak with him. He added that only a few questions would be asked and stressed that all answers would be helpful. They could play a part in solving the homicides. Listening, I realized Patrewski's strategy was to ask the easy and the obvious things first, like how long Hahn Ly had been a member, what did he do on the temple's committee. The detective was gathering a sense of the monk's pattern, responding to safe, non-threatening questions. The monk's replies were softly spoken, usually brief, but Sang's interpretations often varied in length, leaving me to wonder how much editorial license he was taking.

I had moved my chair back to better watch Sang and Chhun, which positioned Patrewski slightly ahead of me, and I hoped, made him the focus of the other men.

The monk had answered the detective's questions politely, but with his gaze fixed on some spot beyond the detective. Only his physical self dealt with our intrusion. I sensed the monk had lofted the core of himself above the room and the conflict we brought.

Patrewski moved into his hard-edged questions when he asked, "Do you know if Hahn Ly had a gambling habit?"

Sang interpreted, "He say that many Asian people gamble. It is part of the culture. It is a way to relax and be with friends."

"Ask him if Ly was involved in illegal gambling."

Sang listened to the monk and said, "He does not know the personal lives of his people like the ministers of religion in America. He does not hear confessions."

Patrewski didn't appear to be deterred by the non-answer. "Does the temple support its operation with gambling or dice games?"

Chhun had been sitting with his legs crossed, hands overlapped on one knee, following the questions with interest until Patrewski dropped the last one. Then Chhun stiffened in his chair, his face a disapproving mask.

The monk and Sang conducted a rapid exchange before Sang answered.

"The temple obeys all American laws and would not influence anyone to do bad or illegal things. The steps to enlightenment do not include hurting anyone."

Chhun spoke up. "We are only wanting peace."

Patrewski turned to him and asked, "How does the temple pay its mortgage and provide food for its monks?"

A current of anger raced from Chhun to the detective.

"You do not understand our customs. We support the temple with our contributions. Many of our people have successful businesses, and they give because they are grateful." He shot the detective a contemptuous look.

Patrewski ignored Chhun's outburst and said to Sang, "Please tell the Venerable Tuch that I humbly respect what he has said, and that I believe he has great insight into the character of a person. Was Hahn Ly a good or bad man?"

The monk listened to Sang and redirected his line of sight from over Patrewski's shoulder to contemplate the detective's face. When he answered, his words fell like padded footfalls.

Sang interpreted the monk's response. "He say, every man has opportunities and temptations in life. Hahn Ly was very important man in my country. He had power in Cambodia. If he had power, he could have done very good or very bad thing. When Hahn Ly come to America, he had small power. He would want it to grow, so he would try to make some here."

Patrewski nodded. "Please tell Tuch that the nature of power forces people to its will. Therefore, I am led to believe that he is saying Hahn Ly, who wanted power, had bad character."

Chhun jumped up and shouted, "You don't know what you are talking about. Hahn Ly tried to help my people. He wanted good government in Cambodia. He organize many people. Give much money to help our cause."

The monk spoke sharply to Chhun in Khmer, who settled back into his chair. The three men talked while Patrewski and I waited.

Finally Sang spoke, but his voice held a dreamy quality and his eyes seemed unfocused. The monk's last words seemed to have acted like an

61

opiate on him. "Tuch say you have good idea about power. But it have no life. Only the holder of power give it life. A man is like a tree. If he is bent and you want to know why, then look at the earth he came from and the wind that blew against him. But don't forget a twisted tree can have fruit."

"Please tell him thank you," Patrewski said formally.

I thought the interview was about over and had picked up my purse when Patrewski turned back to Chhun.

"Tell me more about the 'cause' that Ly was involved in."

Chhun crossed and uncrossed his legs. "He raise money to help government at home."

"Did you support the same cause?"

"I am not political. We help the poor people of my country. We raise money to send to them."

"So how did you and Ly get the money to send home?"

"People have us send money to their families in Cambodia and ask us to find relatives that they lost in the Pol Pot times." Chhun's goatee quivered with his earnestness. "We never charge them."

Sure, I thought, but if Patrewski was skeptical, too, he didn't display it. Instead, he said in mild surprise, "Yesterday you told me you were not good friends with Ly although you worked with him. Today, I find out that you and he were on the same temple committee and members in the same political organization. Sounds to me as if you two were close."

Chhun waved his hand to erase Patrewski's assumption. "No, no, you do not understand. I help people, and I help Ly. But he was not special to me," he said, shaking his head over the notion.

Patrewski might have asked more, but Tuch spoke up and Sang jumped to his feet, saying, "The interview is over. It is time for prayers." The monk rose, touched his hands to his chin and moved toward the door. We shoved back our chairs and quickly bowed. Chhun was already at the door, holding it open for the monk. Before they left, Patrewski asked Chhun, "By the way, who do you think is the better leader in Cambodia?"

Chhun drew himself to his full five-and-a-half feet. "I am a royalist. Sihanook was father to my country, and only a Sihanook should rule," he said, turning to follow the monk out of the room.

Sang led us back toward the entrance in silence. When we turned the corner into the front hallway, we heard the falsetto whispers of kids trying to be quiet and someone shushing them down. We saw Phourim trying to quiet a group of teens from SEAAA.

His chin dropped at the sight of us, and he glanced around as if looking for a quick way to exit. As we approached, he appeared to resign himself to the inevitable.

"Hi! I'm surprised to see you here," I said.

"The kids need to know about their culture. The monks teach them," he said nervously.

"You remember Detective Patrewski, don't you?"

The two shook hands. Phourim looked everywhere but at Patrewski. Poor guy. He might just as well have worn a tee shirt that read, "I'm crooked. Arrest me!"

"I saw Rick earlier. Is he with you?" I asked.

Visibly relieved that I hadn't asked him something like was he doing any illegal bear grass picking these days, Phourim answered, "No, I have not seen him today."

"Well, perhaps he had business here."

"Maybe he came to talk about the Cambodian New Year on Saturday. We help the temple. You will come?"

"Is the celebration taking place here?"

Phourim shook his head. "It is at the neighborhood center by SEAAA. We will have much food and music. Please, come be with my people at a happy time."

I smiled to reassure him. "I had already planned to drop by. Sovath invited me but forgot to mention where the celebration would be held."

Phourim and I looked at Patrewski. Did he want to come? I thought he'd say, "No way." Spending Saturday at a community festival didn't seem his style. I was wrong, though. He said, "I'll be there. I expect I'll learn something."

For Every Action a Reaction
Chapter 9

Patrewski and I talked over coffee at a Starbucks close to the police station. We probably had the only two seats available in the popular chain of coffee bars. For Pacific Northwesterners, lattes and espressos are daily addictions.

The eager young thing behind the counter had sighed with deep regret when I asked for a plain American decaf "and throw in a few ice cubes to dilute it." She perked up when Patrewski ordered a triple shot mocha special with enough caffeine to push his adrenaline into the red zone.

Over the rim of his cup, he said, "Okay, give me your reaction."

"First, the monk. I think he knows more than he's saying. Your chances are probably nil that he'll tell you, even if you could get an accurate interpretation."

"Slim to none. I agree."

"But I also think that there are moneymaking deals going on at the temple, and he either knows or suspects it. It sounded as if he reprimanded Chhun, maybe to stop him from letting out information that might get Chhun or the temple in trouble."

Patrewski nodded. "King County had jurisdiction before Seabell incorporated. I'll tell Morales to see if KCPD has a file on the temple."

I noted Patrewski's used "tell" instead of "ask" Morales. It seemed a distinction that Morales would prefer. He seemed unaware that she might feel more gofer than full-fledged partner. Though, judging by her actions at SEAAA yesterday, she would challenge her status despite Patrewski's seniority.

"Mind if I ask how long you've been in the cop business?"

"Mind if I ask what's it to you?" he said, keeping his tone neutral.

I wagged my head sideways, a kind of apology. "I was just thinking about you having a new partner on this case--and how many partners you've probably had over the years."

"You don't remember?" he said.

Flustered at my mistake, I said, "Sorry, you did say. Twenty-seven years, right?"

He nodded, a faint smile rolled across his face. "Let me take care of my business. Okay?"

Clearing my throat, I nodded back.

We sipped, watching the people who sat on the high stools at the window bar. At least, Patrewski hadn't told me to get lost.

I spoke up first to get back on track. "About Ly. The monk did point you in a direction."

"You mean, the earth and wind stuff?"

"Don't forget the fruit, too. Basically, he was saying check out Ly in Cambodia. But how? Through Immigration Services?"

"There's a tri-county Asian crime task force. I've got a call into them already."

Patrewski pulled out a small wire ring notebook and began writing with a rosewood fountain pen.

Glancing up, he said, "What about Chhun?"

"I think he and Ly were running something shady. Chhun probably was corrupt in Cambodia, and I don't think he's changed his ways here. At least that's my sense."

"So what did they have going?"

"Maybe brokering for money or extorting the vulnerable and scared in their community. Bribes are a way of life in a lot of countries like Cambodia--"

"Yeah. And America," Patrewski interrupted, grimacing at either the thought or his latte.

In a way it was comforting to hear and see Patrewski back in cynical form after my gaffe about his partner. At the temple he had downplayed his usual jaundiced outlook. I was more used to his crankiness.

I went on. "What I mean is that in the past some of the refugees paid money to middlemen to get on SSI or welfare, or to get green cards to work. In reality, the help was available for free. But the newcomers didn't know that or were coerced into paying. They'd never tell the police, though. I don't think there's a Khmer translation for "Go tell Officer Friendly your problem."

Patrewski grunted at my humor, and said, "Welfare reform has dried up that market."

"You're right, but old habits recycle into new situations. Chhun obviously was a supporter of King Sihanook and now of his son, Prince Ranariddh who's maneuvering for his power base in the country. That could be Chhun's political cause. Probably it was Ly's, too. The two could have used the temple as a base to force the faithful--and the fearful--to give. The men would probably skim off the top. It would be an easy way to avoid records and taxes, or the regulations of some governmental agency."

"Okay, suppose that's true. What's the connection to the homicides?"

I shrugged. "It could have been a falling out. Chhun wanting all, not half. Perhaps Ly was going to blow a whistle to one of the agencies. I know that Chhun acts like a man who's had authority, and he gives orders like a military officer. Sovath says that in the old days he was powerful in Phnom Penh. His SEAAA job can't get him that kind of lifestyle. So we need to know if he is doing something illegal to get his power back."

"Speculation doesn't make a case."

"Well, you asked my opinion. Investigating is your job, remember?"

"Don't get testy."

This time, I grunted.

Patrewski let the last exchange settle before asking, "Why were you so interested in what Rick Howard was doing at the temple?"

"I can't figure him out, and I was curious. I saw Rick drive up to the temple, stay ten minutes at the most and leave. Then there was Sang. He told me that he didn't know who I was talking about when I asked if Rick was a member." I looked up from my coffee to make sure Patrewski was paying attention. "Sang's a very frightening man."

"What do you mean?"

The fact was that when Sang had turned and stared at me in the temple hallway, I had felt a moment of utter helplessness. Sang had seen my fear and savored it. His mocking smile had suggested that there would be another time for us.

The explanation was too dramatic to express out loud. I shrugged Patrewski's question off, and said, "Tell me about Rick. Was he cooperative in the interview yesterday?"

"Morales said that he doesn't like cops. So what's new? And she thinks he's sweet on the director."

"I don't think Sovath returns the feeling. In fact, she seemed pretty cold to him at the staff meeting I attended."

"Do you think the two had anything to do with the Lys' killing?" Patrewski asked.

I shook my head. "It's hard to see how, unless Ly was going after Sovath and Rick was jealous. But I knew Ly, and I can't imagine Sovath attracted to him. Mindy, yes; Sovath, no."

"Woman's opinion? Or do you know?"

I shot him a withering look. "Besides feminine instinct, I have empirical evidence. First, Sovath was Ly's boss. In his culture, being her lover, too, wouldn't work. His Asian male ego wouldn't have allowed the combination. Secondly, they were from different social classes, and that's another no-no. Finally, she wouldn't become involved because he was married. Sovath once told me that her husband had cheated on her, and she couldn't understand how any woman could knowingly go out with a married man."

"You think her saying so makes it a fact."

"Yes. I do," I said firmly.

"What if Ly was making a move on Sovath that could hurt her or cost her job? What would Rick have done?"

"Now you're speculating, Patrewski. In that case, I could see Rick protecting her. I suppose that might stretch to killing Ly, but not his wife."

"He would have, if he had no choice. It looks like the wife got it because she witnessed Ly's shooting."

"Don't any of the agency people have alibis?"

"The ME places death between ten p.m. and two a.m. last Sunday. Everybody swears to being tucked into bed or in the bosom of their family during those four hours."

I'd given up on the coffee and pushed the cup to one side. "Why didn't Ly's wife show fright or terror in the photo you showed me? She must have known she was about to die."

"Maybe she had no fear because she knew the killer. Besides the victims' faces won't necessarily show anything. More important is that neither one of the couple had defensive marks on their hands or arms."

"Could it have been a murder-suicide?" I asked.

"'Not unless one of them disposed of the gun after he or she died," Patrewski said dryly.

I went over the interviews again in my mind. Had I missed anything about the monk or Chhun and Sang that I should tell Patrewski? The image of Phourim's round, perspiring face popped up, but I decided not to bring up his name. Let his past stay buried.

I held up the palms of my hands. "Can't think of anything else to tell. I'm afraid the temple visit didn't produce much."

Patrewski sounded philosophical. "We threw a stone in the pond, and we'll get ripples. If we're really lucky, something or somebody may even jump out."

Symptoms and Symbols
Chapter 10

After we left Starbucks, Patrewski walked me to my car. He held the door open while I slid in. "You going to the funeral tomorrow?" he asked.

"I'm not sure. I have a couple of appointments I shouldn't miss. Are you?"

"Yeah."

"Why? Do you think the murderer or murderers will show up? How will you know them if they do?"

"I'll read their body language ..." he paused. "I'm good at that."

I did a double take. He had noticed my reaction in the temple's parking lot. "Well, don't forget the second part, about keeping your mouth shut at the same time," I said, more tartly than intended.

He grinned briefly. "What's good for the goose is good for the gander, right?"

I smiled back. Patrewski had a sense of humor.

As I put my key in the ignition, and he added, "Besides, I'll be a cop presence, which may dampen the proceedings but could help Dak. Those gang kids might force a showdown with him at the funeral. If they do, it would intimidate the hell out of everyone there."

I shook my head at the thought of Dak, dealing with the gang's threat and his grandmother and Lily. Before I could reply, Patrewski patted the car's roof twice, said, "Thanks for coming," and walked off.

I drove away slowly because it was five-thirty, and traveling I-5 would be like inching out of the parking lot after a Seattle Mariner's game. I toyed with the idea of grabbing a bite to eat while traffic thinned out.

I also thought about Patrewski's interest in Dak, an interest that verged on the personal. My instincts told me Patrewski was good at his job. His effectiveness undoubtedly hinged on his objectivity. In the long run, getting emotionally involved with the victim's family would blow his detachment. If my assumption was correct, then why had he gone out of his way to see about Dak getting transferred to another school, and why did he want to protect the boy especially at the funeral?

I knew nothing about Patrewski personally beyond the fact that his wife was a professor at the UW. Idly, I wondered if they had a son and tried imagining the natty cop in Levi's and baseball cap playing catch with a younger version of him. The picture wouldn't focus. I gave Patrewski the benefit of the doubt. Maybe his interest in Dak was part of his own unique way of conducting an investigation.

Heading for a restaurant near the freeway, another thought nagged until I voiced it: I should check out SEAAA. I glanced at my watch. The agency's regular business hours were over, but I knew that Phourim and some of the kids could still be there. They would probably hang out for a while after returning from the temple. Besides SEAAA was only a few minutes from the freeway entrance. Perhaps Rick would be there, too.

I took a right at the next intersection and drove to SEAAA, though I didn't have the foggiest notion what I was going to say or do when I arrived.

There were only three cars in the parking lot, and one of them was Rick's gray Saab. I parked next to it.

The front door was unlocked, but no one was in the staff's open work area. From the rear of the building, where a rec room with ping pong tables had been set up for the kids, I could hear the clicking sounds of bouncing balls and kids laughing.

Sovath's and Rick's offices were straight ahead, and Rick's door was ajar, the light on. I knocked twice and stepped inside his office.

Rick looked up from his computer keyboard, which was on a table placed at a right angle to his desk. He swiveled in his chair to face me. "What are you doing here?" He asked, more sullen than curious.

As usual, he wore a white shirt with the sleeves rolled up, with an olive-green vest over it. His forearms were thin, and he had the spare build of a long distance runner, angular. He needed fattening, but I suspected that Big Macs never crossed his lips. Right now, he stared, very guarded, at me.

Up to that moment, I hadn't known what reason I would give for dropping in after office hours. Thankfully, some part of me had already worked out a response.

Ignoring his sullen greeting, I said in a chirpy voice, "Sovath said you probably could help me. I tried to reach you this morning about Dak's sister, Lily, but you were out. I was in Seabell on business, when I drove by and saw your car..." I grinned and shrugged. "Well, here I am."

Rick turned back to his computer, tapped a few keys and clicked the mouse until the screen saver came on.

"Are you working on something for the Cambodian New Year?" I asked, sitting on one of the visitor chairs.

"No," he said.

"Oh, I thought maybe you were getting final details ready. I heard you were working with the temple on Saturday's festivities."

"I don't know where you got that idea. The New Year's Celebration is the staff's project with the monks and the community. This is the second one in two months, and it's tying up too much of our staff's time."

I smiled. "I have friends who are surprised that the Cambodians celebrate their New Year in April instead of February like the Vietnamese."

"Yeah, well that's the way things work. Besides, I've got three quarterly grant reports due by the fifteenth and a mare's nest of problems," he said, as if reminding me that he was too busy to visit.

"I haven't heard that expression in years. You must be referring to the murder investigation."

"That and other things."

"Is there anything I can do to help?"

Rick leaned back in his chair with his hands clasped behind his head. He had dark shadows under his eyes, and his skin was pale under the fluorescent lighting.

"You could talk to Sovath," he said.

"About what?"

"Get her to turn over some of the administrative details to me."

"Such as?"

"The personnel issues, for one thing. She's too soft and too vulnerable."

I said, "Are you talking about Mindy and Chhun? Sovath mentioned Mindy might sue the agency and that Chhun's threatening to quit--although that may be a blessing to the agency in the long run. He strikes me as more liability than asset."

"Mindy's a troublemaker, and her husband's driving her. She has a backbone of mush around him. The guy probably thinks the agency has deep pockets and will pony up bucks to avoid ugly publicity..." Rick straightened in his chair and slammed the desktop so forcefully with his hands that I jumped. "Don't blab any of this to the cops. Remember you're under contract to the agency."

I almost snapped back, but didn't because he might stop talking. Instead, I said calmly, "You need to remember that the only reason I'm involved with the police is because Sovath asked me as a special favor."

The fact that I had a training contract with SEAAA didn't mean that what I knew about the agency was privileged information to be kept from the police. On the other hand, I had an ethical gyro that kept me centered, give or take a few degrees, and I didn't need Rick's warning. In my mind, I had reserved the right to sift through the circulating speculations and suspicions. If I found something of substance, I'd turn it over to Patrewski.

71

I said, "If the Nguyens file a suit, it becomes public record, anyhow. Unless the suit has a bearing on the homicides, the police won't care. Or are you telling me that Mindy is involved in the Lys' deaths?"

"It's a possibility."

"I sense you think that it's more than a possibility."

Rick rolled a pencil back and forth on his desktop.

I said, "Mindy and Ly could have had a thing going between them. The lawsuit about emotional damage is frivolous, and it makes a great diversion. If Mindy had an office romance with Ly, her co-workers wouldn't talk about it now. The last thing they would want is to be dragged into court. By wailing loud enough and pointing her finger elsewhere, Mindy keeps her jealous husband defending her, not sniffing out the truth about the affair."

Rick appeared indifferent. "It's your story. An interesting one, at that."

I felt my opinion about Mindy's connection with Ly was on the right track. I was glad that Patrewski and I had already discussed it. The ball was in his court to follow-up.

"What did you think of Ly?" I asked.

"He was a con artist who would have one hand in your pocket, another up your skirt if you were a woman, and a toothy smile all the while."

I hadn't cared for Ly, either, but had chalked my impression to the fact that he resented taking instructions from me. My work had included making sure he and the other caseworkers brought their client files up to standard. One-on-one, he would say, "Yes, yes, I know how to do." At the workshops, he was bored and showed it.

"But Mindy liked him?" I persisted to keep Rick talking. If I could get him comfortable, he might ramble and reveal more than he intended. Being a listener--and curious--came naturally for me.

"Yeah." He admitted. "If something glittered, Mindy loved it. She always had on gold necklaces and earrings. I guess most of the Southeast Asian refugees put their money into things they can wear and sell fast in case of bad times. There must be a jewelry store every four blocks in the Cambodian and Vietnamese communities around here. Even their babies have gold studs in their ears."

I've noticed that. But about Mindy ...?"

He leaned back, his hands behind his head, peering over the tops of his glasses. "Anyhow, one day Mindy came in with an emerald and diamond bracelet, showing it off to everybody. She said she had bought it for herself. On her salary? Who was she kidding! Then later, I had to go around the back of the building to check on something--that's where the smokers go. Mindy and Ly were there, and I saw her admiring the bracelet and saying to him, 'It is so beautiful, you are too good to me.' They kissed and when they pulled apart, they saw me. She ran back into the building, and Ly smiled like he was cock of the walk. I wanted to discipline him--fire him, if I could. He never did pull his own weight."

"But you didn't do either one?"

"Ly was off limits. I knew that, he knew that. Besides, Mindy wasn't going to holler sexual harassment on him."

I asked, "Why was Ly off limits?"

Shaking his head, Rick said, "It's nothing. Just the old cultural thing of who's who."

I digested that tidbit, sensing that the subject was a strict No Go area for Rick. Not wanting the revelations to stop, I took a side route. "Hmm. Well, if Ly and Mindy were lovers, she's probably not the one who killed him. Why would she want him dead?"

"Maybe they weren't lovers anymore."

"You say Ly was a womanizer, maybe he had tossed Mindy away and moved on to someone else."

Suddenly, I thought of Sovath. She was infinitely more beautiful than the younger Vietnamese woman. Stricken, I said, "Oh, Rick. Was he after Sovath?"

"She'd never stoop to his level," he said, his face flushing.

"I'm not implying that Sovath encouraged him. But Ly reported to her, not you. Yet, you supervised all the other caseworkers. Why the difference?"

He said, making an effort to calm down. "I actually supervised Ly on the day-to-day things. Ly's reporting to Sovath on his job description was just some Cambodian thing."

Obviously, the line of questioning had hit a dead end.

I hadn't considered Rick as having any animosity toward Ly. Now I wondered if a tenuous thread linking the two was through Sovath. If Rick thought Ly was after her, then he might have a motive for killing Ly.

Rick picked up a pencil, turning it end over end on his desk, frowning. He said, "Did you know that I applied last year for Sovath's job as director?"

"No."

"Yeah, I was one of the finalists. I've had more experience in non-profit management than Sovath. The board wanted to appoint me as the executive director, but Voueck, the board's chairman, insisted that the head of the agency had to be a Southeast Asian. The board compromised and created the position of program manager for me. Of course after six months, I had to find the money to keep my job going. But that was okay."

He doodled interlocking circles on a pad, and then drew a line through them. He said, "I had planned to spend a couple of years here and move on. I think Sovath had the same idea. She doesn't want to stay any longer than she has to. I guess we each went after the job for the money ... and there were other reasons."

He said, dejectedly, "Sovath doesn't trust me."

"I'm surprised to hear you say that. She relies on you. You're great going after the grant money and getting contracts."

He acknowledged the compliment with a nod, but he didn't appear convinced.

"You know," he went on, "I was persona non grata with other agencies in the state when the SEAAA job came open. I had been with the Coalition for Non-Nuclear Proliferation, CNNP, for three years before SEAAA. One day, seven of us slipped onto the Bangor Nuclear Submarine Base outside of Bremerton. We linked ourselves with chains to block a shipment of nuclear warheads. I spent six months in jail for criminal trespass."

I gaped at him. "How on earth did you get the SEAAA job with a criminal record?"

"The SEAAA board members don't run around in the same circles as other agency boards, and frankly, the group as a whole isn't that sophisticated. The references I gave were friends. They recommended me because I'm good at raising money, and they didn't think I'd be doing any protests working for a small refugee organization. The board ran the typical Washington State Patrol background check on me. But it only covers prior convictions for child molestation or sex crimes. I'm clean on those."

He blurted out, "I don't want Sovath's job. I want Sovath. I think of her as a lotus blossom."

I blinked at his description.

Looking forlorn, he said, "I know. I didn't mean it as a stereotype. Did you know that the lotus flower symbolizes Buddha's teachings because the plant is rooted in mud while its blossom reaches toward the light? Sovath's like that flower. She has come from hell and is rising above that... She's beautiful."

"Have you told her how you feel?" I asked, thinking that she had never mentioned Rick's feelings.

Shyly, he said, "No. Between what happened to her in Cambodia and then her husband running out on her here in the States--she can't trust, yet.

I think she feels I'm waiting for her to stumble so I can take over as the agency's ED."

I sighed. Rick appeared to be a man whose life mission was to tilt at windmills, or nuclear subs and tragedy-driven women.

He said, "Sovath has her pride. She's determined not to be a token in her work, or an also ran because the board couldn't get the Asian man they wanted."

"What man?"

"Hahn Ly. He didn't have the background to run an agency; in fact, his English skills were pretty limited. He couldn't communicate well enough to be a good figurehead. But SEAAA was being pushed by the city and county to have someone from the ethnic community as the agency's director. That's how Sovath was chosen."

I had struggled to get Ly to write case notes that made sense and had to agree with Rick's judgment.

Thinking out loud, I said, "Why was Ly wanted as the executive director if he had so few skills? And how did he end up reporting to Sovath?"

"Ly and Voueck, the board chairman, were related by marriage, so there was the chairman's obligation to family. Getting Ly a job as a caseworker took care of that, although it wasn't as prestigious as heading up the agency."

Rick laced his fingers and tapped his thumbs together. "With Sovath, the board got a Southeast Asian who has an American college degree. She's a woman, so culturally she's expected to be subservient to the board, which wants to micro-manage SEAAA. Then they put me in as program manager because I can keep the agency solvent. Ly reported to Sovath not me, because I'm white, and because the board has more of a hammer over her. Ly was left to do pretty much what he wanted. That was the deal. Not in so many words, but it was clear. Keep Hahn Ly and leave him alone."

"Do the police know any of this?"

He gave a mirthless laugh. "Do you think I'm going to willingly cooperate with them?"

Hoping his answer would be no, I asked, "Could Ly have been blackmailing Sovath? Was she afraid of him?"

"Yes. She was afraid of him and of Chhun, but I don't think blackmail entered into it. She was getting pressure from them to get her daughters engaged and married off. But Sovath wanted the girls to have a different future in America; she didn't want them trapped in her culture like she was."

75

Saying no to the men couldn't have been easy for Sovath. Their insistence would have been unrelenting. Most of the first generation refugees that I knew tried to have their families keep the cultural customs. In that regard, Sovath, seemed to have acculturated better.

"Did she fear him enough to kill him?"

"She could never intentionally hurt anything." He added, "Not like me."

I sighed. "What you're telling me gives Sovath a possible motive. If the police should find out..."

"I haven't told them, particularly not that female cop, Morales. Anyhow, she's due here any moment to ask more questions."

I peered around, half expecting to see Morales. "She's coming here. This late?" I asked, looking at my watch.

"For the next two days I'm in Olympia at a conference. I told her this was the only time I had, since I'm staying to get these reports out. She wanted to go over whatever she had on her mind. She probably needs to eyeball me to see if I'm lying. I figure I can throw her enough misinformation to keep her running around in circles for six months."

"Why not help her instead of muddying up the investigation? It might be a better way to protect Sovath."

"Don't worry. I'll help. To a point. I'll just make sure Sovath's not the one she wants."

I wondered how sharp Morales was as an interrogator, then thought about actually running into her any minute. My energy level wasn't up for it. Besides she might be peeved that she didn't go with Patrewski and me to the temple. I knew that I didn't want to be at SEAAA when she arrived.

Hurriedly, I said, "The reason I came is about Lily. Sovath said you could refer me to another agency with a female caseworker who could help. I'm worried that Lily's grandmother may physically abuse the girl."

"Why not go to her school counselor?"

"I would if I had a contact name, so I didn't get a run around."

"Why did Sovath tell you to call me? She could have suggested Phourim or Chhun."

"Maybe she trusts you. She seemed to feel you would have the answers or know who to ask."

I could see he wanted to believe that.

Rick pulled over a note pad, and scribbled on it. "You know with what's happened, I wouldn't bet on Lily staying in school. Don't expect too much." He tore off the sheet and handed it to me. "The first name and number is of a caseworker with CCS, and the other is a counselor at Lily's school who isn't burned out. She still has some common sense."

Holding out my hand, I said, "Thanks for everything."

He held it a moment, and said, "I talked too much."

I smiled. "Perhaps. But there's no reason for me to repeat anything; not when you can beat me to it, with the next person you're meeting."

Sorting It All Out
Chapter 11

Phourim caught up to me in the SEAAA parking lot, calling my name in a stage whisper and glancing around as if afraid someone might be watching. But no one else from the agency had come outside. Dusk was falling, but I could see that worry had replaced his usual eye-crinkling good humor.

He drew close, his breath smelling of fish sauce. "I saw you in Rick's office, but I wait. Did he tell you?"

I should have said, "Tell me what?" Instead, I said, "Yes," my conscience twinging for a moment. Rick had told me several things, but nothing about Phourim. And judging by the young man's face, he had a problem that he had talked over with Rick.

"He will know what to do about the police. He fix many things for SEAAA. I think Rick fix this, too," Phourim said, but his eyes sought confirmation.

"Rick's smart. No doubt about that. But do you think it will take care of the trouble?" I asked. My conscience jabbed me again. I hadn't the foggiest notion what Phourim was referring to and should say so out right. So much for my ethical center.

"Oh, he can stop Colonel Chhun, and I will be safe. Rick told me the police did not have to know."

"You're not bear grass picking again, are you?"

"No. No. I stopped long time ago, but after Ly die I thought I not have to pay any more. But Ly told Chhun and now he say I must give him money. I cannot pay and bring bride to America. Chhun is bad man, like Ly." Phourim shook his head in resigned disgust.

Shaking my head, too, I said, making the idea a statement of fact, "The two did many bad things together, hurt many people."

"They tell people to pay temple each month or they will have Nor Sang put spell on them." Phourim straightened to stand taller. "I do not believe, but the old people are afraid and say Sang has strong spirit power."

Rational or not, a creeping sensation ran up my back. I agreed with the old people, at least some ancient Irish ancestor in me did.

"I can understand that, Phourim. But does that have anything to do with Rick helping you?"

"He tell Chhun to stop or the police will learn about his bad things."

In reality, Phourim should have gone to the police, but I understood why he didn't. He needed someone running interference for him. If Chhun knew the young man had tattled on him, then Chhun had nothing to lose by turning Phourim in or Sang having friends do worse to the young man.

"Why didn't Rick stop Ly from forcing you to make payments?"

"I not say anything to him before Ly die. Maybe I lose job. Then Chhun go after me. I don't know what to do, so I tell Rick."

"Had Rick known for a long time about the two men doing this kind of business?"

"When I told Rick, he get very mad and say he suspect but not sure."

Mentally, I translated "suspect" in Phourim's statement to mean suspicious.

I asked, "Were you from the same place in Cambodia as Hahn Ly? Did you know him there?"

"No, no. He was much older."

"But you know where he came from? What did he do in Cambodia?"

Phourim gingerly nodded, as if agreeing would lead him into a direction he didn't want to go. "He in government."

"Whose?"

"What you mean?"

"Well, was he in King Sihanouk's, or one of his former ministers in government?"

"Oh, it was long ago. I don't know," Phourim insisted.

"How about Chhun?"

Phourim shook his head.

"Sometimes you've called him the colonel. Sovath says he served in the royal army under King Sihanouk."

Phourim smiled in relief that Sovath had supplied an explanation to me. I asked, "If I wanted to find out more about Ly or Chhun from the old days, how would I find the information?"

"I don't know," he said, edging away.

"You must have some idea." I touched his arm lightly, "The more Rick and I know, the better we can free you from Chhun's power." As a woman, touching Phourim was a gamble, but Phourim was familiar enough with American mannerisms, and me now, to accept my gesture as concern.

Hesitating a long time, Phourim finally said, "Ask Voeuck wife, she know about Ly. Her sister marry Ly brother. They divorce after they come to America."

He looked at me reproachfully. "I go now."

I started to apologize to Phourim when a car pulled into the lot and parked. We both turned to see who it was. Detective Consuelo Morales stepped out the car and walked toward us.

She strode over in black leather pumps, black skirt and a flamingo-colored linen blazer. The fashion-impaired would never make it as a Seabell detective, I thought. They would have as much chance as a rhinestone ring in Tiffany's window.

Morales nodded hello at us. "Mrs. O'Hern, what are you doing here this late?"

"Call me, Bridg." I smiled. "I dropped by for names of counselors who can help Lily and her family. Rick is still inside."

"I didn't think you were a social worker?" she said.

"I'm not, but the family's going to need a lot of assistance. The SEAAA staff can't do it all."

Morales stood with one hand resting on her shoulder bag. "I understand you went with Patrewski to the temple?" Her expression was neutral, but my gut feeling told me she wasn't pleased about the excursion.

"He asked me to observe and give my opinion. Did he have a chance to fill you in? I asked diplomatically.

"Not yet. I was out following other leads. So, what went on?"

I said, "Nor Sang interpreted. He's the other liaison sent by the temple. Have you two met?"

Morales shook her head.

"Well, Ban Chhun from SEAAA was there, too. Both Sang and Chhun are on the temple's board. But Patrewski probably wants to tell you the rest--put his spin on it."

"Sure, but I'd like to hear it from you. What are your thoughts?"

Actually, my thoughts were that I didn't care for Morales and that I was probably being unfair. Unfortunately for Morales, she reminded me of Cindy. Cindy's go-gettem drive had won her a promotion and hooked John while he was still married to me. At the very least, Morales could be less brusque when she talked to me--and make an effort not stand so close. She pressed too hard. I laughed to myself. My age showed.

When two women meet, at a subliminal level they quickly determine if there is a relationship potential. Can she become a friend? Or will she become a competitor? Somewhere on that spectrum, Morales and I were positioning each other. Pending more input, I was trying to place her in neutral; Morales was sticking me into the competitor slot. Her turf was Patrewski's, her new partner. From the little I had seen and heard, he

81

wasn't giving her much positive reinforcement. In her view, I was an unwanted intrusion.

Coming to that realization made it easier to respond to her. Glancing at Phourim, I said, "I can hang around and fill you in later."

She looked at him as if she'd forgotten he was standing by us, and then nodded.

Phourim had been shuffling his feet, staring at SEAAA's front door and probably seeing it as refuge. He appeared to be at a loss as to how to politely break away. Suddenly, the front door opened, and a handful of teens burst poured out. They called to Phourim, one hollering, "Hey, man, we want to go home. C'mon!"

The exterior lights of the agency and in the parking lot had come on, and I could see the kids clearly. I knew a few by name, and most of them by sight, except one youth with a shaved baldhead. The boy stood in profile to us until the other kid called out, then he turned in our direction. With a shock, I recognized Dak.

I asked Phourim, "What happened to Dak? Why did he cut off all his hair?"

"His grandmother said he must show respect for father's death. It is the old way for first son to mourn. His grandmother say he must do it so family has honor at funeral."

"I didn't see him at the temple with you. Was he with your group there?"

"Yes. That where the monk shave his head."

Dak stood staring at us; his thin face was a pale wedge under the overhead light. He had an impression of nakedness about him, as if more than his head had been exposed when he had shaved it. In his new homeland, shaved heads were a fad or a convenience but not part of a ritual to honor the dead.

Morales swung back to me. "Look. I want to talk with you, but I need to meet someone inside. Give me your number."

"Didn't Patrewski give you it?" I asked, fishing a card out of my purse and handing it to her.

She didn't bother replying, except to say, "Thanks." She pocketed the card and went into the agency.

Phourim started to go, too, but I stopped him. "I'm sorry for putting you on the spot earlier. I shouldn't have pushed you so hard with questions."

He didn't look at me. With a deep pang, I knew the apology was too late.

Suddenly, loud, popping noises in quick succession burst near us, and Phourim lunged forward, wrapping his arms around me. I fell backward from the momentum of his weight. The kids standing in front of the building were screaming. I tried to pull loose from Phourim as we lay tangled, but he kept his head buried in my chest, his arms clutching me close. I twisted around on the asphalt and peered over his shoulder. A car with dark-tinted windows was slowly driving by the kids. From the rear passenger window, a hand snaked out and threw something in the direction of the kids who were sprawled on the ground, their hands and arms shielding their heads. The loud, rapid popping sounds repeated again, and I saw small puffs and dancing sparks as a string of firecrackers went off. A tinny, high-pitched laugh trailed from the car as it picked up speed, then tore down the street and around the corner.

Phourim's arms convulsed around me. Awkwardly, I stroked his back, murmuring, "You're safe. It's over."

Gently, I pushed against his chest until his arms relaxed, releasing me. I sat up, and he rolled over on his side, his face away from me. I pushed myself up with my hands and stood on wobbly legs. My sleeves were torn, and I had asphalt burns where I'd skidded on my elbows.

Rick and Morales had come outside and were inspecting the kids to see that they were okay. Two girls cried hysterically. I didn't see Dak, but then I still was dazed.

I held out a hand to Phourim. He took it and hauled himself upright.

"Thanks, you could have saved my life," I said.

The moistness in his eyes reflected the light and also his shame. He hung his head and mumbled, "It was not for you. For me. I was afraid. It sound like Khmer Rouge guns."

We walked slowly over to the kids who appeared to be okay, and I looked around for Dak. Morales came over and asked, "Did you get a license number? Description of the car?"

I shook my head. "It all happened too fast."

She made a face, "It figures," and hurried off, presumably to find better eye witnesses.

Rick had sent the kids inside, but Dak wasn't with them. He was giving directions to Phourim, who looked even worse than in the parking lot, and Morales was on the phone. I stood in the doorway and looked up down the street. There was no sign of Dak.

I closed the door and went over to Rick, pulling him aside. "Do you think that was an attempt to scare Dak?"

"What are you talking about?"

83

"I mean, were those gang kids?"

"Probably."

"Why do you think they did that?"

He stared over his glasses. "Showing off. What else?"

"Why here? Why now?"

He shrugged.

Apparently, Rick didn't know about the gang wanting Dak to join them, or that Patrewski thought they might make a show of power at the funeral tomorrow.

I said, "Please check on Dak. He was with the kids, but I don't see him anywhere."

"Maybe he took off for home," Rick answered.

"I hope so. But it's pretty far to go on foot. How did Dak get to the temple? Did Phourim pick him up at his house?"

Rick's irritated expression told me that I'd shot off too many questions.

I put a smile between us, to make amends. "It might help to find out whether or not Dak rode a bike or drove his father's car here."

Resigned, Rick sighed. "Okay, I'll ask Phourim."

I looked around for Morales who was busy questioning one of the kids. Deciding that our "talk" about the temple visit wouldn't be high on her priority list now, I decided to leave.

I walked over to Rick. "I'm going home, but please call me, when you find Dak, even if it's late. Call collect. It's okay." I pointed to Morales. "If she asks where I am, tell her I've left. She has my number at home, too."

Rick walked me to my car and waited nearby until I locked all the doors and had started out of the parking lot. As I turned right onto the street, my headlights caught the briefest movement in the alley opposite me. I should have stopped to investigate or gone back and told Rick. But I took too long to make up my mind, finally convincing myself it would be silly to turn around. Besides, I was afraid the gang kids in the car were still in the area and might follow me.

All the way to St. Mary's Corner, though, I wondered if it had been Dak in the alley.

"Mom, this detective guy, Patrewski, sounds okay but he's a maverick."

Why wasn't I surprised?

Danny had followed up on my request to check on Patrewski's reputation. I listened to the rest of the message. "He use to be with Seattle PD and had a good arrest clearance rate but was kind of a loner. Apparently he was a tough you-know-what on women and rookies, too, until they proved themselves. What's going on, Mom? Call me."

After I arrived home, the first message on my answering machine had been Danny's. C. J. had left one, too. The others were business ones that I'd return in the morning.

I didn't call Danny back because it was easier to reach him in the morning before he left for work. I did phone C. J.

When I moved to St. Mary's three years ago, he and I were the only newcomers to the small community since the Edsel was a hot item. We naturally gravitated to each other. One time while he was recuperating from surgery on his leg, I picked up groceries for him, and called back later to see how he was doing. The visits continued and our friendship grew.

C. J. liked hearing about my different assignments, vicariously walking in my size seven-and-a-half shoes. I was his doorway to places he couldn't enter. In turn, I learned from him and enjoyed his desert-dry humor, when I wasn't the brunt of it.

Now we had fallen into the routine of regularly checking in with each other.

Over the phone, I chatted with him about the visit to the temple and the drive-by scare. C. J. listened more than commented, except at the end. After I had asked him to surf the Internet to find links to Cambodia and find any available information on Ly and Chhun, he fired off a question that ricocheted around in my head the rest of the evening.

"My dear, the police have resources to research this, and the SEAAA people sound competent to handle the kids. Both beg the question: Why are you staying involved?"

"Because ..." seemed a pretty weak response. I muttered, "C. J., I don't have to have some special reason, do I?"

"You know the answer to that better than I, although the word *perseveration* does come to mind. It's a condition you seem predisposed to," he said, with a gravelly chuckle. Then he assured me he'd give me the results of his search on the Net and hung up.

Of course as I got ready for bed, I looked up perseveration to double-check its meaning. My Webster's said: "The continuation of something to an exceptional degree or beyond a desired point." I put the dictionary down and said under my breath, "Darn you, C. J. You got me!"

The call came at two-oh-seven a.m., and I snapped on the bedside lamp. Narvik stood up from where she had been sleeping on the floor, her ears pricked forward at the strident ringing.

My first fearful thoughts were of Mary Rose and the children, and I answered with a tremulous hello, but it was the operator asking if I'd accept a collect call from Rick Howard. I accepted the charges.

He said, "We found Dak. He's in the hospital. You wanted to know."

Even my sleep-fogged brain picked up his petulant tone, but I didn't know if it was because he resented calling me or because he had to deal with Dak's situation.

"What happened?"

"He's been beat-up. They're wheeling him into x-ray now, but the doc thinks he'll be okay. They're making sure his arm isn't fractured." Very briefly, a solicitous concern rose in his voice.

"What on earth?"

"The police found him in an alley about six blocks from the agency. Dak wouldn't give them his grandmother's phone number, but said he'd been on a field trip with kids from SEAAA. The police found our emergency' phone number on the door and called Sovath. She called me, and here we are."

"Was it the kids in the car who shot off the firecrackers? Did Dak say they had done it?"

"He said four kids jumped him, but he didn't know them."

"Do you believe him?"

"How should I know? I'm not his keeper."

"Okay. But what are you going to do?"

"Nothing, except wait. When Dak can leave, I'll drive him home. Sovath phoned his grandmother to tell her know he was okay."

"Why wouldn't Dak let the police phone his grandmother? She must have been worried sick. Well, maybe he felt their call would upset her a lot more than his arriving home late, injured or not."

"Yeah, I guess," he said. "What I'm upset about is Sovath being pulled into this mess. At least Dak's covered under med coupons. Otherwise I could see Sovath suckered into paying the hospital bill."

"Did the police--?"

Rick cut me off. "Here. Sovath wants to talk to you," and I heard the muffled sounds of the receiver being handed over.

When Sovath came on, she was tearful. "I am so sorry that Rick disturbed you in the middle of the night."

I thought for a moment before answering. Rick needed all the brownie points he could muster with Sovath if he wanted to win her. But it was tempting to agree with her that he had been surly. He'd never woo Sovath with his thorn-in-the-paw attitude, but maybe he soft-pedaled that side around her. Sovath did seem vulnerable; maybe Rick could protect her.

Deciding I shouldn't be a roadblock to love, I said to Sovath, "Don't be angry at Rick. I was the one who insisted that he telephone no matter how late. Tell me, how did his grandmother take the news?"

"She was angry and very hard to talk to. She kept saying that Dak had to take her to the funeral. I think she was confused about what time it was. She kept saying, 'It is over, it is over, they are dead.' Then she'd say, 'Where is my *chmaa*,' which is a child's way of saying 'the little tiger that eats the fishes.'" I think she meant Dak."

"Will she be all right? Is anyone with her?"

"No. I was surprised that she answered the phone. I kept asking to speak to someone else. It is not our custom to leave the elder alone at such a time. She should have many people with her."

"Then Lily must still be with the aunt. Perhaps that's just as well. The grandmother might have taken her anger out on the girl." I exclaimed, "What was Dak thinking of to leave his grandmother alone? I can understand wanting to be with his buddies, but not the night before the funeral. He's more responsible than that."

Sovath lowered her voice, and said, "In the hospital emergency, they put Dak in room four. I told them to move him. In Asian culture, four is sign of death. Too many bad things have happened, and I will not take chances."

In the heavy silence that followed, I realized that despite Sovath's college education, the old cultural beliefs still clung.

While we talked, I put on my robe and carried my portable phone into the kitchen, flipping lights on as I went.

Furtively, Sovath asked, "Do you know who is here, too?"

"I haven't any idea."

"Detective Patrewski."

"Why? I thought the patrol cops brought Dak in."

"They did. But somehow he found out and came. He wants to take Dak home. I think it is our responsibility. I should make sure the grandmother is all right."

I picked up the teakettle from the stove and held the phone between my shoulder and ear while I filled the kettle from the faucet. "Where is Patrewski now?"

"He is talking with Rick here in the waiting room. Ohhh. No! They are looking this way. Rick's face is so red. He is angry. I must stop him before, he says something he shouldn't."

"Stay calm, Sovath. Rick's probably trying to keep him from bothering you, but Patrewski won't take any guff. Stop Rick!"

"Just a minute ..." Sovath said, dropping the receiver with a clunk.

I strained to hear, but only caught indistinct voices in the background. I turned the burner on under the kettle, poured water in a mug, popped in a tea bag and sat down.

The call was growing more expensive and more frustrating by the minute, but I didn't hang up. I wanted to know what was going on.

At last, the receiver was picked up and Patrewski came on the line. Without preamble, he said, "How come they contacted you?"

Grumpy gets as grumpy gives, I thought, tempted to reply, "Why do you want to know?" But figuring that two wrongs weren't going to make one constructive conversation with Patrewski, I said instead, "I asked Rick to call when they found Dak. I was at SEAAA when he disappeared. Why were you called?"

"Morales told me about the gang scare--the fake drive-by---and that Dak had taken off. I monitored the scanner and heard the report when they picked him up."

It seemed a peculiar way to spend his off duty hours, but then Patrewski was anything but predictable.

"Sovath thinks she should take Dak home. She'll want to talk to his grandmother and. reassure her. Apparently, the woman is alone and that's a big no-no considering what she's gone through."

"I'm driving Dak home. We'll stop at a Denny's and talk. He's tired, sore and scared. He may open up to me. My gut says he's holding back information on his parents' homicides. So tell Sovath to go on ahead if she wants to be with the grandmother. We'll come later."

Patrewski had Sovath back on the line before I could say, "You tell her."

I shook my head, but told her what he had said about going to the house without Dak. "It's up to you." I said.

She answered, "I will go, although Rick doesn't want me to. It is the right thing to do. He can choose his own way."

Afterwards, I wondered if Rick had any idea of the strong will that lay behind Sovath's delicate beauty. Wouldn't it be ironic if he turned out to be the vulnerable one, and she the protector?

The Loneliest Time
Chapter 13

Three o'clock in the morning has to be the loneliest time in the world, when fears constrict the heart and hope flickers. The windows in my neighbors' houses were dark, and it seemed as if the entire world slept. Except for me. That's why I turned on the lights when Rick called: to keep away "the wee beasties who lurked in the night." At least my grandmother had said that they lurked and could slip into one's restless thoughts.

After the phone call, wisps of depression seeped around me, and I stood up, waving my arms to disperse them. I quickly went into my office and grabbed a pad of paper and pen.

With so many things to think about, I couldn't sleep. Besides, the call had seeded uneasiness. I could take pills to bring on sleep, but I had struggled too hard to get off them. Instead, I had an alternative remedy.

In the past, I'd overcome insomnia by setting down what was bothering me. When my mind strayed, I would bring it back to task, looking for cause and effect, rational explanations. I'd write my version of Twenty Questions and answer them until my eyes drooped closed.

The idea of writing down what was bothering me gave me purpose, putting me back in control of the night. I padded into the kitchen with Narvik at my heels, freshened my tea and got to work.

First, I put down Sang's name and that bony finger of fear trailed up my spine again. I could understand Sovath's reverting to superstition about the number four meaning death. I was only two generations away from a grandmother who believed in the little people. Just thinking about them made me glance around to see if one was perching on top of a kitchen cabinet.

I wrote, *Why are you so afraid of Sang? Because of Sovath's talk, saying he has the 'evil eye. He could rob me of my mind.* I stared for a long time at the paper, then scribbled defiantly, *Says who?*

When depression descended on me after John's death, a gray fog had filled my mind, making it impossible to think. For days at a time, I had lain in bed not caring about eating or dressing. The months had dragged on, my mind and body chained by depression. I wanted to die and be out of my misery. Meeting Sang had rattled that old, stored-away chain.

I could almost hear grandmother Kate saying, "Bridget, face your fears and they'll flee."

I scrawled, *Sang has no power over me unless I grant it to him.* I could sense grandmother pat in approval; though in reality, I'd have to work hard on that thought.

The next name I jotted was Morales's. Though she didn't look like Cindy, she reminded me of her. Why? *She's sexy, younger and pushy. You're not.*

This was not pleasant to write or read.

I took the description apart.

Sexy. Did I want to swish my hips when I walked and have a bosom that strained the buttons on my blouse? Truth to be told. No.

Younger. Would I want to be thirty again? Yes, but only if I knew as much as I did now. I wouldn't make the same mistakes.

Pushy. Morales went after what she wanted and didn't care about who got in her way. The counterpoint voice in my head, said, "Do you know that? For sure?"

No, but I envy her self-confidence. Morales waved no flags of self-doubt. On the other hand, I was two people: the one who put up a confident front in public, and the one inside who ran scared, always questioning herself. It would be nice if the two merged into a whole. The insight helped, and I drew a line through Morales's name.

Now I could get onto the creative problem solving exercise that I had in mind. On the left side of a new sheet, I wrote down the names of the agency people that I had been with in the last three days. They included Sovath, Phourim, Rick, Mindy, her husband, and Chhun. Trusting my subconscious to surface information, I left space under each name for notes. Drawing three columns to the right, I labeled them *Method, Opportunity* and *Motive.* The intersecting lines made a grid with boxes. By each name, I would assign a number between 1 and 10. The number would reflect the probability of the individual being the killer. I would add up the numbers from the three categories and high score won--or was the most likely suspect.

Opportunity. According to Patrewski, all of the persons on my list were at home at the time of the murders, so I assigned 3's to all but Mindy and her husband. It seemed likely they would cover for each other, particularly Mindy out of fear. I gave her and the husband, 4's.

Method. I considered who might have access to a gun, and who would have used a gun as the means to kill the Lys. And who would have been able to kill the wife in cold blood? Sovath's painful experiences under the Khmer Rouge made it unlikely that she would own a gun or be that calculating in the style of execution. Months ago, Phourim had mentioned that he wouldn't have a gun in his home. But he worked with some streetwise kids who could have sold him one. However, I suspected that Phourim's hand would have shook so much holding the gun, that he would never gotten off the clean shots that killed the Lys. And if Rick was a true pacifist then he shouldn't own a gun or know where to get one. Though, he could have bought one from a kid, too. Rick had a temper and a record to prove it. How strongly he felt about protecting Sovath was an unknown. But if his feelings were aroused enough--who knew how far he would go?

Then there was Mindy and her husband. I thought it likely that Mindy's husband would have a gun in his home, though that was guesswork. Still, he seemed hot headed enough to have one and use it. It was possible that Mindy might have taken the gun. But I ran into a wall believing that either she or her husband would have been invited or gotten into the Lys' house without a fuss. Of the six names on my list, I felt Chhun was the most likely to have a gun: he was as an ex-military man, and he would have reason to visit Ly as his friend, and apparently, business partner.

Not much to go on, but I assigned numbers anyhow. Under *Method*, Sovath and Phourim had 3's; Rick, a 5; Mindy and her husband, 6's; and Chhun, a 7.

Motive. Assessing each person's motive was harder to do, but I put brief notes under the names:

Sovath–pressure to marry off her kids, how serious the threat?

Phourim--possible blackmail, could get in trouble with law, lose chance for bride.

Rick--love twisted, has passion for causes, criminal record.

Mindy–fears husband's wrath or jealousy, could be mad at Ly for dumping her.

M's Husband--jealous with ego to defend, quick tempered; and

Chhun–most to lose? Wants money and power, has history of it.

Under *Motive*, I quickly weighted my opinions and gave Sovath and Phourim, 5's; Rick and Mindy, 6's; Mindy's husband and Chhun, 7's

Tallying the three categories, Sovath and Phourim tied at 11 each, Rick, had 14; and Mindy and her husband were at 16. Chhun scored 18, the high total, which still made him the best suspect in my book.

I looked at the chart and notes. Nothing conclusive there, but I felt satisfied with the work. It had cleared my mind and also made me sleepy.

Stretching my arms, I glanced at the clock above the kitchen window. A quarter-to-four! I stacked the pad and sheets together, put my cup in the sink and began turning lights off.

Before drifting to sleep, the answer to C. J.'s question came to me; the one about why was I staying involved in the Lys' investigation. I had to assemble parts of the puzzle before letting go, to make cosmos out of chaos. C. J. would like that explanation. Rolling over, I hoped that I would remember the explanation in the morning.

Talking It Over
Chapter 14

Sovath called early in the morning as I was dressing and asked me to go with her to the Lys' funeral.

Her request took me off guard. I had assumed she would go with her staff, the members unified in paying their respects to the family and showing their esteem of Hahn Ly. It would be expected of them and also wiser, maintaining face for all in the Cambodian community.

I said, "Won't Rick and the others from the agency be there?"

"Yes. But I am asking you."

I waited for her to elaborate but she didn't, and in the long pause that followed, I sensed her hope that I would agree to come.

"You don't want to go with him?"

"No," she said firmly, and waited for my response.

Prompted by sympathy, not reason, I said yes.

Later, I chided myself for not asking her why she didn't want to be with her staff. But Sovath would have told me if she wanted me to know. I had learned that much about her.

However, I did ask her about Dak and his grandmother. "How late did you stay at their house?"

"It was almost four-thirty this morning. I am tired."

"How was Patrewski with Dak?"

"Detective Patrewski pretends to be very tough. But I think he is like the *durin*, sharp to the touch but with soft goodness inside."

I laughed. "Don't tell him that. He might arrest you for ruining his reputation."

"He gave Dak his pager number and said to call him if he is in trouble, no matter what time of the day or night. Then before he left, he put his arm around Dak's shoulders and said, 'You'll make it, kid.'"

Sovath's comment reinforced my own conviction that Patrewski's interest in the boy had crossed from professional to personal.

Dak's actions that evening still bothered me, and I asked, "Did the boy say why he left his grandmother alone?"

"He said she wanted the old customs followed, and he went to the temple to pray for his parents and to honor his father by having his hair cut off. He did it, although I can tell he believes it is a strange custom. Dak has no memory of Cambodia. He was young when his family came to America."

"But he obeyed her about having his head shaved. I saw him afterwards at the agency. He looked like a skinny ten-year-old."

"Yes. I can tell he is very respectful and cares for his grandmother. He insisted that she go to bed when he got home and fixed her a special tea to make her sleep. That is why I cannot understand him leaving her alone all night."

"Did you ask him?"

"Yes. He said his grandmother told him to go. She wanted no one with her while she mourned for her daughter."

"But not mourn her son-in-law?"

"The grandmother said that he had brought shame to her family."

"How?"

Sovath hesitated. "She talked first of the happy times with her family, before Pol Pot. She had seven children, but only her youngest, Dak's mother, survived after the Khmer Rouge came. The rest of the grandmother's daughters died of illness or starvation. Her husband and two sons were killed. Soldiers shoved them in a line in front of the village. Then they made her stand by her husband and sons. The soldiers shot her husband and then her sons. When her turn came to be shot, the head soldier moved close to her, aimed and fired, but the bullet went by her ear. He laughed, and told her that he had saved her so she could dig her family's graves. He made her do it with a sharp stick and her bare hands." Sovath's anguish spread across the line, thick and palpable. "I think to remember is to be crazy."

Neither words nor time would ever heal the grandmother's experience--or Sovath's.

Groping for some way to move past the images, I asked, "When did Ly marry her daughter?"

Her words dragged out. "It was in a Thai border camp. Did you know that Hahn Ly had also been married to the grandmother's oldest daughter?"

"No. I had no idea."

"I had not known, either. The grandmother wept and clutched at her breast as if she wanted to pull her heart out. I was afraid she was going to hurt herself. But she talked on and on until she dried up and sat like a statue.

"The grandmother said that one night when they were in a Khmer Rouge labor camp, the soldiers came and took Hahn Ly away. His wife--her oldest daughter--was pregnant. They had very little food, and she died in childbirth. The baby didn't live long after. Then the Vietnamese invaded Cambodia and the Khmer Rouge were going to destroy the village

96

where the women had been taken. The grandmother and her last daughter fled, walking for weeks to reach the Thai border and a refugee camp. They found Hahn Ly there. He told them he had escaped from the Khmer Rouge and had hidden in the jungle. He married the daughter in the camp. But he had no dowry to give the grandmother. The grandmother was bitter that he had lived and her oldest daughter, his wife and baby, had died. The marriage was a way for the grandmother and her last daughter to survive. It meant they had a man to protect them in the camp, and families with a husband and wife had better chances of being accepted by the U. S. as refugees. Ly was their way out."

Sovath sighed. "These memories are like a tight yoke on a water buffalo, hurting at every turn ... Bridget?"

"I'm listening," I said quietly.

"Thank you for going with me this afternoon. I do not want to be alone."

After Sovath hung up, I returned Danny's call from last night. He wasn't at the Public Defender's Office, which didn't surprise me. I left a message thanking him for finding the information on Patrewski and told him all was well.

When I left the house, a gray drizzle had set in that made it seem more like February than April. I stopped off at C.J.'s on my way to Seabell. The day's soup special would be potato leek with garlic chives, definitely a comfort food. I wanted to cheer myself with it and happier talk.

C. J. had a dark blue kerchief tied around his neck and looked jaunty. I smiled hello and talked weather with a couple of the regulars seated at the counter.

Helping myself to a bowl of soup, I said to C. J., "You look perky." Then I grabbed some utensils and the soup and carried them to a booth. I sat down, leaving the other side available where I knew C. J. could stretch out his bad leg.

He came over with two mugs of coffee, eased himself into the booth, and said, "Women are perky, and men are rakish."

"Actually, I was thinking raffish."

He nodded. "Better than perky. I tried calling you this morning, but your line was busy."

C. J. knew I wouldn't put call waiting on my phone because I hated the annoying clicks when another call came in. Also, it seemed rude to put the first caller on hold.

"Then I'm glad I stopped by."

"I thought you might."

97

"What do you mean?"

"It's the P word."

"What? Perseveration? Which, by the way I don't like having as a label."

"No. Predictable was the word I had in mind."

"That's as bad. Who wants to be always predictable? Besides, it was just by chance that I dropped in," I said.

"Actually, predictable also means consistent, which is an admirable trait."

I laughed, shaking my head. "I'm going to quit while I'm ahead. What were you calling me about?"

"My progress on the names you gave me. It was rather intriguing to be in chat rooms with college youth exuding idealism, albeit in the Net's strange idiom that passes for grammar. There are a surprising number of Cambodian web pages, including those done by student associations. I traversed them last night."

"They're so young. How would they know about Colonel Chhun or Hahn Ly?"

"The students regularly access Cambodia through the Internet, and they trade stories among themselves. One enterprising young woman asked her father about Ly because she thought his name was familiar, that she had heard her parents talk about him. She e-mailed me this morning."

C. J. leaned back, apparently enjoying the suspense he had created.

"So, what did you learn?"

"This Chhun was something like a deputy minister of the Royal Cambodian Army, and got out of Cambodia before Phnom Penh fell to the Khmer Rouge. But apparently he's doing business now in his former country and is tied in with a company that's clear-cutting the teak forests. Also, your Colonel Chhun's been active in Long Beach and New York at political meetings, raising money to get King Sihanook's son, Prince Ranariddh back in power."

"I didn't know about the business interest," I said. "But the rest fits. With Ranariddh in, Chhun probably figures he can go back and get some high position in government and continue wheeling and dealing. Did you learn anything about Hahn Ly? Did the two know each other then?"

"There's an interesting twist to that. It seems Ly was Khmer Rouge, which should have put him and Chhun at odds, don't you think?"

I stared at C. J. "Are you sure?"

"The father of one of my Internet correspondents lived in a small village in the interior of Siem Reap province. There was a secret prison built there for high-level dissidents. According to the girl's father, a Hahn Ly ran it. No one who went into the prison came out alive. The young woman said that when her father drank too much, he told the story of the terrible 'man of death.' I gather that when the Khmer Rouge began losing, the guards and soldiers blew up the village, the prison with it. Only a few of the villagers made it into the hills, this girl's father was one."

I stared out the window at the dull, dripping sky. "Sovath told me this morning that the Khmer Rouge took Hahn Ly away but that he had escaped. He lived in the jungle before he could make his way to a refugee camp."

"Well, he did live in the jungle. Perhaps he struck a deal and turned against his people in order to save his own skin."

I said, "How on earth did Ly and Chhun hook up together if they were at opposites politically? Or didn't Chhun know about Ly's past? Then again, what if he did find out and killed Ly?"

C. J. stared at me quizzically. "How do you know who's on first and who's on third in Cambodian politics? What can you say about a country that has two co-prime ministers, and one's a prince! And you have Chhun backing the prince who's aligned himself with a Khmer Rouge faction in order to gain control over this other Prime Minister, Hun Sen."

I answered, "It's probably beyond our American psyche to figure."

"Obviously, my baseball analogy was too simple," C. J. said, raising one shaggy eyebrow.

I rubbed my temples and looked at him. "Thanks for researching this, but I'm not sure what to do with the information."

"I presume you'll give it to your sheriff?"

"Detective," I said absent-mindedly. "And yes, I will."

"Keep in mind," C. J. said, "we may not have the right persons. I presume that Ly and Chhun are common names in Cambodia like our Smith and Jones."

I nodded and thought of the scraps of fact and innuendo collected so far. Following them was like falling in the rabbit hole in *Alice in Wonderland.* I said, "Mutual greed might have brought Chhun and Ly together. And with no loyalty involved, Ly might have double-crossed Chhun on a business deal."

C. J. eased out of the booth, pausing a moment until his gimpy leg took his weight. He reached over and took my empty soup bowl and the mugs. He said, "Follow your instincts. Just be careful doing it."

That was as close as he would get to telling me what I should do, which is one reason why C. J. made such a good friend.

Before pulling out of the parking lot, I took out my cell phone and dialed Patrewski's number at the station. St. Mary's had its own cultural norms, and I would have broken one by using the phone from the booth. My farmer neighbor sitting at the counter inside would have hooted about my big city airs, showing off in public what I could have done in private.

Patrewski wasn't in, so I left word for him to call me. I needed to let him know what C. J. had discovered and give him the name of Ly's former sister-in-law. I'd forgotten to do that earlier. If Patrewski attended the funeral, maybe we could find a corner and talk. Over the last few days, I felt that I had glimpsed the underlying reason for the Lys' murders but had ignored its significance. Talking to him might etch in the sketchy impression.

Uncertain Futures
Chapter 15

When I met Sovath in front of the funeral home, she had her twin daughters with her. She hadn't mentioned bringing them along, but in a way I wasn't surprised. Having her family with her would show great respect for the Lys, and the girls would be added insurance. Her staff couldn't box her in with the three of us hanging on her.

The girls were identical twins and, and the only way I could tell the two apart was that Srey's eyes darted about like a curious junco at a bird feeder, while Saray kept her head down, her long lashes veiling her eyes. After we were introduced, the shy twin took her mother's arm, and her lively sister linked arms with me as if I were an old friend.

Patrewski stood on the entrance steps off to one side in sartorial splendor: tan raincoat, leather gloves and a fedora. He seemed to be keeping an eye on the mourners hurrying up the steps to get out of the rain and also on the cars discharging their passengers in front of the funeral home. I glanced back at the street, looking for gang kids. None were converging on us, which eased my earlier concerns. I looked back at Patrewski who hadn't come over, and caught his eye, mouthing, "let's talk." He nodded.

Inside the foyer, Sovath greeted people she knew while we queued up to sign the guest book. There were a sprinkling of Americans but it was packed with Cambodians wearing cultural and Western-style clothes, or a combination of them: long skirted sarongs hung below Pacific Trail jackets and krachumpa scarves, in rich fuchsia shades, brightened the white shirts worn by some of the men.

Near a large peace lily by the chapel's double doors, I spotted Morales. In a dark green pantsuit, she looked as lush as the plant. Like Patrewski, she was keeping an eye on things.

A group of five girls in the line chattered among themselves, loud enough that the older people near us stared with disapproval. The teens affected an exaggerated indifference. They were Asian, about Lily's age and probably her classmates. Their eyebrows were plucked and penciled into half-moon arches, and they wore a blackberry shade of lipstick that aged their youthful faces. I sensed that the drama of the funeral setting excited them.

While we waited in line, Mindy and her husband came up and Sovath acknowledged them, briskly, as if to discourage further conversation. But

Mindy's husband grabbed Sovath's hand, shaking it vigorously and smiling. He said how pretty the twins were and joked that it was too bad he was married or he'd take one of them for a wife. The people near us looked away.

I felt with absolute certainty that Mindy's husband had created the scene to achieve a purpose: he wanted everyone there to see him, to know that he had come, and that he had nothing to hide.

Perhaps he didn't, but Mindy did.

Under her heavy makeup, I could see the puffy discoloration of a bruise on her cheek. She had hung back while her husband talked to Sovath, but she covered her cheek with her hand when she caught me staring. Then she moved next to her husband and murmured in his ear. He broke off his conversation with Sovath, and saying good effusively, took Mindy by the elbow into the chapel.

I almost said something about the bruise to Sovath. Instead, because of the anger in her eyes, I stepped up and signed the guest book. She didn't want to hear anything about Mindy or her husband.

We had started for the chapel when we heard someone calling Sovath's name and saw Rick and Phourim hurrying toward us. Rick came up first and put his arm around Sovath's shoulder in a friendly way. He greeted the girls who appeared pleased to see him, and Phourim spoke to them in Khmer. They laughed, the shy one blushing.

I said hello to Rick and smiled at Phourim but didn't say anything. The last time we saw each other, he had knocked me down and lain on me in the agency's parking lot. The embarrassing memory might be too much for him. For an instant, though, he smiled, and then he looked down at his shoes.

It was a start.

Sovath had slipped out from under Rick's arm to stand between her daughters, and he blinked behind his wire-rimmed glasses. "You okay?" he asked.

Feeling like a chaperone who had neglected her duties, I started to run interference between Rick and Sovath. Perversely, I stopped. Now that they were actually together, I had the urge to see the situation play out. Besides, Sovath was doing okay without my help. In fact, the encounter with Mindy's husband seemed to have stiffened her backbone: She was steely control in a serene wrapping. Rick, on the other hand, was confused distress in a wrinkled suit.

Sovath said, "No. You go on in. We'll wait for a while out here."

"Who are you waiting for?" he asked, glancing around the room. She started to answer, but he turned back, eyes frightened behind his glasses, and grabbed Sovath's hand. "We need to hurry in or we won't find enough seats together," he said. Over Sovath's protest, Rick herded her and the twins into the chapel with Phourim tagging behind.

I looked around to see what had galvanized Rick and saw Chhun and Nor Sang bearing down. Chhun wore a cold, imperious smile that opened a pathway through the crowd of people. But it was the confident malevolence on Sang's face that sent me rushing after the others.

We crammed into a row near the back with two teenage boys. Phourim sat next to them, Rick beside him, and Sovath between her daughters. I sat by the aisle, the chatty twin to my right.

When Chhun and Sang walked by, I focused on the monks praying by the two caskets on the raised platform near the front. The chapel had old style pews, and the front rows were full except for the first one on our side of the aisle. I assumed it had been left vacant for the immediate family. The men, though, easily found two seats on the other side because an older couple gave up theirs.

The caskets sat high on skirted trolleys banked by huge baskets of flowers, many of them Asiatic and Cana lilies. Their cloying fragrances fought with the incense that infused everything. I pulled out a handkerchief and held it to my nose, hoping to filter out the smells inflaming my sinuses.

The people around us rustled in their seats, and we turned toward the chapel's entrance. In the doorway stood Dak, his grandmother and Lily. They all were dressed in white, the color of mourning in their country, although Dak's arm was in a blue sling. His grandmother appeared as frail as a dry reed. She leaned on Dak, and he supported her with his good arm. He looked so ill, though, that I thought he might buckle under her weight. Lily stood a pace behind them.

While pain lined the faces of her brother and grandmother, Lily stared straight ahead, chin thrust forward. She wore no makeup, but there was something different about her. She had shaped her eyebrows into two pencil-thin arches like the girls I'd seen in the lobby. I could understand her wanting to be like her peers, but I hoped she wouldn't lose the defiant individuality she had shown in her home.

As the three walked slowly to their seats, the grandmother wailed along with the monks' chanting voices.

Throughout the ceremony, and then as we filed downstairs afterwards to the crematorium, the chatty twin provided running color commentary. Sovath's outspoken daughter had no conformance problems; she was an independent thinker. And when I wasn't busy saying, "Oh? Why not?" I was thinking, "Stand by world for this one!"

She had done a term paper on Cambodian customs, she said, and with 16-year-old candor added, "My mom wouldn't help me research the death stuff. It made her cry."

After the ceremony ended, my young commentator pointed at Lily who was sprinkling grain from a basket as she walked in front of the pallbearers. They were carrying the caskets to the crematorium downstairs, led by the monks, followed by the family with the rest of us spilling out of the pews.

"Can you believe it? " the twin whispered. "I bet her grandmother came from a really backwards village. This is old stuff."

Our row was among the last to get up and join the crowd. I lagged behind, having no desire to be stacked like firewood with everybody in a dismal room, watching the Lys' final trip into a 4,000-plus degree oven. I already had throbbing sinuses and a headache that three Sudafed and two Tylenol hadn't touched.

Anyway, I had my talkative friend to explain everything.

She said cheerfully, "Did you know that cremating is better than burying the body, 'cause the body's ghost will smell better?"

I shook my head, hearing ringing in my ears.

"Know why Lily's throwing the wheat down?"

I thought it probably wasn't wheat. Wheat didn't grow in Cambodia. But I wasn't feeling up to the effort to make the point. "No. Why?" and pressed my forehead to see if the pain would shift to a new spot.

She confided, "The daughter of the dead person has to put grain on the ground to the burning place because it represents food for the person who died. Their ghost has to eat." She went on wide-eyed and earnest, "When someone dies and is burned, the older people believe that the body's ghost wanders around for three days. It gets thirsty and tries to drink but it has no middle finger. The middle finger is the 'ghost' finger. When the ghost tries to get a drink from a spring and cups its hands to scoop the water, the water runs through. It can't drink!"

She paused for effect and said, "That's when the ghost realizes its dead, and it can go on to its next life."

While she told her story, we had become separated from Sovath and the others and had slowed until we were well behind the throng. Sovath, however, came back for us and let her loquacious daughter know that she didn't approve of her behavior. I told them to go on ahead, that my allergies were kicking up. I would join them later at the reception upstairs.

I started back the way we had come, but saw an exit sign at the end of the hall and decided to slip outside. I had to get some relief from the sinus headache, and the damp fresh air would help. The door opened onto a garden courtyard. A tall black wrought iron fence enclosed the area that ran about fifty feet down the side of the building and was probably half again as wide. Tall arborvitaes rimmed the fence, providing privacy. Two screened arbors at either end of the garden created meditative settings, and evergreen clematis and climbing roses covered the sheltering latticework. The rain had changed to a refreshing spritz, and I pulled out a crushed rain hat from my coat pocket to keep my hair from frizzing.

I was in the arbor toward the backside of the courtyard when I heard a door open and voices. Not being in a social mood, I stayed where I was.

The people spoke in Khmer. I recognized a few words, but not enough to know what they were saying. I couldn't help but listen to them, and with a sinking sensation, knew the voices belonged to Chhun and Sang.

I looked around for a way out but the gate in the fence was across from the door leading into the building. Either way, I'd be seen if I left now. A whiff of smoke and the direction of their voices, told me that the men were standing by the door. Rather than strolling around, they probably were under the roof's protective overhang while they smoked and talked. My best bet was to stay put, and I sat down on a damp bench, huddling to make myself smaller behind the arbor's screen.

Along with the few words of Khmer that I recognized, I heard them say Rick's name several times, once accompanied by laughter that was anything but pleasant. They also mentioned the word Richmond several times as if there was some joke connected. Their tone was arrogant like John's had been often. Arrogance crossed all cultural lines.

The door opened again and for a moment, my hopes rose. Maybe the men were going back inside, or the service was over and people were coming outside to look around. If that happened, the two would probably visit with them, and I could slip out.

Unreasoning panic enveloped me when I thought of confronting the two men, especially Sang, especially here by myself. The talk of ghosts by Sovath's daughter had affected me more than I realized, stirring fears hidden so deep that I couldn't consciously identify them.

The last few years, I had pulled together the pieces of my fractured ego, but I was a work in progress. Sang, through his sixth sense, knew of this vulnerability, and each time we met, had probed for it. In my imagination, Sang coiled like a viper waiting to strike.

I strained to hear above my own breathing, afraid the sound of it carried in the moist air. I shut my eyes to hear better, then opened them, pulling back my coat sleeve carefully to mark the minutes as they passed on my watch. Five minutes. Let five minutes pass to be sure they had left, and I was safe.

Only muffled street noises entered the courtyard. Nothing rustled, no sounds of feet crunched on the courtyard's paths. I exhaled deeply. I was alone.

Shivering, I pulled my raincoat tighter about me, making up my mind. I would find Sovath and tell her I had to leave, and if I found Patrewski, I'd ask him to go somewhere else to talk. But I wouldn't hang around.

Then I sensed rather than saw Sang first, acutely aware that my heart was pounding so hard that he must be able to hear it.

He stood in the arbor's archway, a small man, yet somehow growing larger in presence as I looked at him.

Fear trapped me.

"I thought someone was here. It is pleasing it is to see you," he said, his eyes mocking his words.

"I--I didn't realize anyone else was here," I lied.

He took a step closer. "You do not have your policeman friend with you. He is gone, you know. He left with the other woman." A smile crossed his face, then his expression changed to regret.

"You are afraid. Don't be, we need to help each other. The police look to us. Remember, at the police station? Talk to me about what you have found out. What you have told the police about my people?"

I tried to get hold of myself. I could scream or stand up and walk out. He didn't have a gun, and if he did, why would he use it on me? But I couldn't move, my legs were like wooden posts, stuck in place.

As he stepped closer, a memory surfaced. I was a little girl and my big brother had shut me into a dirty, cold closet in our basement because I had tattled on him. He said I couldn't leave because I had been bad. The door wasn't locked but, too terrified to try and get out, I stood in the dark, crying, waiting for him to come back. When he did, he made me promise not to tell our mother or he'd do it again.

Now, like in the closet, I waited, helpless, for Sang. He said, "Who does the detective think killed Ly? Is he checking on Chhun?"

He moved closer, stopped, and began swaying, a rhythmic side-to-side motion that almost seemed comforting. All the while, he held my gaze.

"What did the detective say after you left the temple? You want to tell me," he said softly. "I see you are tired. Tell me, and you can go."

Dully, I said, "I don't know what he thinks. He doesn't confide in me."

Sang stood in front of me now, silent, appraising. Then he leaned forward and stroked me on the shoulder, and I felt my will power ebbing. Triumph gleamed from him.

Shame swept over me, too much to bear, and the voice of the little girl within cried, "I don't deserve this." A roar of outrage broke free.

"Get away from me." I shouted, pushing him backwards. "Don't you ever, ever threaten me!"

He stumbled but caught himself. Crouching, he sneered. "I do not have to touch you to make death come in your house. Death walks with you."

"You're right. But there are worse things than dying." When I said that the thunderous pounding of my heart slowed.

Sang stood up, brushing his pants, and looked troubled. My meaning was obscure to me, too. I only knew that compared to a moment ago, something shackled had been released.

Sang hesitated, then tried once more to gain control. "You are woman and put ideas in the policeman's head. You are no good for my people."

I watched, fascinated, as his black eyes glinted and his face filled with loathing.

Suddenly, I thought of Benjy, my three-year-old grandson, and his game of scary where he'd growl and make faces, then I'd cringe, cross my eyes, and yell, "Boo!" Benjy would tumble back, and we'd both laugh, immensely pleased.

Before I knew what I was doing, I crossed my eyes at Sang and said, "You know, I'm not buying this time."

Shaking with fury, he pointed his finger. "You are here because of Sovath. But she will be gone from agency. She is not Khmer. Rick will be director, and he will do what we say. You will go, too."

When I had pushed Sang, an intoxicating rush had gone through me; the high helped me defy his spellbinding attempt. But caution quickly sobered me. Offending Sang could have bad repercussions on Sovath. I rearranged my face into respectfulness and gestured around me to take in what had happened in the last few minutes. "I'm sorry. Perhaps I didn't understand your intention. As you said, you are helping the police, too."

"I think you forget that. My people look to me, not you."

"Yes. You care for them."

Standing straighter, Sang said, "They need me."

"Yes, of course. Don't punish Sovath for my mistakes. She only asked me to help the police because she didn't have any other American name to give them."

Sang shrugged. "The reason does not matter."

"What did you mean that she is not Khmer?"

"Sovath is not Cambodian. Her mother was Chinese," he said, his contempt clear.

"But her father was. She was born in your country. She suffered under Pol Pot."

He smiled as if the idea pleased him. "She has served her purpose."

Sang had successfully used my concern for Sovath to regain the upper hand. His power, though, didn't come from his so-called evil eye but from his ability to prey on people's fears and weaknesses. He had found mine and manipulated it. Had I cost Sovath her future?

I stared at Sang, willing him to believe me. Lying with conviction, I said, "The police are watching agency staff to make sure no one else gets hurt or dies. They have Sovath's family under surveillance to make sure she stays safe. I'll confirm that with Detective Patrewski before I leave."

In mock acquiescence, Sang bowed at the waist. "I am sure she and her daughters will be safe. But as you say, there are worse things than the dying."

There Are No Trivial Occurrences
Chapter 16

Upstairs in the reception area, I looked around anxiously for Sovath but didn't see her. Tables covered with white linen had been set up against one wall. They were laden with food and fruit, apparently brought by friends because much of the food was ethnic Khmer. Usually after a Cambodian funeral, everybody would have gone to the family's home, but the Lys' apartment was too small to hold this crowd, though people would drop by later.

Dak's grandmother sat on a high backed chair placed on a riser at one end of the room. She seemed even more wizened than when she walked behind the caskets to the crematorium. Dak, his aunt, and a swarm of women attended to her, fussing and urging her to eat.

The room had a surreal quality to it, partly because my senses were bombarded by scents that included incense and perfume, partly from a bad case of shakes after the confrontation with Sang. People talked in noisy clusters, competing to be heard above each other. Sovath, though, wasn't with any of them. She had to be told about Sang's threat and the danger to her; Patrewski, too, then I'd leave.

I walked among the crowd searching for Sovath and Patrewski, or Morales even. I didn't find them but spotted Lily with the girls who had been in the guest book line. She was staring across the room at her grandmother and the people around her. Lily obviously wanted no part of them and judging by the bitterness on her face, perhaps not of her grandmother, either.

Lily had changed from her simple white outfit and sandals into a tight black mini-skirt and blue blouse. Her block-shaped high heels made her two inches taller. She looked again at her grandmother and Dak, who seemed to sense her gaze, turned around. He waved and beckoned her to come over. But she swung away from him and began talking to her friends.

I walked up to her.

"Hello, Lily." I smiled at her and then the girls. "I see your friends came. That's good."

For a moment, the shy young girl I'd sat with in her bedroom appeared glad to see me. Then aware that her friends were gawking at us, she asked, "What d'you want?"

Her buddies turned from Lily to me to see how I'd handle her response.

Probably disappointing them, I said, "I'm concerned about you. Your brother and grandmother seem to be getting all the attention. Do you need anything?"

Lily shook her head, but once again, looked over at her brother and grandmother. Her mouth quivered. I guessed that she wanted to be with them but didn't feel she would find what she needed there.

I wanted to hug her, to tell her it was okay to cry, but she didn't want me in her private world. She stepped back.

Thinking of my own teen years, trying on adulthood and finding it a hard fit, I smiled with sympathy. I hoped she would take it as I meant it.

The moment didn't last, because Dak interrupted us. He had walked over, and begun speaking sharply in Khmer. He grasped Lily's arm, but she jerked away, answering him in quick, angry bursts.

He said, "Look at you! Why do you embarrass our name? You should be with grandmother. I told you that we cannot leave her alone. One of us must always be with her." He had switched into English, and I wondered if it had been for my benefit. Perhaps he hoped that I might help him persuade his sister.

Lily leaned toward her brother. "You are her *chmaa*. Her defender. She likes you best. You think you are my boss, always telling me what to do: 'Stay home. Don't talk about our family.' Who cares what grandmother says. She's crazy. I'm sick of listening to you! I don't have to do the old ways anymore. Our parents are dead, or didn't you notice? Oh, yeah. I forgot. You were too busy being the man of the house!"

Trembling, Lily glared at him and then stomped off. Her friends hesitated, unsure of what to do, and then followed her.

The color had drained from Dak's face, and he appeared about to be sick. Ignoring the startled faces of those near us, I led him over to a couple of empty chairs and brought him juice. He sat holding the glass between his hands, staring into it.

I sat beside him. "Give Lily time. You both need each other, and she will make up."

"What am I going to do?" he whispered forlornly.

"About Lily?"

He shook his head. "My grandmother..."

I stood up to see if she was all right. Someone must have convinced her to eat. She had a tray on her lap and was eating from a bowl with chopsticks. I also saw Chhun talking with her, probably trying to get the funeral gift money. He would take it and promise to send her daughter's ashes back to Cambodia for a proper ceremonial interment--for a good price, no doubt. I hoped the aunt hovering near the two would guard the grieving woman's interests.

"Your grandmother's eating. That's a good sign."

"Lily's right, she is crazy." He amended. "Just a little."

"After what the elders went through, most of them are depressed, or worse."

He nodded. "I can't protect her. I can't watch her all the time."

"We can find a home aide through an agency. You need to stay in school, Dak. That's the best way to help your family."

"I want to, but grandmother..." I could see tears welling in his eyes, and he blinked them away.

He said, "Lily doesn't like it, but I *am* the man of the house now. And you know something? The job sucks."

Sovath said, "It's begun."

She had found me and sat down after Dak returned to his grandmother's side. Sovath pointed to Lily and her friends standing at the far end of the banquet tables.

"What has begun?" I asked, glancing at them.

"She has left her family and goes on a slippery path."

Lily stood talking, animated, one leg thrust out, and hand on her hip, like a model posing.

I said, "Dak's upset about her. She just read him off for being too controlling. Right now I'd say she wants very little to do with him or their grandmother. That ceremonial walk with the caskets was probably her last obedient act for a while."

Sovath tightened her mouth, shaking her head.

We observed the girls silently. I wondered if Sovath was thinking of how one act of defiance by Lily might irretrievably alter her life. Right now, reason didn't rule the fourteen-year-old, just peer pressure and emotions percolating with hormones.

While we watched, two young men joined the girls, and I did a double take. One of them was the gang leader who had dropped by the Lys' apartment and given Dak the AZ jacket. I almost didn't recognize him: the slouch was gone along with the sagging, baggy pants. Instead, he wore a suit and had his hair neatly pulled back into a ponytail. At nineteen, or whatever his age, he was too old and too dangerous for Lily. He laughed and talked, and she leaned toward him like a sapling to the sun.

Turning to Sovath, I saw my own concern reflected in her eyes.

"That teen with Lily wants Dak to join his gang. Do you know him?" I asked.

"No, but I know what he desires with her."

Patrewski had been wrong about the gang causing a ruckus at the funeral. Their leader was using a more devious means to get to Dak.

I glanced around, hoping to see Patrewski or Morales and saw Dak staring at Lily. His shoulders seemed bowed under an invisible weight. He looked down at his grandmother for a long moment, then at Lily again, studying his sister almost dispassionately. Finally, Dak broke off his somber reflection and turned back to the old woman huddled over her soup.

Lily never even noticed.

Sovath had also been watching Dak, and she said, "He must choose the grandmother."

"Why not Lily? Can't he do both?"

"It is Asian way. The elder has more value than the young, even though both are loved. The grandmother you must always respect. She cannot be replaced when she is gone. But more children can be made. I think the grandmother holds the boy tight to her. If Dak must help either his sister or his grandmother, he will choose the grandmother."

"I couldn't do that," I murmured.

Sovath smiled. "What would you do?"

"I'd go for the one most hurt and get someone else to help the other one."

"How practical... and how American," she said, but there was no criticism in her voice. The gang leader had separated Lily from the other three girls who were gathered in a giggling cluster around his buddy and was edging her toward the door leading to the hall and foyer.

Sovath touched my arm. "Let us be Dak's helpers."

Gratefully, I followed her.

We weren't more than a few feet from the two when Patrewski appeared next to them. The people who had been chatting close by melted away, apparently sensing trouble, leaving the three alone. Sovath and I kept our distance, too. Morales had sidled up to the buddy and his flock. I didn't know where the two detectives had come from but admired their quiet efficiency. After some low earnest talking back and forth between Patrewski and the leader, the young man jerked his head at his buddy and they stormed out.

Patrewski tried to keep Lily talking to him, but she started crying and ran out.

Sovath and I went after her, searching the hall, in the restrooms and outside on the front steps, but we couldn't find her.

I asked, "Do you think Lily went with the gang leader?"

Sovath shook her head. "Let us hope her friends are with her and not him."

For a while, the drama with Lily had taken my mind off Sang's threat, but I had to tell her. I asked her to go with me where we could talk alone. We found a private visitation room with an old-fashioned settee and cushioned armchairs and sat down.

I asked, "Where are your daughters?" Putting off for the moment, what I had to tell her.

"With Phourim." A rare lightheartedness crinkled her face. "I told him he would lose his job--and his head--if anything happened to them. He almost has the money he needs to bring his bride here. He will not risk his job."

"Sovath..." I stopped.

It wasn't only Lily who might be altering the course of a life because of an impulsive action. When I had stood up to Sang earlier in the courtyard, I'd committed the ultimate offense: I made him lose face. Briefly, I'd even broken his power until he gained the advantage by threatening to fire Sovath. How could I explain what I had set in motion?

My friend watched me with the wariness of someone expecting bad news.

"Sovath, do you remember when you came back and got Saray, and I went outside? I ran into Sang. We had a kind of fight, and well... I humiliated him. He may hurt you to get back at me. He said they--I think Chhun and Sang-- are planning to have you fired."

Sovath had listened without any expression. I took a breath, and said, "There's more. Sang said that you had served your purpose. He didn't say anything more specific than that, but I feel you could be in harm's way."

She shrugged slightly. "It was only a matter of time."

Her reaction threw me. I had expected anger or tears.

Almost as an afterthought, she ask, "Tell me exactly what he said."

I went through everything: that she wasn't Khmer, about Rick being made head of the agency, and Sang's resentment at my meddling with the police because Sovath had brought me into the picture.

I stood up and paced in front of the settee where she sat, her hands crossed, palms down in her lap. "I tried apologizing, and at the end I warned him that the police had you and your family under guard. I thought it might scare him off."

She asked, "What was this humiliating thing you did to him?"

"Pushed him away when he tried his mesmerizing act."

Sovath gasped. "He put a spell on you?"

I shook my head, smiling sheepishly. "Actually, I crossed my eyes at him. Like this! It broke his concentration."

Sovath's musical laughter rippled in the room, its sadness echoed.

Sighing, she drew slender fingers over her brow. "Do you think that is the end of Mr. Sang's power with you?"

"I think so, because I am an outsider and because I'm in contact with the police. However, for the Cambodian community... As long as it remains insulated and filled with superstition--I think not. Am I wrong?"

115

She leaned her head back against the settee, and said, "Please stop walking, Bridg, and sit down."

I plunked myself in the chair across from her.

Sovath straightened in the settee and began talking as if giving a recitation.

"When I joined the agency as its director, I wanted to make a difference for my people, to find them jobs, help our children stay in school. For many kids, this is hard. They do not see themselves as wanted by the teachers; they do not see their lives in the books they read. Why do they care about a prince named *Hamlet* who culturally lived in a time and place as far away as another universe? Even if their parents speak English, they cannot read the language well enough to assist their children do homework. The mother who has bad nightmares does not understand why her son needs Nike shoes to be like other kids, or why he joins a gang to belong.

"The adults may live in Seabell, yet they are prisoners here just as much as they were in Cambodia under the Khmer Rouge. Only now they are prisoners to old traditions that separate the parents and the children. Many of our clients came from the rural villages, not the cities of the rich or educated who Pol Pot killed. The lives of the country people were simple and good. The children obeyed and parents arranged marriages. Love came afterwards, over time, and everybody knew their role. If a man was not good to his wife and drank too much and beat her, the relatives and the village solved the problem. Sometimes it was as easy as the neighbors standing outside the house of the family. The man would not beat the wife for fear the noise would bring his neighbors' disapproval. No one wanted to be shunned and cast out of the village's circle. Here in America, that is all gone."

Sovath leaned forward. "Sang will be able to control because the old ones need him. He is part of their past that they hold onto for good or bad. Change will come only with the young, the second generation. Hasn't that always been true for the newcomer to your country?"

"And your daughters, too?"

"They are my hope. I died in Cambodia. My new life lives in them ... Hold my hands, Bridg."

She held them out. "Take them. Look at them."

Holding them, I realized that we had never shaken hands before because I would have remembered the rough striated ridges and fibrous welts on her palms. When I turned them over, ugly red and gray translucent scars crisscrossed her palms and fingers, as if a sharp knife had repeatedly slashed them.

Sovath said, "I cannot straighten my fingers without pain, these hands made by the Khmer Rouge. When I danced as a girl, I could bend my fingers back until they curved like the crescents of new moons. This was very important because when we danced in the temple, our hands told the sacred stories of our people. But the Khmer Rouge did not want us to remember them. They cut our roots, and they cut my hands."

She pulled them away. "I can endure, but I cannot hope for myself anymore."

We stayed in the room for another twenty minutes, some of it waiting while Sovath wept. After a while, we talked about what to do next. I sensed a relief in Sovath, as if the waiting for what she had feared was finally over. She began making plans, confident that with her bi-lingual skills and bachelor's degree she could find other work. I promised to hook her up with contacts in Seattle's nonprofit community.

"What about Rick?" I asked. "He's in love with you, you know."

"Poor Rick. He does not know that he hangs onto a tiger's tail at SEAAA."

"He really wasn't after your job."

She nodded. "He is nice in many ways and smart in some. But he will not last. Chhun and the board will use him until they have the person they want. Then Rick will be gone, too."

"Maybe he needs you beside him because you can be tough where he is not."

"I have been married two times. My heart is too dry to be good for a man anymore."

I thought for a moment about how I was pushing Sovath into Rick's arms and realized that I might be trying to matchmake her to a murderer.

I blurted out, "Sovath, do you think Rick had anything to do with the Lys' deaths?"

She didn't answer right away. "He has a secret part to him, but it came with him to the agency. As Ly's supervisor, he was fair. I told Rick I did not need his protection, and that he should not make the second guess about my decisions."

I smiled inwardly at Sovath's quaint way of telling Rick to back off.

"Would he have killed Ly because he was pressuring you to marry your daughters to his friends? Rick told me that Chhun and Ly were doing that."

Cold amusement shone in Sovath's eyes. "I took care of that. Ly and Chhun believed that I have accepted a large dowry for the girls from rich Americans who live in New York. I said that they were very powerful, something like the Mafia, and would do terrible things to Ly and Chhun if the girls were spoiled in any way. I said that the Americans weren't like Cambodian men and wanted the girls to finish their schooling before they married them."

I laughed. "You are a ferocious, scheming mother hen."

Sovath reflected for a moment. "You asked me if I thought Rick was involved in the Lys' deaths. The answer is no. Hahn Ly and his wife were shot, and Rick would never use a gun. He does not believe in weapons of war. He would not be friends to anyone who used guns. I am sure," she added, with a decisive nod.

I agreed that her assessment tied in with Rick's history of coming from an anti-war group.

"What about the others in the agency, Sovath? You must tell the police your suspicions. What you know about Ly's relationships. Or let me tell Detective Patrewski what you told me. It's the fifth day since the Lys died. If the police don't get leads now, I don't think the murders will be solved."

"I know. The longer the truth lies hidden in our community, the deeper it will be buried. Perhaps now I am free to talk."

Feeling we'd successfully hurdled an obstacle, I told Sovath that I was meeting Patrewski, and she gave her permission for him to call her at home.

Suddenly, we heard loud, excited voices and running footsteps in the hall. The door flew open and Rick burst in. "Thank God I found you!"

Sovath sprang up, her hands to her mouth. "My daughters! Something has happened to them."

Rick rushed to her. "No. No. I didn't mean to scare you like that. They're okay. I gave Phourim twenty bucks to take them to the Starbucks on 35th."

He put his hands on her shoulders and guided her to the settee where they sat down.

"It's Dak's grandmother. I think she's dead."

"What?" Sovath and I said together.

"I guess she had a convulsion and passed out. The two cops are doing CPR on her. But they can't get a pulse. The paramedics are on their way."

Rick's hands were shaking and Sovath, without thinking, cupped his hands in hers.

A haunting fear in his eyes came out in a hoarse whisper. "Everything's going wrong, and I can't stop it!"

When we had entered the banquet room, we went immediately to Patrewski, who, with Morales and another funeral home employee, had formed a kind of perimeter around the working paramedics who had gotten there quickly.

Bedlam and babble had broken out with excited versions of what had happened being shouted in Khmer. Apparently, Dak had thrown himself on his grandmother's body and had to be pried off her before Patrewski and Morales could administer CPR. Meanwhile, the aunt, crying and demanding that Lily be found, had sent friends and relatives streaming down halls and out of the funeral home. The din of frightened and alarmed mourners threatened the fragile order that the dark-suited funeral director and his second-in-command were restoring.

The paramedics, their gear spread around them, still attended to the grandmother. Chhun and Sang stood by haranguing people. They could have been telling the crowd to stay out of the way or might have been keeping the hysteria going. I was glad that Sang was focused on something other than me. Somewhere, though, in the midst of the crowd, a sound began swelling like a tsunami until it washed over the room, leaving stricken faces in its wake. *Pset puhl*!

Patrewski turned to Sovath, "What'd they say? What's going on?"

She had turned as pale as the porcelain bowl lying upside down near the grandmother's body. "*Pset puhl* means poison, poison mushroom. They say she had bad karma and is dead from mushroom in the soup."

Patrewski looked at Morales who had moved closer to hear the answer. The two of them went to the paramedics, who had stopped working on the grandmother. Patrewski said something, and the one paramedic shook his head. Patrewski and Morales came over to us. He said, "We gotta get these people back into the chapel and seal off the area."

Morales nodded. "We'd better call in the crime scene unit."

Patrewski hesitated a second then jerked his head in agreement, muttering, "I hope to God this is a false alarm."

Morales spread her arms, moving people back and toward the door. She looked at Sovath, "Can you explain to everybody that we need them to stay and to wait in the chapel?"

Sovath said, "We will help." She pushed her way to Chhun and spoke sharply to him. With an imperious lift of her chin, she also rattled something to Sang standing next to him. The men didn't move, and she repeated herself, eyes blazing. Finally, Chhun backed away and started herding people. Sang stood his ground, but so did Sovath. Slowly, acting as if it wasn't worth the argument, he relented and started gathering up people. I turned away quickly, so that he wouldn't catch me watching.

Rick was already moving through the crowd, his face calm, politely explaining the situation to those who spoke English and leading them to the chapel.

Patrewski grabbed me and said, "Get the kid. Take him somewhere safe while we investigate what's happened. Dammit! If this is a crime scene, it's already contaminated. We could be here for hours. Look, I want to talk to Dak before anyone, including his aunt, changes his story." Squeezing my arm tighter, Patrewski added, "Don't ask him anything about what he saw. I want it fresh."

I didn't need his pincer grip for emphasis. "Do you want us to wait here in the building?"

"No! Get him away from here. Maybe he's next."

Patrewski rejected the idea of Dak and me hanging out at the SEAAA offices or staying with anyone connected to the agency. In the end, we agreed that I should check the two of us into the Stouffer Madison in Seattle and leave the room's phone number on Patrewski's pager. He'd get to us as soon as he could.

"In the meantime, don't talk to anyone, don't say anything," he warned.

Patrewski needn't have worried about Dak's talking; the boy didn't say a word in the car, in the hotel lobby when we registered, or in the elevator where he stared at the carpet's fleur-de-lis pattern. When we got up to the room, he slumped in a chair by the window, the shine of youth rubbed dull in his eyes.

How could I console this sixteen-year-old boy whose parents had been shot, his grandmother possibly poisoned, and his sister run off to who knew where? I didn't talk much to Dak, not because of Patrewski's warning, but because I had little to say that could comfort him.

I looked in the mirror over the lowboy chest and saw a tired woman in a "Mother Mary" dress: high-necked, long-sleeved, with lace collar and cuffs. Moodily, I realized that the way I was dressed, it could have been my mother in the mirror. I sighed. The pain in my sinuses made my teeth ache, and I longed to be home, sipping tea and perusing the latest Raintree catalog while Narvik slept by my feet.

122

Dak had his head pillowed on his arms. I would have shucked the whole mess and gone home if I hadn't agreed to be responsible for him. With his shaved head and skinny body, he looked as forlorn as a sheared lamb.

"Would you like to eat?" I asked. "I can order room service."

Dak shrugged one shoulder. I picked up the phone and ordered off the menu next to it, stuff that should please a teenager: a hamburger, French fries, Coke, a cinnamon roll and Caesar salad and tea for me. What he didn't eat, the pigeons could have.

"Would you like to watch TV?"

He didn't answer, but I pressed the on button anyway, found a Fraser rerun on Channel 11 and turned the volume low.

I had not seen Dak cry; not after he had been beaten up, not at the funeral and not afterwards. Except for that scene with Lily and concern for his grandmother, he had hidden most of his emotions. The pain from them, however, had taken a toll. He sat like an arthritic old man whose joints hurt.

I cast about for a safe topic for conversation and decided that getting him to talk about school would be okay. That shouldn't plant any false ideas concerning his grandmother's death.

"Would you like me to call your school on Monday and let them know you'll be out for a few days?"

He mumbled, "No. I can't miss class."

"Your teachers will let you do catch up."

He stirred. "I can't. I've got straight A's so far. Besides, I have to take tests tomorrow."

"It's Saturday. There's no school."

"I'm taking APE tests for advanced placement. If I pass them, then I can take classes next fall that will count toward college. Tomorrow's the only time I can take the tests."

"School's important, but there's your sister and ... all that's happened."

He straightened in his chair. "Don't you think I know? I tried with Lily. She won't listen to me."

He added, "I've got to keep going. My mother and grandmother wanted me to be a lawyer so that I'd bring honor back to our house. My grandmother told me ... she told me," he repeated. "I was the only one left who could make the circle better, to go to a higher level. I must do the right thing!"

"All right. It's all right," I soothed.

123

He waved his hands, brushing off my words. "Don't you see? If I chase after Lily, I can't keep up my grades. The only way I'm going to get into a good college is with high SATs and scholarships. I'm not like the stupid "Cambodes" that Lily thinks are cool. Nothing's going to stop me. Not anymore."

Dak said "Cambode" as a racial slur. Phourim had told me that the Cambodian kids who fell behind in school usually dropped out by eighth grade, making fun of their friends who remained.

He explained once, "The bad ones in school are like a bucket of crabs. When one try to climb, the others pull it down."

Dak said, "Most of the parents want their kids to be doctors or lawyers. How many do you think will make it?" His mouth twisted into a sneer. "This many?" He held up one finger. "Just me," he said.

I sat down on the side of the bed close to his chair and touched his shoulder. " Dak. I'm sure your parents knew how hard you worked and were very proud of you."

"I don't care what my father thought," he said, his voice rising. "What I did was for my mother ... my grandmother," he said, and started sobbing.

Dak's stored-up anguish gushed out. He cried with wrenching gulps, trying to stop, then breaking down again only to cry harder. Gradually, his sobbing slowed until he hung his head, exhausted.

His story came out halting and low. "My father was a bad man. Lily liked him because he made her his favorite, his little pet. He bought her pretty things, but never my mother. When I was a kid, he hit my mother all the time when she did things he didn't like or fixed his food wrong. He'd get drunk and talk about his other women and tell my mother she was ugly. He said he only married her to get to America. He called my grandmother names, *sapchech*, a cockroach. That is a very bad thing to do. One night when I was twelve and he slapped my mother, I started to call 911, and he stopped because he was afraid of the police. I told him I would report him if he ever hurt my mother again. He knew I would call." Shuddering from the after effects of his crying, he added, "He made my mother grow old and sad. I hated him."

We sat without talking, until room service brought our food, setting it on the table in front of Dak. He ate a few bites of his hamburger, and I drank my tea. We were both too upset to eat much.

It was close to seven o'clock, almost two hours since we'd left the funeral home, and Dak was exhausted. I said, "Why don't you lie down and rest? You'll feel better afterwards. It might be another hour or more

before we hear from Detective Patrewski. I'll wake you when he comes."
I pulled down the bedspread.

Dak didn't need urging. He slipped off his shoes, lay down on his side, and was asleep in minutes. I tucked the spread over his shoulders and sat down at the table.

I picked at my limp salad while thinking about what to do. I didn't want to go downstairs. Patrewski might call. Besides, if Dak awakened and found me gone, he might take off.

Feeling anxious in ways that needed sorting out, I picked up my purse and went into the bathroom, leaving the door ajar so I could hear Dak's steady breathing. I put down the toilet seat lid and sat on it. Taking out my cell phone, I tapped the speed dial number to C. J.'s. I needed to bounce some troubling ideas off his hard Norwegian noggin.

"And how is St. Bridget doing?" C. J. responded. "Overwrought from too much soul saving?"

I had just recounted the sequence of events that had led to me calling him from my cell phone in the bathroom. "It's bodies, not souls, we're trying to save--or keep alive," I answered. "Besides, Buddhists don't believe in a one-shot heaven or hell deal. To them, souls are on a wheel, reincarnating until they can get off in Nirvana. Then they're released from misery and all desires. I have to believe, though, that Dak's mother's soul is at peace. His grandmother's too, if she did die." I sighed. "Right now it's the sleeping Dak that I'm concerned about."

"What does your viscera say?"

"You mean my gut instinct?" I countered. While C. J. could be blunt, he also enjoyed playing with words for effect.

I went on, "Dak's smart and almost obsessive, living up to his family and cultural obligations. I feel sorry for him and Lily, but I'm also getting some disturbing vibes. You know, it never entered my mind before to think of the kids being connected to the murders. However, in the last few hours..."

"You've learned something?"

"No, just bits and pieces of information. Lily apparently doted on her father, so I can't see any reason for her to want him dead. Dak, though, just told me he hated his father, and it was he who came home and discovered his parents. Could he have killed them?"

"Could your imagination be getting the better of you?"

"Yes. It could," I admitted.

"Where is the logic in what you've learned?"

"Bless me if I know. The sticking point is his wife. Why was she killed? Ly had enemies. He was involved in illegal deals and headed up a death camp. He would have enemies. But his wife? In a way it's almost as if she was a nonentity: a captive most of her life to events. Her marriage was one of convenience and her husband abused her... and you know the saddest part?"

"No."

"I never heard her name--and didn't ask. She was just Ly's wife or Dak and Lily's mother. Not her own person. She passed through life barely wrinkling it."

C. J. waited a moment before venturing, "So why was she shot?"

"I've asked myself that question over and over. She showed no signs of struggle. Other than the bullet hole in her forehead, she looked peaceful enough ... perhaps she had a look of resignation."

"Is that Celtic hyperbole at work, again?"

"Don't rile me with fancy words. It comes down to the fact that she was not the primary target. It was Ly. She was with him and was killed because she was a witness. Maybe all her passive conditioning made her accept this last act of fate."

"Could her husband have killed her, and then the boy shot his father?"

Reluctantly, I thought about that possibility, and said, "If Dak caught his father in the act, he might have retaliated and somehow got his father's gun away from him. Or had one himself. But I can't imagine a man who ran a death camp calmly letting his 16-year-old son shoot him." I shook my head at the flood of images, including the one of the Lys and others of Dak over the last few days. "I don't think the boy's guilty of shooting his father," I said. "He's been distraught, mostly worrying about his grandmother and his responsibilities."

"So you don't think you're holed up with a murderer at the Stouffer-Madison?"

C. J.'s question was a reminder to be careful, but he'd never say the words directly. To do so would have broken one of our friendship's taboos: telling the other what to do.

After a quick mental review of Dak's appearance and whether his clothes had shown the bulky outline of a gun, I said more confidently, "That's right. Besides, he looks like a famine relief poster boy. I could push him over and sit on him if he gave me trouble."

"Have you anyone else in mind for all this villainy?"

"Rick is acting as if he's under some kind of strain. After he reported about the grandmother keeling over, he said, 'Everything is coming apart.' I think he was talking about his life. My sense is that Chhun and Sang have something on him. Sang told me in the courtyard that he and Chhun were going to get rid of Sovath and put Rick into the ED spot. Apparently, the two men feel they can control him. Rick is probably afraid of being exposed and losing Sovath."

"You have no idea what his secret could be? Or if it's connected to the Lys?"

"I've wondered if Rick has a wife somewhere. He knows Sovath would never tolerate going with a married man. Or maybe he embezzled on his last job. He said his friends gave him the references for the job at

SEAAA because his former employer wouldn't. Rick was part of an anti-nuclear protest at the Bangor Submarine Base that got out of hand. But maybe that wasn't a true story. He also said SEAAA was just a transition job to help him clean up his employment history." Thinking out loud, I added, "If Patrewski ever calls, I'll ask him if he ran a check on Rick's background."

I had filled in C. J. about the possibility of the grandmother being poisoned. C. J. brought the subject up by saying, "Sang sounds quite capable of poisoning an old woman."

"I wouldn't trust him if he were looking me straight in the eye. Especially then." Shuddering, I said, "I never want to test his hypnotizing powers again."

"How do you feel about that?"

"Surprised ... and relieved. "I don't think I'd have the courage to try it a second time, though."

"The mind is a powerful instrument."

I didn't know if C. J. was referring to Sang's or my own. My stomach tightened, and I blew out my breath to relax. "Let's get back to Rick. On a scale of one to 10, his mysterious motive scores a seven. But, as far as shooting Ly or his wife, I've given him a six. After all, he was involved in the peace movement."

"That's no guarantee." C. J. snorted.

"Perhaps. However, Sang and Chhun are a different kettle of fish. More like piranhas."

"Is that more opinion or fact?"

"It's a mix of smoking guns and patterns. The smoking guns are in Sang and Chhun's hands pointing to the illegal activities they're involved in, at least according to Phourim and Sovath. Phourim hints of blackmail. I know Ly had threatened to expose Phourim's unreported earnings from picking bear grass and now he fears that Chhun will do the same. With Sovath, she's uneasy that Chhun might be engineering welfare scams, the kind the newspapers write about every couple of years.

"The patterns are the under-the-counter schemes that spring up with every new wave of immigrants or refugees. Their members become invisible in cultural enclaves. The more enterprising ones like Chhun and Ly and Sang size up the American systems and work them illegally."

C. J. said, "You're not saying anything new. It's the immigrant story--except maybe for the Norwegians."

I moved over to sit on the side of the bathtub and took off my shoes, wiggling my toes, wishing I had my overnight bag with me.

I said, "Now wouldn't that be a good Internet project for you--ferreting out the underbelly of Norwegian America?"

"Not likely, dear."

"At any rate, it's a good bet that Chhun and Sang brokered services on how to defraud welfare and extort hush money from their customers afterwards. The two could launder the money through the temple or just keep the cash under their mattresses." I stopped, trying to catch an idea that flitted by, but wouldn't pin down. "The temple would make a good base of operations, though I don't think the monks are involved."

C. J. said, "You have no proof."

An unfortunate reality, I admitted.

I said, "Working at a hand-to-mouth social service agency and presiding at pre-wedding ceremonies and funerals won't cut it for Chhun and Sang. They're too hungry for power. That's why I think it's possible they killed Ly. He was a partner with them. He could have double-crossed them or held out money. Maybe Ly had gambling winnings in the apartment. Of course, the kids said nothing had been stolen."

"You believe them?" C. J. was beginning to sound testier. His leg must be bothering him.

I stood up and traced the pattern on the floor tiles, heel to toe. "If it turns out that the grandmother was poisoned, then it could have been Chhun. He was by her while she ate. Though poisoning does seem more Sang's style."

"Why would Sang go after this poor elderly woman?" C. J. sounded indignant.

"Because the grandmother saw him kill her daughter and Ly. But if she did, why didn't he silence her at the same time? With his power, it would have been easy to subdue and kill her. She was getting feeble, even senile. Perhaps he thought he could intimidate her to stay quiet, but then found she was becoming irrational. Then again, why wait and risk her talking? Why poison her food in the middle of the funeral reception?"

C. J. said, " I saw on the Net that NASA researchers are mapping images that indicate a 1,000 temples in Cambodia are buried or obscured by the dense forest. From the images, the researchers speculate that the Angkor had a million people around 1100 A.D." Sounding worried, he added, "Don't underestimate a culture that old. We round-eyes have a poor track record when it comes to understanding other cultures."

"I know. What is, is not what it appears to be."

"That's so enigmatic, it sounds like me."

"You know, C.J., the first time I met Patrewski, I said that to understand the Khmer people he should study their fables. That they had one like Little Red Riding Hood, only the wolf was a tiger. At the time, I was referring to Sang and his seemingly innocent offer of help. You're right about Americans having a hard time understanding the Asian mind."

C. J. chuckled. "I can imagine his reaction."

"It wasn't pretty to see." I laughed.

"Do you believe in Jung's theory of a collective cultural consciousness?"

"I guess I do," thinking of the Irish melancholy that permeated my way of looking at life.

C. J said, "Knowing the collective consciousness of the Khmer might be a key to the killer's motive."

I nodded though he couldn't see me. Remembering our conversation in the cafe, I said, "Maybe control is a big part of the Cambodian consciousness." Embarrassed, I laughed. "Or it might not be."

C. J. caught his breath as if in pain.

I asked, "Is the leg bothering you tonight?"

"A bit."

I had planned to ask him feed Narvik; we lived less than five minutes apart, and he knew where I kept my extra house key. But I didn't want to ask him now.

He volunteered instead. "It's getting late, your detective hasn't come, yet. Why don't you stay in Seattle tonight? You've already booked the room. I'll go feed that magnificent mutt of yours. I might even bring her home with me if she fusses for company."

I smiled, knowing that it was C. J. who wanted the company. He'd probably let Narvik sleep in the bedroom with him. He might grouse, but she would climb up on the bed, stretch out next to him and ease his pain with her warmth.

Which was more consolation than I would find tonight.

You Can't Outdistance What's Running Inside You
Chapter 20

Talking to C. J. brought balance to my outlook. He restored perspective because he didn't rattle. In a world that seemed to have as many flakes swirling around as a child's Christmas scene globe shaken upside down, C. J. was solid.

While I was in the bathroom freshening my face, a light rap on the hotel room door startled me. For a moment, I panicked thinking someone, the killer, had come after Dak. However, when I looked through the door's peephole, I saw Patrewski and let him in.

I put a finger to my lips and nodded at Dak fast asleep. Patrewski looked at him and said in a low voice, "Where can we talk so he won't hear?"

"It's either the bathroom or outside in the hall," I answered, covering my surprise at the change in him since the afternoon. The whites of his eyes had a dingy yellowish cast to them, and the color of his face didn't remind me anymore of fresh-turned earth in the spring but of yesterday's ashes. "Are you feeling okay?"

He shrugged. "I've felt better. Let's step out for a minute."

I slipped my cardkey into my pocket and took it with me. In the hallway, Patrewski leaned against the wall beside the closed door, fished out a cigar and stuck it unlit in his mouth. Wearily, he asked, "How's the kid?"

"Worn out and pretty upset. What have you found out? Was the grandmother poisoned?"

Patrewski said, "We think so, but it will take a couple of days at least for the toxicology report. We sent in the mushroom pieces we found in the spilled soup. Right now, we're in a wait-and-see mode."

"No one else got sick from eating at the party?"

"Nope. There was some hysteria and stomach pains. But if someone ate a poisoned mushroom, they'd should be in emergency by now." Jerking his head toward the room where Dak lay sleeping, Patrewski asked, "Did the kid say anything?"

I appraised him before answering; weighing what he needed to know and what should stay with me. A stubble of gray whiskers covered his chin and cheeks, and I realized it was the first flaw I'd seen in Patrewski's grooming since I'd met him.

"Just school stuff," I replied. "He has to do exceptionally well in order to hold up the family's honor. My sense is that in someway he feels he has failed his grandmother, and he's determined to make up for it. He's also sure that Lily's fallen in with the wrong kinds of kids--probably gang types, and ... his father had abused Dak's mother, at least until the boy stood up to him one night and said he'd call the cops on his dad."

There. That was the truth. If Patrewski saw a lead in the information, he'd follow it. I wouldn't mention C. J's theory that Ly might have shot the mother and Dak the father. Patrewski must have thought of that possibility already.

"Yeah. It figures. In a homicide, the first person we look at is the spouse and whether there was an abusive relationship. Usually, though, jealousy or money is the motive behind the killing. In Ly's case, he would have had a primo reason; he was the beneficiary on his wife's half-million dollar life insurance policy. It was taken out four months ago. He had big gambling losses; the insurance money would have covered them. Too bad he got knocked off, too. It ruins a perfect motive."

"Will the insurance go to the kids now?"

"Probably. We found the insurance policy in his papers at work. But we didn't find a will." He paused, and added dryly, "If he left money to his kids, then I guess they didn't need my fifty bucks at that bereavement ceremony, after all."

I glanced at Patrewski, but it was his sardonic humor speaking. Guiltily, I realized that I'd been a piker compared to him. I only gave twenty.

He went on, "We've questioned the aunt, Sovath, Chhun and others. None of them knew of any will, for her or Ly. It's not something usually done in their culture. 'Course he might have left a bundle to one of them, and who'd tell? It would give the person a motive. We've got someone over at the Lys' apartment going through everything again, at least to see if a lawyer's name or an accountant's name turns up."

I had been facing him as we talked, but now I shifted position and stood next to him, my back to the wall and arms folded across my chest. I asked, "Do you think someone is trying to kill the whole family? Are the kids in danger?"

"We can't rule out the possibility. Except the daughter and grandmother were in the apartment when the Lys were killed. Why weren't they shot, too? We've got too many inconsistencies in this case."

Inconsistencies. C. J. had been on target: straight-ahead thinking would never work. The trail to the killer was a spiral path. Still, I felt that we were on the path, not off it. The end just wasn't in sight.

"Did you find Lily?" I asked.

"No. Morales pushed Lily's girl friends hard to find out where they thought she might go. It's a good thing they hadn't left the funeral yet. Our best bet is that Lily will call one of them and say where she is. Morales 'counseled' the girls about obstructing an investigation and advised them to call us when Lily made contact." Patrewski shrugged. "It may work."

I said, "I've found out some information and a name that might help. Not about Lily, but her father."

"What is it?"

"Apparently Ly ran a death camp for the Khmer Rouge in the jungles of Siem Reap Province. Most of the people in that kind of place where tortured and executed for no more reason than that they wore glasses or had been a teacher and were considered an intellectual. Any surviving family would have been glad to revenge their loved one and kill Ly."

"And painfully so," Patrewski said, looking even more weary than before. "The memories don't stop. They play tricks sometimes, but they jab at you until you do something about them. That part of the world gets under your skin like a parasite--like malaria. It can lay quiet for long periods, but you never get rid of it completely."

"You were there? Vietnam?"

He nodded. "Two tours. I was dumb and young and came down with this. Patrewski gestured toward his jaundiced face.

"You have malaria," I said, making it a statement. "Shouldn't you be in bed or a hospital?"

"I'm taking medication." Then he added, as if I were the cause, "Aggravation doesn't help, and I've got a lot of that now."

It didn't take much analyzing to know that Patrewski would have rejected any demonstration of sympathy so I answered, "Not from me, you don't. In fact, I have my own aggravation including that fact that I'm sharing a hotel room with a sixteen-year-old kid and at my expense."

"Yeah, well, I'll see what I can do about that. You do kind of have him in protective custody."

"Why didn't you tell me that first day at the police station that you knew something Southeast Asian cultures? You must have been there the better part of four years."

"I don't talk about that time. It's history."

"This case has to bring some of it up," I said, and watched Patrewski chomp hard on his cigar. The twinge of sympathy I'd felt for him gave way to a greater curiosity. "Did you get into Cambodia at all?"

He straightened up from his slouch against the wall and glared at me. "What is this, quiz time? Just give me your information, the name you have."

Pushing Patrewski for personal details was only irritating him, so I stopped. I didn't want anyone nosing around in my past, either. On the other hand, maybe his stint in Vietnam was linked to his concern for Dak that went beyond pure duty. I nodded for my own benefit. Patrewski might be a great cop, but I'd spent forty-eight years figuring out people and what made them tick just so I could get along with them.

I'd bide my time, but I'd have my day with Patrewski.

Ignoring his anger, I said, "I wanted to talk to you at the funeral because I've learned a couple of things. The first one may be nothing, but I overheard Sang and Chhun. They were talking in Khmer, but they included the word 'Richmond' several times, and each time they said it, they snickered. I thought it was odd."

Patrewski looked skeptical. "They snickered. You got anything more than a hunch?"

I answered, "No. Maybe it's a place where they've got contacts or a doctor whose dirty, involved in their welfare scams. It just didn't sound right," I added, knowing my answer sounded lame.

"What else do you have?"

"Ly's former sister-in-law. She's married to the president of SEAAA's board. She should be a good source to know about Ly's life. Even if she's not close to him, I think the Cambodian rumor mill would keep her updated about him. I'm not sure how much English she has. You may need an interpreter--but don't take Sang."

"You still have a hang-up about him?"

"I do. But it's buried history, too. What's important for you to know is that he is supposed to have the evil eye, the power to use bad spirits. If the woman becomes afraid to speak up or fears you because of Sang, you'll get nowhere. I've got her name and address inside. I can get it for you."

Patrewski nodded, and said, "Okay. Let's go back."

I took out the cardkey from my pocket and moved to the door. Over my shoulder, I asked, "What happens next?"

"I talk to the kid, you talk to Morales. She's waiting downstairs in the bar. You don't mind?"

I minded. Not the bar, but chatting with his partner. "What for?"

"We need to question Dak and you. We didn't have time at the funeral home. I don't want her handling the boy. I've made progress with him; he's opening up to me. The two of you can talk. Maybe woman-to-woman, something enlightening will come out."

"I wouldn't say that she and I were ready for a cozy girl chat. Why can't I wait for you to interview me?"

"She's a little spooked right now, thinking she's on the back burner in this investigation. She's new in the department, looking to make her bones on a case that could become high profile, get media coverage. I don't want Morales rattling bars--or people--before a few more pieces start to jell. She thinks you and I are tight, so you're my trade off. I do Dak and she does you."

Patrewski's comment about being tight was some sort of concession, although I wasn't sure over what. Realistically, I couldn't refuse to be questioned by the police, but I hunted for some leverage in the situation. After all, I had a vested interest in the case, including the whopping bill for Rick's collect long distance call from the hospital and paying for the hotel room to stash Dak away safely. I deserved some answers.

"I'll meet her, but I'm not volunteering information, and I want to talk to you afterwards."

Inside the room, I leaned over Dak and shook him gently. "Wake up. Detective Patrewski's here."

Dak bolted upright, flinging my hand to one side as he did. He rubbed his face and then saw Patrewski standing at the foot of the bed.

"It'll be okay, Dak," I said. "I'm going downstairs to talk to Detective Morales. I'll be back shortly."

With scared eyes but sullen face, Dak said, "I don't want to talk to anybody. I just want to go home."

Patrewski planted his cigar firmly in the corner of his mouth and said, "You'd better talk to me kid. The way things are looking, I'm the best thing you've got going right now." Then he looked at me and motioned toward the door.

I hesitated, though, and rested my hand on Dak's shoulder. "The two of you won't leave before I return, will you?"

Patrewski shook his head, but added, "It's your call. After you finish with Morales, you're free to go home. This situation is getting messy."

With a sinking heart, I had to acknowledge that he'd given me an exit line if I wanted to take it. And maybe I would have--if I'd been smart. After a moment, the only thing I could think of to say was, "In for a penny, in for a pound."

I didn't want to be interviewed by Morales. Despite my recent insight as to why I felt antagonism toward her, it didn't prepare me to cope with her officiousness. Especially not on the spur of the moment and wearing a high-necked shirtwaist dress that made me look like her spinster aunt.

On the way down in the elevator, between the twenty-second and fourteenth floors, I worried about how to handle myself in the interview. Between the thirteenth and seventh floors, I rallied and told myself to get some gumption. Descending the last six floors, and alone in the elevator, I hitched up my panty hose, and smoothing my dress over my hips, straightened up my act and me. When the elevator door opened with a discreet whoosh unto the lobby, I was ready. Morales's bust size and career plans were her business. I wouldn't get into a hissing match with her--not on either front and smiled at the double entendre as I strode toward the lounge.

The Stouffer's bar is divided into two distinct areas: one has an enclosed dark ambience, cozy enough for romantic assignations; while the other side is bright enough to read a newspaper by and opens onto the lobby. Morales sat at one of the small tables there. She seemed to have a penchant for placing herself near shrubbery and sat next to a large ficus, its drooping branches and leathery leaves an effective visual screen to the next table. She also sat with her back to the wall, which gave her a wide-angle view of the room and lobby. She waved me over.

After I sat down, the bartender came to our table and I ordered a Bailey's. Morales already had a glass in front of her and refreshed it with mineral water from a blue Ty Nant bottle. Unlike Patrewski whose face had sagged with fatigue upstairs, Morales's was crisply controlled. She still had on her Nordstrom's suit, and nary a crease in it or her face admitted to a long, tiring day.

While the bartender set my Bailey's down and made change, Morales looked around, and I couldn't help but contrast her to Sovath. In my mind, they were night and day: Morales all bold energy, charging the atmosphere with her presence, her hair reflecting iridescent colors like sunlight on a blackbird's wings; Sovath was rod-thin steel wrapped in soft compliance, subdued like moonlight on deep and murky waters. I wondered how they'd match up in a confrontation and decided it would be even money.

After the bartender left, Morales turned toward me and pulled out a pad and pen. She eyed me for a moment, taking in my dress and lace collar.

"Patrewski tell you what this is about?"

"He said you needed to question me about what happened at the funeral. Apparently, the grandmother was poisoned, but you haven't confirmed it, yet. And you don't know if it's an accident or murder."

"Anything else?"

I shook my head and caught a brief look of annoyance on her face. I swirled the swizzle stick in my Bailey's, cautioning myself to watch where her questions led. I didn't want to incriminate Dak, or anyone else unnecessarily, and frankly, I didn't want her to get a head start over Patrewski in the investigation. Although the two were a team, I didn't think Patrewski was rushing to judgment; I wasn't sure about his partner.

"What did the boy talk about with you?"

"Nothing about the funeral, just school."

"Did you ask him?"

"You mean about his grandmother's death? No."

Morales tapped her glass impatiently with manicured fingernails. "What do you think happened?"

"I really don't know. It could have been an accident. The Cambodians pick mushrooms all the time in the Cascades and foothills. A bad one could have gotten in the batch."

"If they pick them all the time, then a person should know the difference between good ones and bad ones."

"It seems that way."

Morales sipped her water, but kept her gaze steady on my face. She put her glass down and said, "There are something like twenty-five hundred kinds of mushrooms that grow in the region, and only five are deadly. The odds are long that one of the bad kind would end up in the soup."

I gave a noncommittal shrug, although I was impressed at what she'd found out.

"Who made the soup?" I asked.

"The aunt," Morales replied. "Do you know if Lily and Dak ever went mushroom picking with the family or friends?"

"I don't know. You'd have to ask them or their friends and relatives."

"We are," she said, tapping her fingernails again on the glass. "We asked Sovath to find out why the other Cambodians thought she'd eaten poisoned mushrooms. Do you know why?"

"No. Everything happened too quickly."

"They said it was because the grandmother had been sweating and shaking, complaining of stomach pains, and went into convulsions. I checked with the toxologist. She said that normally it takes several hours for symptoms like that from mushroom poisoning to show up. It could have happened faster though, because of her age and poor health. Her heart would never stand the strain."

Alarmed at the implications, I said, "You're saying she was poisoned before the funeral?"

Morales took another sip, before replying, a mannerism that was rapidly becoming irritating. Perhaps she did it to give herself time to think, or perhaps she thought it made me anxious, left me hanging, waiting for her next question. Finally, she said, "It's likely."

"Did you ask the aunt if the grandmother had eaten beforehand? She would have been at the apartment. The grandmother should have had a lot of people with her before the funeral."

"We're checking on that, too. Did you talk to the grandmother at the reception?"

"No. I planned to go over but got waylaid. "

"How was that?"

"First, Dak came over to talk to me and then Sovath dropped by and we chatted. After Lily ran out of the room crying, Sovath and I went looking for her. Then we came back inside and found a quiet place to talk. That's where Rick found us. He said the grandmother had passed out."

"What did you think?"

"I thought she'd had a heart attack."

Morales moved onto another direction with her next question, but I was willing to bet that like an IRS agent at an audit, she would circle back around to this point.

"Did you get anything to eat from the banquet tables?"

"No. Not even coffee."

"Who did you see at the tables?"

"Of the ones I knew, Lily and her girl friends, the two teens that had been at the Lys' apartment after the mourning ceremony. One of them was the AZ's leader." But then Morales would know that since she and Patrewski hassled the two at the reception. I presumed that he also had told her about the incident at the apartment with Dak and the AZ gang leader. And, Patrewski did send Morales to check out the gang connection to the killings.

Morales wrote on her pad, shielding it with her other hand.

I said, "Do you think the gang was involved in the murders?"

141

She ignored my question and asked, "Who did you see with the grandmother at the reception?"

"Dak, the aunt that I met at the apartment, others that I didn't know. Oh, yes, I did see Ban Chhun from the agency. He was leaning over her and talking."

"You don't like him."

"I didn't say that."

"No, but your face did. Would he have any reason to get rid of the old woman?"

Quickly, I decided that while I had wanted to go over my ideas with Patrewski first, maybe if I talked more freely with Morales, she'd return the favor. I needed to know what she'd found out checking with the gang task force.

"I'm betting that Chhun and Ly had a falling out over their business deals, and Chhun, with his buddy, Sang, are the most likely candidates for having killed the Lys. Maybe the grandmother found out and Chhun killed her, too."

"Why didn't Chhun kill the grandmother that night, the daughter, too? Two people or four. What would it have mattered?"

"I don't know," I said. "Perhaps the men thought the two were sleeping. Perhaps they thought Dak was coming home any minute, and they wanted to leave quickly. Or maybe they threatened the grandmother and she kept quiet to protect the kids. At any rate, I think the grandmother knew who killed her daughter and Ly and was silenced because she was losing it and beginning to babble."

"You seem sure of your theory."

Not that much because I could see the flaws.

I said, "Well, another possibility is that it was a gang home invasion because of the way the Lys were killed. What do you think? Is that still viable? You're the gang expert."

"Says who?'

"Patrewski."

For a bare second, she looked pleased, then slipped behind her professional mask of detachment. "The scene doesn't fit a home invasion. The place wasn't tossed and nothing was stolen. At least that's what we've been told by the kids. Add to that the fact that neither Lily nor the grandmother were raped or tortured. Of course, Lily could have been in on it with the gang."

"I can't believe that," I said, pushing my glass away from me.

"Patrewski says you know Lily and her brother pretty well. You took her side against the grandmother at the apartment."

"I wouldn't say it was taking sides," I answered, wondering if Patrewski had really given her that impression.

"Tell me about Lily's relationship with her father."

"She was close to him from what Dak said. I know she was very upset with Mindy Nguyen and repeated the events that happened at the apartment." I said, "I don't think Lily's her father's killer, though. What would be her motive?"

Morales ticked off a short list. "The parents were too controlling. She couldn't live her own life. Lily wouldn't be the first kid to shoot her parents because she couldn't get her own way. Or maybe she did it for money."

I looked away, then down at my drink, sipping it slowly. What had been so elusive when I talked to C. J. came back with frightening clarity. Guns. Most Cambodians did keep their money hidden in their homes--although not piles of it· like Morales inferred. They also kept guns. Phourim had said that he was one of the few Khmer people who wouldn't keep a gun or knife in his home. Why hadn't I thought of that before? Patrewski said no guns were found in the apartment. Didn't he find that suspicious? Did Ly have a gun there, and was it used to kill him and his wife? If so, who used it? Who has it?

Dak and Lily's faces popped up in my mind. I went back to what Morales had last mentioned. "Why would Lily need money? She's only fourteen years old."

"With a nineteen-year-old boyfriend who heads up the AZs. He could have put her up to it, or she let him in the apartment."

"No! She might run away with him, but I can't believe that she'd participate in her parents' murders. I nodded to myself, reacting more on instinct than reasoning and leaned back in my chair.

Maybe I seemed too smug in my conviction, because Morales snapped, "I can't believe you. You're so naive ... How can you be of any use to Patrewski?"

At least a dozen hot answers ran through my mind, but in the end I said none of them. I needed Morales as an ally in the investigation, so I could find out more. Besides, as a practical matter, she outweighed me. So, I said mildly, "I haven't the foggiest. You ask him."

Her face flushed and she turned away to stare out at the lobby. Morales appeared to regret her outburst, and I let that work on her for a bit.

Stretching out an olive branch, I said, "Patrewski seems to respect your knowledge about gangs."

"Did he really say that?" she asked.

"Pretty much," I assured her. "You've not been partners long, I gather."

"No. This is our first case together. He has a reputation for being a loner. Too bad he doesn't like having partners."

It was easy to laugh. "Particularly female ones, I bet."

She raised her eyebrows as if to say, "Isn't that the truth."

"I do get the impression that a person is excess baggage unless she measures up to a standard ... known only to him," I added.

"He was the same way at Seattle PD. He never kept a partner very long. The old-timers say one year working with Patrewski is better than three at the academy."

"Why did he join Seabell's Police Department?"

"I don't know. The story I heard was that he took leave three years ago to go to Vietnam with a couple of guys he served with in the Marines. Some say Patrewski flipped out while he was there. When he returned to Seattle, he resigned from the force. Said he needed a change. He joined Seabell after they got their own police department going. Guess he didn't know how to be anything else but a cop."

"How long have you been one?"

"Eight years. One year with Seabell PD."

"Have you always wanted to be in police work?"

Morales shook her head.

I looked down at my empty glass, and then motioned to Morales's. "Do you want another?" She nodded, and I signaled the bartender.

I said, "There's another theory I know of. It's about how people pick their vocations in life, that it begins with some triggering event at a certain age when they're young. For instance, you find out what a woman wanted to be when she was a girl of nine; for a man, you find out what he wanted to be when he was twelve. Whatever captured their fancy at those ages, what they wanted to be when they grew up, will play some part in what they actually do in later life."

Morales seemed amused and expansively tolerant. "So, did I want to be a cop when I was nine? No-oh," she said, stringing out the syllables. "But I'll play. You tell me first, though, what you wanted to be when you were nine."

The first woman explorer to go all the way down the Amazon." I laughed, and added, "But I'm scared of snakes, don't like humid climates, and haven't been further south than San Diego. Now you."

The bartender brought over our drinks. After he left, she said reflectively, "I haven't thought about this in the longest time." She seemed almost shy when she spoke. "I wanted to be the first woman mayor of San Antonio. The first Latina woman mayor. My third grade class went on a field trip to city hall. I got to sit in the mayor's chair in the city council's chambers. I even pounded his gavel and told everyone in my class to sit down and be quiet. It was the greatest feeling."

"It could still happen--your goal," I said. "Mine won't, and thank goodness."

"If your theory holds up, then you have to be doing some kind of exploring in your current work. What is it?" Morales asked, with a hint of challenge.

"The simplest explanation is that I go into agencies, figure out a way through the muck and dead ends blocking their progress and clear a path."

She nodded. "I guess that's what you've been doing with SEAAA. Ever think it might be a dead end you can't clear away. Well, anyway, I'm working on my masters in public administration at Seattle University. With my law enforcement experience and an advanced degree ... who knows?" She shrugged, and for the first time since we had met, smiled with warmth, although it quickly frosted over.

Nonetheless, it was a small victory. I smiled back.

After a moment, I said, "Do you really think the gangs were involved in these killings?"

"The AZs are into auto theft and small time drug dealing. If they did the shootings in the apartment, it would be a first--that we know about, at least. You're asking a lot of questions about the gangs. Why don't you talk to Dak? He has his own clique, even if he says it's a school club. That's why the AZ's wanted Dak; get him, they get his followers." She smiled cynically this time, "But I guess you already knew that."

Before I could respond, Morales peered at her pager that must have vibrated for her attention because I didn't hear anything. She turned it off, pulled out her cell phone, punched in some numbers, and said, "Morales." She listened, then said, "Okay," and hung up. She fished around in her purse, took out a couple of dollar bills and threw them on the table.

"C'mon," she said, "Patrewski's on his way down with Dak and wants us to meet in the lobby. Lily's been found. Her boy friend got shot, and she was with him. They're holding her at the county juvenile detention center. Patrewski wants me to go over and talk to her. Take you, he said."

I threw down money and followed Morales, concerned for Lily, but also thinking that Patrewski's timing couldn't have been worse. So much for my bonding girl chat with Morales.

Within minutes, the four of us were in the lobby. Patrewski deposited Dak on a settee and said to Morales, "Stay with the kid. I need to talk with O'Hern for a minute."

Patrewski guided me behind a pillar where we could talk without Morales and Dak overhearing. Touching my arm for emphasis, he said, "I'm worried about Dak. The way he's sounding, I think he's contemplating suicide."

"Whoa! I didn't have that impression when he was with me upstairs," I replied. "What'd he say to give you that idea?"

"He said his people would be better off without him around because he'd only bring them shame."

"Do you think it means...?"

Patrewski broke in, as if he knew the rest of my question, and said, "I asked the kid point blank, did he shoot his dad. He said no. My gut says he's telling the truth; my head says he should be on our short list of suspects."

"I can't believe it."

"Yeah. It'd be nice if this were a kid we could salvage. Talk to him. He talked about bringing shame, then he clammed up."

"That's not surprising. It's against his conditioning to focus on himself and spout about feelings, particularly a cop."

"Just talk with him. Tell me if you get the same reading on him as I did. Afterwards, I'll take Dak to stay with a friend of mine, an ex-cop with a big family. I checked with the aunt, she says it's okay. She wants Dak safe. But I don't want to put my buddy in the situation of waking up to find the kid hanging from a closet door."

I started to protest that I didn't know what to say, that I wasn't a counselor, but then Patrewski said, "Please," with a flicker of pain, or perhaps discomfort from having to a favor.

How could I refuse someone whose eyeballs were turning yellow right in front of me? I threw up my hands. "I'll try."

We went back, and I switched places with Morales on the striped settee. She and Patrewski walked behind the pillar.

I placed a tentative hand on Dak's shoulder and said, "You must feel that your whole world has caved in on you."

He didn't answer, but sat crouched over, elbows propped on his thighs, his head in his hands.

What could I say in five minutes that could help this hurting boy? Or help me understand if he was seriously thinking of doing himself in?

I said, "Do you want to talk?"

He didn't answer.

We sat close, yet remote. I thought about my own struggle with John's death. It had been the final blow on top of the divorce and his remarriage. My reality had splintered into too many pieces to pick up. Maybe talking about my experience would open Dak up. I didn't know what else to try.

"I can't understand exactly what you feel. But I can tell you how it was for me when my husband died suddenly. The pain. The thinking. I kept going over things that were said, that should have been said. Finally, I just wanted to shut down. Everything. Is it like that for you?"

He didn't raise his head, but nodded, struggling not to cry.

"One night after my husband John died, it was so bad that all I could do was pace back and forth in the dark. I thought about taking my own life. It seemed the only way to escape the pain."

Dak crossed his arms and cradled his elbows.

I plunged on. "Know why I didn't?"

He glanced at me, and then hung his head again. "No."

"It wasn't the preachy things people said like 'give it time' or 'you have so much to live for.' None of those things made me change my mind..." I stopped, crushed by the memory of that night's agony.

He straightened up. "You okay?" he asked uneasily.

"Yes. Now I am." Taking a deep breath, I said, "It was this--being able to breathe, to live, not deny life. I wasn't ready for nothingness."

Dak seemed to be taking in what I'd said; at least my words didn't seem to bounce off the protective wall he'd had around him when we first started talking.

"You ever sorry you changed your mind?" he asked.

"No, though truthfully, there have been some bad times since then."

He stirred and said, "Do you think suicide's a sin. I mean, like would a person go to Hell?"

I thought a moment, wanting the answer to be right for him and honest for me. "That's a tough question, Dak. I don't know exactly what Buddhism says about suicide and sin except that all life in whatever form is special and not to be hurt. For me, I think God sorts out the why of our actions and knows our hearts. In the end, nothing's hidden. Maybe the greatest sin involved is the suffering brought on the family. The ones left behind face a living hell."

Dak shifted, and began tracing the red stripe on the settee cushion beside him.

Without warning, a prickling sensation began crawling across my shoulders, and I turned to scan the room because I knew as surely as I could feel my heart thumping that someone was watching me. I glanced at the hotel's entrance and saw the doors shutting behind a small Asian man dressed in black. Sang! I was sure of it.

Through the hotel's front window, I saw him cross Madison Street on the green light, and then disappear from view. He must have followed us or maybe Morales. Was he after Dak? Or me?

Rattled and eager to turn Dak over to Patrewski, I said, "Are you thinking of killing yourself? You don't have a gun hidden somewhere, do you?" Horrified at what I'd said so bluntly, I wanted to grab the words out of the air before they reached Dak's ears.

He jerked away. "Why are you asking me that? What kind of a friend are you?"

He tried to get up, but I held his arm, restraining him. "If a friend cares, she will try to help if she thinks you're about to make a terrible mistake."

He pulled his arm away. The damage was done, the words out, and I couldn't take them back, though I tried to soften their impact. "I was wrong to ask you like that. I'm sorry. It's just that Detective Patrewski's worried about you, and I am, too. You have had too many losses in too short a time ... Dak, do you have a gun hidden somewhere?"

Dak looked me in the eye, then away. "No," he said.

I didn't believe him.

My badgering had pushed Dak into a corner. He wouldn't level with me now no matter what I asked, but still, I considered other approaches. As I did, an ugly thought reared up: What if he did have a gun and planned to use it on his parents' killers? Or his grandmother's murderer? I cast about for something that could make him want to see tomorrow come, something that could give him hope, a reason for living. I said, "Upstairs you said that the test tomorrow was really important to you. You'll be staying tonight with a family Detective Patrewski trusts. I could stop by in the morning and drive you to school. Make sure you get there on time. Okay?"

Dak let out a sigh, the kind that seemed to come from somewhere around his shoe tops, but finally he nodded.

149

"Let's go tell Detective Patrewski. He can give me the address where you'll be."

When we stood up, Patrewski and Morales walked toward us. Patrewski had a cell phone to his ear, and he was talking fast and angry into it.

Morales met me and said low enough that Dak couldn't hear, "Lily's gone. KCPD screwed up and so did the juvie center. After she gave her statement, they were supposed to hold her for us. There was a shift change and the word didn't get passed. She called someone, a girlfriend we hope, then walked out of the place. If she's the killer, she's loose and running. If she's not, she's could be easy pickings for the bad guys. Let's hope we don't have a killer whose goal is to wipe out the whole Ly family. We have to find her."

Patrewski pocketed his phone and hurried over. He looked at Dak, then me. I turned to one side and he stepped closer so Dak couldn't hear me. "I think he's okay. He wants to go to school tomorrow. That's a good sign. He's taking an advance placement test. I'll stop by for him, if you'll give me your friend's address."

"You sure he's okay?" Patrewski said, pulling out his notebook and jotting down the address.

"He seems together considering what he's been through. But I'm no expert. Maybe he'd be safer at the detention center."

Patrewski shook his head. "It might do the opposite. Push him over the edge." He hesitated. "I'll ask my buddy to keep a close watch on him."

I eyed Patrewski for a moment and said, "You're pretty far out on a limb, aren't you, helping Dak like this? Are you sure you know what you're doing?"

His face said, *I hope to God I do.* Out loud, he said, "I'll call you later. How long you planning on staying here?"

"Overnight. I'll be out of here by ten in the morning."

Patrewski seemed distracted. Maybe it was the medication he had taken to fight off the reoccurring malaria. My gut feeling was that he had no intention of contacting me later. And I wanted to talk him about what I had been finding out, some of it confirming my suspicions. I asked him again, "You're sure you'll get back to me?"

His tired smile barely limped across the space between us, "Yeah. I want to bounce some ideas around with someone who has a receptive ear and a closed mouth. You're elected," he said. Spinning away, he hustled Dak out the hotel door.

I realized after they were gone that I had not told Patrewski about Sang watching Dak and me in the lobby.

What to do? Patrewski had left with Dak, intending to plant the boy safely under his buddy's watchful eye. Morales was on her way to chew out the juvenile detention center staff and determined to pick up Lily's trail. Neither detective wanted me along. In fact, as Morales rushed away, she had said over her shoulder, "There's no need for you anymore."

I was free, but to do what?

With a tone reminiscent of John's, my critical self scoffed at my reaction to seeing Sang and overrode my fear. But just to be sure he was gone, I went outside and scanned the street. I ventured to the intersection of Sixth and Madison. Even under the streetlights, I could tell that the pedestrians on the sidewalk were too tall. I was okay.

Inside the hotel, the clock behind the registration desk said eight o'clock. I asked the clerk if I could make it to Nordstrom's before it closed. She reassured me that I had time and that the store had a great sale on until ten that night.

Nordstrom's had remodeled the old Frederick & Nelson building on 3rd and Pine, and it seemed a nice treat to shop there for a nightgown and underwear. No washing undies out in the hotel bathroom. I didn't bother to get the car out of the hotel garage; parking would be a hassle. Walking to the store should be safe. I'd convinced myself that Sang's visit had been to check on Dak not me. Since Patrewski and the boy were gone, so should Sang.

I didn't linger on Nordstrom's first floor, although its ambiance with a pianist playing light classical music made it tempting to browse. I went up the escalator to the lingerie department where, between the teddies and bras, I ran into Rick. He shrugged at my surprise and said, "I'm here with Phourim," and pointed at the checkout counter. Behind it, a sales clerk was shaking out the folds of a lacy red negligee, readying it to go into a silver-and-gold-edged gift box. In front of her stood Phourim with the look of a kid who's peeked at his birthday presents already.

My mouth dropped open and I turned to Rick. "What--"

"I know," he said. "Who would ever have thought?"

I was surprised not only to see Phourim buying sexy lingerie but also to see both men shopping as if nothing extraordinary had happened earlier in the day. Finding them at the store seemed too frivolous, too full of life as usual. But then I was here shopping, too.

On closer examination, though, I could see that the accumulation of the last few days' events had impacted Rick. The groove lines that ran down either side of his nose and mouth seemed deeper, his face more angular, and the skin over his cheekbones had an unhealthy pallor.

Rick said, "I thought you'd be home by now."

"No. It was too late to drive back. I'm staying overnight at a nearby hotel," I said, deliberately not naming the hotel.

Phourim had paid for his purchase and walked over with bag in hand, his broad face beaming, and his smile at full candlepower. "Hello-ooo, Bridget. I am glad to see you," he said. He held up the bag. "It is for my wife. She comes tomorrow from Cambodia. I buy her the best."

"Wife? Wait a minute. I thought you were getting married here in the States!" I said. His announcement differed from the story Phourim had told me on the phone days ago.

Phourim shook his head gently and smiled as if I'd made some silly mistake.

"No, no. We marry in Cambodia when I there in January. She could not come to U. S. unless we were right."

"But you said you didn't have the money to bring her over."

"I have money to pay her family," he said.

I took that to mean that he had paid her family a dowry. "And you had enough for her airfare, too?"

He smiled expansively. "I have money to show government I can support wife."

I stood flatfooted, feeling dimwitted. My impression of Phourim struggling to save enough money to bring over his bride-to-be sometime in the future was way off base. Using a few hocus-pocus words, Phourim had been like a magician who shows his audience an egg and transforms it into a white dove. In Phourim's case, while I had listened slack-jawed, he had produced a wife, a dowry, and an expensive airfare. What had changed in just a matter of days?

With resignation, I realized that challenging Phourim about the discrepancies in his stories would do no good. Phourim probably saw no conflict between what he had told me on Monday and this version on Friday. Culturally, I doubted that he could understand that I felt duped and uneasy about trusting him now. Had he told me other half-truths wrapped in wistful stories that garnered my sympathy but blocked objectivity? When he said he had nothing to do with the Lys murders, was he playing a game of 'King's X'?

Phourim didn't seem to pick up on my doubts, and with innocent enthusiasm, he pulled out a paper from his jacket pocket. "Here is invitation to my wedding reception. It is in two weeks. You come?"

I looked at the folded photocopy, which had the date, time and place in Khmer and English. "I'll have to check my calendar," I said absent-mindedly. I made one more attempt to clear away my confusion. "You said a few days ago that you didn't have enough money to bring your wife over. What changed?"

Phourim's sunny expression dimmed. "I get loan. My wife family need money now. They very poor. Times bad in Cambodia."

Too little sleep and nerves strung tight had left me short on patience. I'd already lost my normal reticence about confronting someone, wanting to let them save face. When I had asked Dak about whether he intended to kill himself, I had breached that barrier. Bullying Phourim now for answers came easier. Sadly I thought, what you permit, you end up practicing.

I asked, "Who gave you the money? Was it from a bank, a person?"

He wouldn't look at me but answered, "Chhun loan me."

"How much?"

After some visible struggle within himself, he said, "Five thousand dollar."

"Oh, no!" I turned to Rick for confirmation, who shrugged again as if to say, what can you do?

Phourim appealed to me. "It is only way to get my wife Malati here."

"How will you pay the money back? Chhun's probably charging you a hundred percent interest."

The three of us had moved away from the sales clerks to a quiet corner near the elevator.

I realized that the only good part of learning about Phourim's borrowing the money was that it meant that he had no motive to rob the Lys, and by extension, no reason to kill them. Unless Ly had been blackmailing him.

Phourim's good-humored outlook had vanished with our talk. Even so, I still couldn't convince myself that he was capable of committing a violent act.

I said, "Look, with everybody still a suspect in the Lys' murders, anything unusual could be taken against you, especially suddenly coming into a lot of money."

Phourim almost wiggled with earnestness when he said, "I can explain. Rick helped me. I will have new job and my wife will work. We can pay back the money."

"What job? Where?" I asked, acting more and more like a schoolteacher grilling a student. Phourim's innate politeness kept him answering. That, and the fact, that he liked me as a friend ... or had.

"I go to the Cham Muslim School in Olympia. Malati will watch children at the pre-school and earn money"

"You're Cham?" I said, wondering how many more surprises Phourim was going to spring. My mind seemed to be working in slow motion, sorting through what I knew about the Chams. I knew that the Chams, who were Muslim, had conquered the Khmer people hundreds of years ago, and later their land became part of Cambodia. The Khmer Rouge had tried to wipe out the Cham because they weren't ethnically pure Khmer. Supposedly, the Cham had come from Polynesia. Phourim did have a stockier build and wavy hair that might distinguish him apart from the Khmer – or not.

"Did you know all this?" I asked Rick.

"About him being Muslim? Yeah. It's been hard on him when he has to take the kids to the temple. He didn't want the others in the agency to know he wasn't Buddhist. Especially not Sovath. He was afraid he might lose his job."

I thought back to when Patrewski and I had visited the elder monk. "Phourim, when you were at the temple with the kids and saw Detective Patrewski and me, you acted frightened. Why? Was it because of the policeman?"

"No. I do not want to be in the temple. The monks expect me to pray with the kids. It is bad for me to do that. I cannot follow Mohammed and be at that place which has spirits."

Rick spoke up. "The Cham have started their own private school for the Cambodian Muslim community. I helped Phourim with his resume and the interview. He's going to be their youth program coordinator."

I said to Phourim, "All right. You'll be able to pay back Chhun. But you're afraid of him. Why borrow money from him?"

"Because he is rich. Everybody know he loans money." Phourim seemed surprised that I didn't know the obvious answer.

Of course. What bank would loan a refugee young adult five thousand dollars on an unsecured note?

"Where does Chhun get his money? Not working at SEAAA."

Phourim shifted the bag to his other hand, looked down at the floor and then at Rick before saying, "People sell him things they steal. He sell for bigger money, and he force people to pay him to keep mouth shut. Sang help him, and people very scared of *ahjah sar*."

Using any assumed authority I could muster, including the fact that I was taller, older and fed up, I said, "Tell me the absolute truth. Has Chhun blackmailed you? Ever? Have you ever paid Chhun or Sang money to be quiet?"

Surprisingly, it wasn't Phourim who squirmed but Rick.

Phourim answered with a quiet dignity, suggesting a strength I'd not seen before. "No. I have not done that."

Rick had been quiet during this exchange between Phourim and me, but he had a troubled expression.

"Rick, what do you know about Chhun's schemes?" He might tell me off, but I thought he wouldn't. My sense was that he wanted to say something.

"I heard the Thrift Store across from the temple might have hot suff, stolen goods. The temple owns the store and uses it as a money maker."

Chhun and Sang fencing stolen goods? Why not?

"Has either of you told the police about Chhun?"

Phourim definitely paled at the suggestion, and Rick glared with a stubborn set to his mouth.

"Does everybody in the Cambodian community know about what Chhun and Sang have been doing except the police?"

Neither man answered, so I took that as a yes. "Was Ly a partner in the fencing?" I saw Phourim's puzzled expression, and added, "Selling stolen property for a profit."

Phourim nodded.

From the beginning, I had felt that the community would know before the police who had committed the murders. And I asked now, "Who does the Cambodian community think killed the Lys, and maybe the grandmother? Does the community think it was Chhun or Sang?"

Phourim spoke up, as if anxious to give an answer that might satisfy the schoolteacher and stop the rush of questions. "People say the Ly family has bad karma."

"But do they talk among themselves and give the name of the killer or killers?" I locked in on Rick. "Have you heard anything?"

He said, "Everybody's too scared of Chhun to say anything. I think he's capable of it, but you won't get any Cambodian to testify against him – or go against Sang."

"Would you?" I asked.

"Leave me out of it," he said, raising his voice. A nearby salesclerk looked over at us.

"I have a feeling you're already in it, Rick. Maybe your best bet is to talk to the police."

"What do you mean?"

"You act spooked, as if you're concealing something. If I'm aware of it, the police must be too."

"I don't have to stay and listen to this."

I grabbed his arm. "Look, I'm going to give this information to Detective Patrewski. He'll want to know how I learned it, and I'll tell him. You two. He'll want to ask you questions, but he can talk to others in the agency and community so that you won't be singled out. He'll protect you."

"Protect us? Where do you come off? You think the police will care?" Rick's voice had risen again. The sales clerk looked at us uneasily.

I smiled at her and turned to Rick and Phourim, "Keep your voices down." I said, "Patrewski cares. I also overhead Chhun and Sang laugh when they talked about a place called Richmond. If you know anything about that, say so and tell Patrewski."

Rick pushed his face forward, inches from mine, and said, "You keep your goddam mouth shut and me out of this." He stomped off, leaving Phourim and me staring after him.

Phourim said, "He very upset because he like Sovath and think he will lose her."

"He may not have her to begin with. And lying won't be the way to get her."

Phourim seemed to think about what I'd said, or maybe it was something else. After a moment he smiled and said, "Now that I have wife here and will go to good job in Olympia, I think I be okay. You tell police, I will talk to them."

I was tempted to ask why he hadn't done that before, but the serene look on his face stopped me. He was proud. I could see it in the way he carried himself, the way he looked directly at me instead over my shoulder or at the floor.

I nodded, smiling back at him. Then apologizing again for his friend, Phourim left with his wife's red negligee gift in its Nordstrom bag. Red, for good luck. I watched him and suddenly felt happier, for him not me, and I wasn't sure why. But something good had happened.

Hurriedly, I bought underwear and the first nightgown that had a decent price and one where the straps wouldn't fall off my shoulders in the middle of the night, leaving me half naked.

Walking back to the hotel, I mulled over the subtle shift in Phourim's demeanor. Finally, as I headed up Madison toward the hotel, I realized what had occurred. Phourim had let go of the scared, insecure refugee kid, the one who had been unable or unwilling to acculturate into American ways. Why hadn't it registered? Phourim had been wearing a Ralph Lauren polo shirt with its embroidered pony symbol, Docker pants and Nike shoes with telltale blue swoosh. The clothes were a change for him, not the off brands that I'd usually seen him wear. These clothes not only fit his body, they also fit his new persona. A new job and wife also seemed to have given him more substance, a stature. I'd heard the expression Cuppie used to describe a Cambodian version of Yuppie: Young, Urban, Professional, and maybe throw in Protestant, too. Phourim was becoming a Cambodian Urban Professional--although no Protestant tag. He was on an upward path into middle class America. I chuckled. Good for him!

Pleased about my insight, my thoughts switched to Rick and whether Patrewski would get back to me tonight. I was abreast of the alley that cut through the last block before the hotel. I checked for cars but saw none, just the outline of dumpsters caught in the shadows. As I started across, someone from behind clapped a hand over my mouth, and strong arms dragged me into the alley.

Rough hands pulled a hood over my head, and someone else yanked my left arm behind me. I was dragged down the alley until one of the men slammed my face into the wall of a building. Even through the material of the hood, the jagged surface of bricks bruised my nose and cheeks. Dimly, I wondered if the material was silk, it was so slick. A hand gripped my hair through the hood, jerked my head back and rammed my forehead against the wall. Lights exploded in my head and a stabbing pain shot through it. I sagged and fell to the pavement, but didn't lose consciousness.

A knee pressed into my shoulders and I couldn't move, even if I had the strength to try. My head was twisted to one side, the hood's material bunched under my face. The material was roughly straightened and then I felt the drawstring of the hood tightened around my neck. The material became damp with my breath and clung to my nose and mouth. My legs had a weight on them, and my arms were pinned behind me. Afraid I would suffocate, I willed my dazed brain to slow my ragged breathing.

A hand pressed my face down and someone leaned over me. His voice was sibilant, a snake's hiss penetrating the hood. "See. You do not listen. Stop helping police. You go away or you and your friends die very, very bad way."

I tried to say I would stop, but only a strangled cry came out. Tears of terror and impotent anger ran down my face. Suddenly, the weight pinning me down lifted and quick hands shackled my wrists behind me and tied my ankles together. Then they shoved me against the wall like a sack of garbage. Their hurrying footsteps faded away, and I heard a car's engine start.

Panic took hold again. What if they changed their minds and came back to finish what they had started? A rolling black tide washed over my mind, and I passed out praying that they wouldn't return.

Making It Through the Night
Chapter 24

As I regained consciousness and breathed slowly, I realized I wasn't going to suffocate. Relief surged through me. So did a throbbing pain that spread from my head into every moveable body part. I hollered for help twice, but the effort made the hood's soft material cling to my mouth. I didn't try to call out again.

A steady rain had begun, and my cramped hands were cold, my fingers stiff and swollen. The dark hood had robbed me of my sight, which made my hearing all the more acute. I raised my head and listened. The rain falling on surfaces made percussive riffs, some tinny, some dull. Water gurgled nearby.

I had been shoved against a building. My guess was that the bulky dumpsters I'd seen earlier hid me. In a reflexive action, I closed my eyes to listen again and then shook my head at what I'd done. Sirens wailed far away and tires hissed on wet pavement.

Judging by the traffic noise, my head was pointing toward the street, my back against a brick wall. My attackers had not pulled me that deep into the alley, I thought. I had been walking uphill on Madison when they grabbed me. If I could only make it to the sidewalk, I'd be found.

I wriggled my body upright using the wall for support and tried to stand so that I could hop toward the street. But with my hands and ankles tied behind me, I couldn't get my balance. After banging my head several times, I gave up. Finally I rolled onto my back and like a crippled inchworm, began scooting my body forward using my feet and shifting weight from shoulder to shoulder for extra locomotion. My raincoat's waterproof coating helped me to slide, that is until the upper part wadded around my waist, caught by my bound wrists.

Sliding the few feet had exhausted me and left my neck and shoulder muscles cramping, I bumped against something hard and pivoted on my rear end until I was sitting up and leaning against cold metal. I was sure it was a dumpster. Like a sightless creature lifting its face to sense what was in front of it, I used mine to carefully feel about, hoping to find something jagged, a sharp corner to tear off the hood. I found the protruding edge of a bolt. It took me long minutes, but finally I positioned myself so that the drawstring of the hood was hooked over the bolt, its end gouging into my neck. I sawed back and forth gingerly. Then tugged downward to see if the drawstring would tighten. It didn't. I seesawed faster and harder until with a ripping sound, the material gave way. I yanked backwards and the drawstring snapped.

I fell over and lay panting, groggily aware that the hood had fallen off. The rain falling on my face seemed like a reprieve from heaven.

The alley's entrance was about seventy-five feet from me, but if drivers glanced into the alley, they probably wouldn't see me on the ground.

Slowly I inched on my back toward the street, stopping every few feet to rest and to adjust my raincoat so I could move more easily. Halfway to the sidewalk, I heard voices and laughter. A couple walked by the alley's entrance, and I screamed loud enough to frighten a banshee.

Seattle's major hospitals are within a five-minute ambulance ride from the Stouffer-Madison. But it took over an hour from the time the couple found me until I was in the Harborview Trauma Center waiting for the emergency room doctor. The hotel's security had called 911 and the police. Soon after that, I had been surrounded, poked, questioned, strapped on a gurney, and questioned some more by a blur of blue-and white-uniformed men and women.

I told the police that I thought it had been Sang and friends who had waylaid me. I also gave Patrewski's cell phone number to an officer, explaining that the detective and Morales were working on a murder investigation that involved Sang. A paramedic found my purse, and to everybody's surprise including mine, my wallet was intact in it. No money or credit cards had been taken.

At the hospital I gave the admitting clerk C. J.'s phone number for an emergency contact--not Mary Rose or Danny's. I didn't want to alarm them. Actually, I didn't want a lecture about putting myself in harm's way. Particularly not from Mary Rose. She would say, "Really, mother! What were you thinking?"

I had been put into a room in emergency that had a draw curtain across the front and opened onto a kind of central command post for the emergency staff. I was on a rolling bed with side rails. The nurse had taken my clothes and put me into a gown, even though I hoped I'd be able to leave after I had x-rays done and the doctor had looked at them.

I grabbed my purse and fished out a mirror to assess the damage. An ugly red line ran across my throat, and an oblong lump was turning midnight blue on my forehead. Pulling my bangs low would partially hide the swelling. So would a lot of makeup. I couldn't baby-sit tomorrow looking like this. But the thought of explaining to Mary Rose was too much. I'd deal with her in the morning, and crawled back on the bed.

The doctor who examined me had said that everything seemed okay, no fractures, although I might have a mild concussion. He had ordered x-rays to be sure. After he left, a CNA with spiky hair and a chipmunk chin came in and informed me that emergency had a full house. "All the usual and a few crazies," she said cheerfully. There had been a three-car smash up on the floating bridge and two gunshot victims. "A typical Friday night," she said, adding that it would be a while before x-ray could take me.

I toyed with the idea of getting dressed and walking out of the hospital but thought that if I did, my insurance company would deny the hospital's claim for treating me. Granted, the treatment so far had consisted only of two Tylenols for my headache, a tetanus shot, and a quick cleanup on my abrasions. Still, I stayed put.

Apparently, one of the aide's crazies was in the cubicle next to mine. At least I thought he was one because it sounded as if he was banging a foot up and down on his bed, its frame rattling in protest while he hollered, "Somebody get the hell in here."

Several of the hospital staff went in to calm him down, but each time after they left he returned to his thumping and loud demands. Following one noisy session, the harried doctor who had examined me rushed in with a nurse in tow. The doctor's voice carried because he enunciated his words with frustration and anger. "What's the matter with you, Booster? What do you think you're doing?"

"I got chest pains."

The doctor answered brusquely, "You're not having a heart attack. Look, Booster, I checked the ER database. You've been to Highline, Auburn General and St. Joseph Hospitals in the last two weeks. You were in here last weekend!"

"So?"

"Do you have a permanent address?"

"What if I don't?" my neighbor yelled. "I'm goddam sick and this is a goddam hospital. You gotta take care of me."

The doctor sounded like he was in Booster's face when he replied., "Not when you've come here to get doped up and a prescription for more. Now where are you living? The Gospel Mission?"

"What if I am? That don't give you no right to treat me bad."

"I'm treating you to a cab ride to the mission. Now get dressed and get out. Take the cab or take a ride with the cops. I don't care. You're out of here."

The curtain to Booster's cubicle flew to one side, rings clattering on the rod and the doctor stormed out with the nurse scurrying behind.

My neighbor mumbled colorful oaths upon the doctor, the staff and the hospital. I also heard him mutter, "Course I come back here," then as if wondering how the logic could have escaped the doctor, he added, "They know me." A few minutes later, I saw Booster shuffle by in dirty UW Husky jacket and camouflage pants.

The doctor came back and stuck his head around my curtain. "Sorry for the ruckus next door. It shouldn't be long before they get you to x-ray."

With Booster gone, I looked around for other entertainment but found none. My own company certainly wasn't stimulating. I didn't want to think, not about the Lys' murders, the death of the grandmother, what kind of future lay ahead for Dak and Lily, or to replay the helpless despair I'd felt in the alley. Like dealing with Mary Rose, I'd think about all of it tomorrow.

The Tylenol had dulled my headache, and soon, half asleep, half awake, I dreamed of Sovath dancing with scarred hands and dressed in shimmering gold. Gold bracelets shaped like serpents encircled her slender arms. The jeweled, ruby eyes of the serpents glittered, enraptured, as she moved. The serpents suddenly took on life and began writhing down her arms and crawling over her body while I watched helplessly. Suddenly, I was in a coffin-shaped closet, unable to see anything but two pinpoints of light that grew larger until they became the glowing eyes of a cobra that coiled itself at my feet, its head raised with hood flared. The creature weaved and its eyes held me spellbound. Then it struck, and its flicking tongue caressed my leg.

My eyes flew open and I sat up with the bed sheet twisted around my chest and the gown hiked up to my hips. I pressed my hands against my chest to calm its erratic beating. My bare leg was wedged against the cold bed rail. I collected myself by straightening the bedclothes and sat up waiting to go to x-ray. I wouldn't lie down again.

The busyness of the emergency room and the jumble of conversations had become white background noise until I heard the sharp syllables of Khmer. Adrenaline surged again, but the voices were female. It couldn't be Sang. A pretty face peeked around the corner of the curtain "door" to my space, withdrew, and then popped back, opening the curtain wider for a better look.

It was Lily.

We stared at each other, and I scrambled off the bed, afraid she might run off and not sure how to keep her there. "Am I glad to see you," I said. "Come in. Are you okay?"

Another face appeared. I recognized her as one of the girls from the funeral home, who looked a little older than Lily. Suspicion clouded her face when she saw me, and she said something in Khmer. Lily's response sounded like a rebuke.

I stretched out my hand, palm up, inviting Lily to come closer. "Are you okay?" I asked again, softly.

She said something to her friend and took a couple of steps toward me. I think Lily's curiosity overcame her caution. She said, "You look awful."

I grimaced and laughed ruefully. "Don't I, though."

"What happened to you?"

"I was mugged, knocked down on the street, but Dak's fine."

Her lips set in a defiant line at the mention of Dak. If I wanted to keep Lily talking to me, I'd better steer clear of mentioning her brother for the time being.

Burying the alarm I felt, I smiled to let her know I was glad to see her. "Okay, my turn. Why are you here?"

Still a kid despite the sophisticated airs she had put on at the funeral home, Lily seemed to relish explaining how smart she was and the trick that she'd played by walking out of the juvenile detention center. She wept telling how she and her boyfriend were in the backseat of the car at a stoplight when rival gang kids drove up and opened fire. Her friend found a tissue box on the counter and brought it over. Lily let me hold her hand.

She sniffled and said, "I'm here to find my boyfriend. They took him away in the ambulance."

It had been at least three hours since Patrewski had gotten the call that Lily had escaped and probably four to five since the shooting. Her boyfriend was either in surgery, moved elsewhere in the hospital--or even dead, I thought.

Her buddy said, "They always bring the drive-by shooting guys to this place."

"Did you ask at admittance where he might be?"

The friend rolled her eyes at Lily as if to say can you believe her?

Lily glanced at her before saying, "We just started looking for him. They're real busy. We acted like we knew where we were going. If we asked about him, the person might turn us in to the cops. Can you help find him?"

I took a moment before answering. Getting Lily into safe custody was what I wanted to do. The trick was how. If I called out for someone, Lily would take off. I couldn't restrain her. She might be the size of a minute, but she had youth going for her. My body had morphed into a mummy--a very sore one--from being punched and thrown around.   Stalling for more time, I said, "What's your boy friend's name?"

Lily said proudly, "It's Sammy. Samovang Virak."

"He means a lot to you, doesn't he?" I said, and risked some probing. "You must feel very sure that he had nothing to do with your parents' deaths."

Lily drew herself up at the suggestion. "He wouldn't do that. He wouldn't hurt my family. He loves me."

Her friend murmured something to Lily in Khmer, and the two giggled. I ignored the by-play because I couldn't leap the generational chasm much less the language one to understand.

I did believe that Lily thought that Sammy loved her. True or not, I wasn't going to dissuade her. She was fourteen and in first love.

Lily said, "I can prove that Sammy didn't do it." She checked out my expression, seemingly to assure herself that I was taking her seriously.

I waited.

"The police said that my parents must have let the killer into the apartment because the locks hadn't been broken. Well, my father wouldn't have let Sammy inside because he hated my boyfriend. We had that peephole in the door. If my father had seen Sammy, he wouldn't have opened the door."

"Maybe Sammy had a gun and forced your father to open the door."

"My dad had a gun, too," she said triumphantly. "He always got it out when someone knocked on the door at night."

"Perhaps your mother went to the door instead of your father."

"No. He never let her answer the door when he was home."

"Did you give the police this information?"

Lily shook her head, and picked at the brown polish beginning to peel on her thumbnail. "Dak said I shouldn't say anything. Say that I knew nothing."

When she said that, a deep sigh escaped from me, though I'd kept my expression neutral up to now. "What's turned you against your brother? Did he do something to you that night?"

She stiffened. "The police already asked me all kinds of questions."

Her friend spoke up sharply, again in Khmer. She appeared to be as much counselor as friend, and I didn't think she liked the direction the conversation was taking. In English, she said, "C'mon, Lily, let's go."

Both girls had been standing near the bed. The only place to sit was a swivel stool. I had sat back on the bed after the girls stayed to talk. Now I scooted over and patted the space next to me. "Hop up, Lily, and have a seat. Before you leave, let's figure out how to find Sammy."

She hesitated, but then boosted herself up to sit next to me. Her friend perched on the stool, swiveling back and forth while watching us.

I said, "Here's the idea. You don't want to be seen in person asking about Sammy. Why not call on the phone?" I nodded at the friend. "You can use the pay phone in the lobby. Call the hospital and ask if Sammy is in emergency. Have the person check with patient information in case he's been moved to another part of the building. Pretend you're a cousin. No one will be suspicious."

"Do it," Lily said, her face excited.

I reached for my purse. "I can give you change for the phone. I bet there's a brochure or a card at the reception area that will have the hospital's phone number."

The friend looked around and spotted the telephone on the wall and pointed to it. "Why can't I use that one?"

"I don't know how to dial out," I said truthfully. "And what if a nurse comes in while you're on the phone?"

I took out my wallet, shutting my handbag quickly. I didn't want the girls to see my cell phone. The friend took the change and a couple of dollars for pop. "Nothing with caffeine in it," Lily said, giving her friend a stern look.

I had only a few minutes alone with Lily to find out what I could and to convince her that the police wanted her for her safekeeping.

"I have a feeling you'd like to tell someone what's been going on, someone who won't tell you what you should do." I grinned. "It's hard to find an adult like that, isn't it?"

"Boy, that's true!"

"I bet you heard or saw things that you never told the police."

"I know a lot," she said in a way that made it seem that the knowledge wasn't easy or pleasant to keep.

"You don't want to tell them because Dak would be in trouble?"

"He's already in trouble."

"How's that?"

She sat swinging her legs back and forth, bracing her weight with her hands on the bed. "Dak had my dad's gun. I saw him sneak it out of the apartment that night."

"Does he know that you know?"

She shook her head. "All he cared about was my grandmother. She cried and cried that night but she never made a sound. She was like a tree dripping rain. Dak just worry, worry over her. He told me not to talk to grandmother. He didn't have to say that. I didn't like her anyhow.

"Do you think she saw what happened to your parents?"

Lily shrugged.

I recalled the bereavement ceremony Patrewski and I had attended at the apartment and being in Lily's room. A thought struck me. "Where did your grandmother sleep? With you?"

"No. She slept on the couch. Sometimes on the floor on her mat."

"Where? In the living room?" I asked, barely concealing my excitement at this discovery. "Did the police ask you where the grandmother slept?"

"Dak said to tell them in my room on her mat."

"And did she that night?"

"No." Lily stopped her kicking and held her feet out in front, tapping the toes of her shoes together. "You know something?"

"Uh-uh. What?"

"That wasn't my real mom that got shot."

I wanted to say, "Are you sure?" Instead, I said, "I didn't know that."

"I wasn't like her at all. She was a nothing person. I think my dad had another wife, and they had me. But my real mother died, so his other wife had to take me."

"How can that be? You're younger than Dak." I had a hard time comprehending what Lily was saying, not the actual words, but whether reality or wishful thinking was behind them. I knew that in the past in rural Cambodia, a man could have several wives. Could Hahn Ly have had several wives Cambodian style here in America? Was there another wife, a jealous one, out there somewhere?

"Oh, Dak was the big, important son in the family. But I knew I was different from the time I was little," Lily said, holding her hands a few inches apart. "My father loved me. This mom didn't."

Like quicksilver warming, Lily's mood changed. She said, "Sammy loves me. He will take care of me."

She looked over shyly, her eyes happy. She pressed her lips together as if to hold a secret behind them. It came out, though.

"I'm going to have Sammy's baby."

My heart sank. A baby having a baby! I put my arm around her shoulders. "This is a surprise. Did you just find out?"

"I'm three weeks overdue."

Matter-of-factly, I asked, "Have you seen a doctor or taken a test?"

"No."

"I can tell you're happy at the idea but so much has happened. Your body could be giving a false alarm."

She pulled away and hopped off the bed. "No, you're wrong. I'm going to have a baby."

I nodded. "Then you'll want to take good care of yourself, for the baby. Think about your safety, Lily. Do you know that the police are worried about you and Dak? They aren't sure, but maybe somebody is trying to hurt all of your family."

"That's dumb."

I wasn't sure that Lily knew that her grandmother was dead. She had left the funeral home before her grandmother's seizure. However, knowing how swiftly news spread in the Cambodian community, I thought that Lily probably had heard. She didn't seem grief stricken, but then she hadn't liked her grandmother.

I asked Lily, "Do you know what happened to your grandmother?"

"Yeah, but nobody would kill her. She was crazy."

"Just the same, I'm going to give you Detective Patrewski's cell phone number. I think he's a good person and can help you. I'll put his number on the back of my business card. Call me, too, and stay in touch."

I got a card out of my purse, wrote on it and had just handed it to Lily when her friend came back looking pleased.

She said, "They operated on Sammy, and he's in the recovery room. He's going to be okay." The girls hugged and did a little dance together. "They told me the room where he'll be."

I might have found out more, perhaps even the friend's name, but the CNA with spiky hair came in, and said, "A Detective Patrewski called and said not to go anywhere. He's on his way here."

I could tell by the CNA's tone that getting a message from the police had somehow raised my status in her eyes but certainly lowered it with the girls.

They took off before I could say, "Wait."

Painful Memories
Chapter 25

The ethical debate in my mind lasted about three seconds. I tattled on Lily. At least where she was. The girl needed help in more ways than one. I reached Patrewski on his cell phone, and he was not happy to hear that she was looking for Sammy in the hospital . On the other hand, he was glad she had been located.

I said, "You'll have to be careful who you send after her. If it's Morales, she'll need to use a light touch or Lily will clam up."

"It's going to be me. I'm pulling up to the hospital now."

By the time I got back from x-ray, Patrewski was sitting on the stool in my area, his eyes closed and a *Newsweek* open on his lap. He startled himself awake with a wheezy loud snore and found the aide and me staring at him. He stretched, took his time looking me up and down, and said, "Gawd almighty."

"You don't look so hot, either," I retorted.

The aide smothered a smile, then backed out with the wheelchair.

Wanting to get our conversation on a higher plane, I asked Patrewski, "Any luck finding Lily?"

"I just missed her. The nurse had chased the girls away because it was too soon for Sammy to have visitors."

"Catching her will be like netting a butterfly."

"More like a honey bee and Sammy's the blooming idiot. She'll keep coming back to him. That's fourteen-year-old thinking."

I made a face in agreement.

"Are you looking for Sang," I asked.

"No. What have we got to pull him in for? You recognize him?"

"No, Not his face. I was grabbed from behind and hooded. But it was his voice."

"Too circumstantial. That won't be enough to hold him. Besides Seattle PD has jurisdiction, and a mugging with nothing taken, just a shaking up isn't going to be a high priority. I can put a scare into him, though, so he'll leave you alone."

"I've been thinking about that. Maybe you shouldn't. He might disappear. If Sang's one of Lys' murderers, you need to keep him around, work with him, until you've gathered the evidence you need."

"Why'd he go after you?"

"He said to stop interfering, but I think he went after me because he had lost face. When he tried to use his evil eye trick on me at the funeral home, I humiliated him. Yelled at him, too."

"You think that was a wise move?"

"I did what I could at the time."

Patrewski nodded, seeming to empathize with how I dealt with the situation. It surprised me to realize how often his thoughts seemed to translate into non-verbal messages. Of course, I could be reading more body language then he was sending. We were both becoming very good at that skill.

Patrewski said, "If Sang stays in the picture as community liaison, you're out of it. It's the only way to protect you."

I started to protest then stopped, deciding to see if I agreed tomorrow when I felt better.

The doctor came in then with clipboard and chart in hand, and the two men shook hands. When Patrewski introduced himself as a Seabell detective, the doctor showed no interest except to study Patrewski's jaundiced face with a kind of clinical detachment. Turning to me, the doctor confirmed that I had a mild concussion. He said that my sore ribs were just that, nothing worse, and yes, it would hurt to breathe deep or move fast. He also said to check in with my doctor and call her if I experienced blurred vision or drowsiness during the day.

As he wrote out a prescription for pain, the doctor glanced over at Patrewski. "Do you know you're sick?"

"Yeah. I'm taking stuff for it."

"Bed rest wouldn't be a bad idea, you know."

"When I've got time for it," Patrewski said, truculent at the unwanted medical advice.

The doctor shrugged. He handed me the prescription, cautioning, "Don't drive for twenty-four hours," and left.

I asked, "Could you give me a lift back to the hotel? On second thought, I'll check into a different one where nobody knows me."

Patrewski said, "Get dressed. You're going home with me."

What could have come out as a thoughtful invitation marched out as a brusque order.

"I can't do that. It's the middle of the night, your wife..."

"She's the one who said, 'John, bring her home.' The barest bit of humor crept into his voice. "If you think I'm tough, try going against Nicole!"

John! I hadn't made the transition from Patrewski to Jack, yet. Learning Patrewski's christened name jarred the pigeonhole where I'd placed him, producing a familiarity that didn't sit well. After carefully keeping each other at arm's length, we seemed to be closing distance and discovering dimensions to the other. Neither one of us knew how to react.

I also stored away the interesting side note that Patrewski's wife called him John, not Jack.

Patrewski left to bring his car around to the entrance. I threw my ripped hose away, put on my shoes, dirty dress and torn coat, clutched the soggy Nordstrom's bag that had been found with my purse, and limped out of the hospital with the aplomb of a seasoned bag lady.

Patrewski stood by the opened passenger door of the car and helped me in. When I fumbled with the seat belt, he leaned across, buckled it and then carefully shut the car door.

On the drive to his house in West Seattle, we stopped at an all night pharmacy and had my prescription filled. I swallowed two pills right away. We drove in silence until we were past the Rainier brewery, when I said, "Do you always take such a personal interest in the people involved in your cases?"

"No. But the least I can do is keep an eye on you tonight. If you hadn't helped me with Dak, you wouldn't be hurt. Come tomorrow, though, you're back to St. Benedict's or St. Theresa's or wherever the hell it is you live."

"St. Mary's Corner. Near Chehalis," I corrected automatically.

I leaned my head against the cold glass of the passenger door window, hoping the chill would clear my fogged mind. "Earlier I had things to tell you, but they're too hard to recall except for Lily's conversation. It's fresh. She's certain that the boyfriend--and I guess the AZ's since he's their leader--didn't kill her parents. According to her, she already was Sammy's girlfriend and that connection made Dak accepted as an AZ. The gang didn't need to intimidate the parents to get her brother to join."

Patrewski didn't seem impressed by Lily's explanation, though he did say, "Morales doesn't think it's a gang crime or a home invasion. The scene doesn't fit."

"Killers, plural? Like Chhun and Sang? Lily says that her father wouldn't have let anyone enter the apartment that he didn't know and trust, which leaves friends, relatives or partners."

"And co-workers."

"Chhun was both, a partner and co-worker."

173

I thought a minute. "If Lily's right, then we can eliminate Mindy's husband. Her father wouldn't have invited his mistress's husband into his home late at night."

"Maybe Ly wanted to show he wasn't afraid, played macho. Then again, maybe it was Mindy who came by." Patrewski added, "Ly knew her well enough."

"Hmmm. But not likely. Suppose the killer came earlier in the evening and waited until Lily and the grandmother were asleep to shoot the couple."

Patrewski shook his head. "It doesn't work. When we interviewed the aunt, she said that her sister, Ly's wife, had called around ten that evening. She had been upset because Ly was drinking and ranting about his gambling debts. The wife was afraid with Dak gone. The aunt said that her sister only had Lily and the grandmother with her at the apartment, and they couldn't--wouldn't--help her. The aunt was afraid of Ly, too. The way she tells it, he was one of those drunks that broods then explodes, hurting the weakest person near him."

I pictured Ly's wife in their cramped apartment, slipping around the edges of her husband's vision to keep his anger at bay and hoping it wasn't stalking her. It was a hard image to shake off.

"Could the aunt have been at the apartment?"

"No. We checked out her alibi. She was home all night. Her kids had friends stay over. She's clear."

Glancing at Patrewski, I hesitated before saying, "Speaking of kids, Dak and Lily lied to the police about their father having a gun in the apartment... Lily said Dak had one that night. She thought it was her father's."

Patrewski jerked his head toward me and gripped the steering wheel tighter. "Fool kid. You're sure Lily actually saw Dak with a gun?"

I nodded. "He took it outside to hide it."

"Think she's telling the truth?"

"Who can tell? She's so mixed up. She didn't seem to have an ulterior motive, although she's mad at her brother. He's been getting all the attention. Lily also has this idea that Ly had another wife who was her real mother. If that's true, Dak's just her half brother."

"Where'd she get that idea?"

"I guess Lily couldn't identify with her mother. Not in any way. She called her a 'nothing person.'"

"Couldn't stand her, huh?" I knew from his tone that he had moved Lily up a notch on his persons-of-interest list.

I said, "Lily wouldn't have killed her father. She was crazy about him. Remember how upset she was when Mindy showed up at the apartment? The girl was jealous of Mindy for stealing her father's attention away."

As with Phourim, the idea of Lily as a killer didn't resonate. In fact, it clanged.

"Lily also said that the grandmother had been sleeping in the living room, though the kids lied about that, too. It means that the grandmother probably saw the shootings."

"Then why wasn't she killed at the same time? Do you have a better answer this time around? We don't know that the grandmother's death is even connected to the Lys'. She could have died from natural causes. We've too many ifs, too many inconsistencies."

I said gloomily "That describes the Cambodian culture pretty well."

"Aw c'mon, keep it simple, O'Hern. Don't get hung up forcing some mysterious cultural angle. The motive will probably come down to money or jealousy."

"What do you mean, don't get hung up?" The pain medication made it hard to be as indignant as I wanted. "Why have I been involved at all, if it hasn't been the so called cultural angle?"

I said as patiently as possible, "Look, you have a Cambodian husband and wife shot point blank in the forehead without any signs of fight. The dead man had killed and tortured hundreds in Cambodia. He probably executed people the very same way he died. A coincidental cultural connection?"

Patrewski said, "I'll grant you that Ly had the capability."

"Well, do you think Ly said, 'Go ahead, be my guest, shoot me?' Okay, think about Ly's partner Sang, who turns out to be a *Krau Khmer*, a person who Cambodians believe casts spells. He's someone who could have mesmerized Ly into standing like a stationary target in a shooting gallery. If he didn't hypnotize Ly to a standstill, then certainly he could have forced that bullied, traumatized wife. To me that smacks of a cultural angle. But I guess you run across situations like that all the time in your convenience store shoot-em-ups."

The sarcasm seemed to be coming from someone else besides me, though I knew it was my voice. Actually for a change, it felt good not to worry about being pleasant or careful with my words.

I said, "You haven't even explored the possibility of Ly and Chhun having a falling out over political loyalties. Chhun is lined up behind Prince Ranariddh, and who knows who Ly backed. He was a Khmer Rouge.

Remember? Ly was a terrible, cruel man, a product of a society gone mad."
I added, "You have to understand the culture."

Patrewski swore under his breath.

"Understand! What you understand is books and talk. They don't
leave you crawling, dirty with running sores. You've never set foot in a
rice paddy, or wondered if the kid you see is a walking booby trap. Ly a
Khmer Rouge soldier? Some Khmer cut out and ate their dead enemy's
liver for his strength and courage. Yeah. That was done and more that
would have you puking on the seat. Barbaric? It's equal opportunity. Race
doesn't matter in that depraved part of human nature; the part you don't let
out because you're scared you'll never completely bury it again."

Patrewski slammed his fist against the wheel and slumped against his
seat. "God, I'm sorry. Forget what I said."

I had recoiled from his fury and the pain driving it. For his sake, I
nodded.

We drove in silence until he pulled into his driveway. He said quietly,
"I'm sorry. You have helped; you got Lily to talk."

"Thanks," I said, glad to get things back to a more normal level. "I
gave your cell phone number and mine to Lily. Said to call anytime. We'd
help." I didn't mention her pregnancy. The revelation could wait for better
timing.

Inside, Nicole greeted her husband with a loving embrace and me with
tsk-tsking commiseration. If she sensed any strain between the two of us,
she didn't fuss about it. She took Patrewski's jacket and my coat while
maneuvering us into chairs by a gas-burning fireplace. Then Nicole
brought us hot Japanese Twig tea. She also gave pills to her husband and
waited while he gulped them down. Then she sat down on an ottoman by
his recliner.

Nicole wore an earth-toned caftan with copper arabesque figures on it,
and the fire's reflected light flashed on them and skin the color of amber
honey.

A feeling of well being seemed to settle on the room as if she'd
decreed it. Patrewski sat contentedly, Nicole's hand resting on his arm. He
could have been her subject, a very willing one I suspected; yet she was
attending to him. Suddenly, I felt incredibly alone.

Perhaps my loneliness projected itself because Nicole said, "Bridget,
I'm glad you're here so we can take care of you. You must be exhausted
and want a shower and sleep. I'll lay out some clothes for you in the spare
room where my sister stays. You're both about the same size. She's a flight
attendant and leaves extra clothes here for her stopovers. I'll also prepare a

poultice for your forehead that will stop that bruise from turning Technicolor." She chuckled at my expression. "I know. Poultices? This one will work. Don't worry, it's not made of mugwort and toad eyes."

When Nicole left, Patrewski and I talked about schedules for the morning. We kept it low key, neither one referring to the scene in the car. I reminded him that I had promised to pick up Dak and take him to school in the morning.

"On Saturday?"

"He's taking a special advanced placement test. He has to be there by eight-thirty. It'll last until noon."

"I'll pick him up. I've got to go over his story again."

I shook my head. "No, I gave my word I'd take him. If you'll drop me by the hotel in the morning, I'll get my car."

He eyed me, and then said, "Okay. But I'll be on point in my car and lead you there. Coffee's ready by five, and you can help yourself. We'll leave at seven forty-five sharp. There's a clock radio with an alarm by your bed."

I had the feeling Patrewski expected to be long gone before I got up. When I got to my room, I set the alarm for six.

The furniture in the bedroom was dark oak, mission style, with uncluttered lines and a solid feel like everything else in the house. The bed looked particularly inviting with bolsters and pillows piled high. I took my cell phone into the bathroom so I could hear it. While I was showering, Nicole set out food on a small writing table near the bed. Feeling a hundred percent better after the shower, I dressed in my new nightgown and a robe she found for me. Famished, I dug into a turkey sandwich.

Nicole rapped on the door and entered with a tray. "One poultice to make you feel better, and a dream pillow with herbs guaranteed to make you sleep well."

She set them down on the foot of the bed. "I'll leave you so you can get to bed." She didn't move, though. Instead she said, "I hope you don't think John is ungrateful to you. He's not unfeeling. On the contrary, he camouflages his sensitivity."

"I'm aware of that. I hit a raw nerve in him tonight that must have triggered bad memories from Vietnam."

"He doesn't talk much about that period in his life."

"Did you know him then?"

Nicole smiled indulgently. "Heavens, no. I suspect John and I were literally worlds removed then. I was in college and very anti-war. This is a second marriage for both of us. After years of bad relationships, we were lucky to find each other. An odd match, but a good one."

"Well, he seems to reciprocate that opinion. The minute he walked inside the door and saw you, I think he got better."

"It's my medicines and potions," she said lightly

Nicole was easy to talk to, perhaps because she was at ease with herself. "Do you mind if I ask what attracted you to Patrewski, I mean Jack? Forgive me, but I'm not used to calling him by his first name."

She laughed. "Oh, I know. You don't get on a first name basis until you've passed his personal litmus test. John is something of a dinosaur, but I love him."

This time I laughed. "You seem to be opposites in personalities. Nice ones," I amended.

"I'm not offended. To answer your question, it's John integrity that drew me. And he's authentic. You have no idea the number of cardboard cutout men there are in academia."

"If I asked Patrewski the same question, what would he say?"

"That's easy. My intelligence, and I don't flutter ... and a few physical attributes are drawing cards--so to speak."

We both smiled.

I said, "Well, your husband's not acting like a stereotypical cop, and you're not acting like a typical cop's wife--whatever those might be. For one thing, it's kind of you to take me in."

With a twinge of anxiety, she asked, "And the other? How is John acting that's different?"

Giving Nicole a half-truth to be polite seemed wrong. "I think Jack's too fond of Dak, the boy whose parents were killed. The problem is that the youth is becoming a suspect."

Nicole sat down opposite me. "He's talked more about this case than any other that I remember. Do you know that Jack went back to Vietnam a year or so before we met? He told me later that he went to 'put old ghosts to rest.'"

"Did he?"

"You'd have to ask him. Jack's walking down his own red road. That's what the Cherokee's call it I can provide this," she said, gesturing around her, "a respite, but he has to walk his road alone."

"Does Jack have children?"

"No." She gave a wry smile. "Do you think he's having a mid-life crisis, missing the son he never had?"

"I think he finds Dak smart and gutsy and in a tough spot ... like himself."

We both pondered on that for a while.

Nicole stood and put the dishes on the tray she'd brought. At the door, she said, "You can trust John's integrity. I'm glad you're involved in this case. Your spirit's different than his partner's."

"The body, too, sad to say."

She smiled. "Be sure to put the pillow under your head, and the poultice on your forehead--not the other way around. You'll have good dreams."

Actually, it was one dream.

In it, Grandma Kate was with Booster from the hospital. The three of us were on a mountainside, green and serene, the air soft and warm. Grandma and Booster were on the opposite bank of a swift-moving stream. Downhill, it flowed faster, spreading wider and finally becoming a turbulent river. Upland, the stream narrowed as it twisted to its birthing place, a spring bubbling from a crevice. I knew it was close but not its location.

Grandma and Booster held hands, which surprised me. Booster repeated what he had mumbled behind his curtain: "Of course I came back. They know me." Grandma's brown eyes bore into me and smiled encouragingly. She pointed toward the path that led up the mountain, and held out her hand for me. Then she turned, and chatting cheerfully, the two began climbing the trail.

"Wait," I called and picked my way across the stream's slippery rocks.

"You beat me to the coffee," I said, walking into the kitchen at six-fifteen a.m. The coffee's aroma had pulled me eagerly out of my room. Of course, it had taken twenty minutes under a hot shower before I could walk not crab-step down the hall.

"I'd hoped you would sleep in," Patrewski answered.

I bet he had. He wanted to be the one to pick up Dak and have first crack at talking to him.

Patrewski sat at a large, square table, a mug at his elbow and a yellow legal pad and pen in front of him. The unhealthy pallor of his face had improved, and for a Saturday morning, when he could have dressed casually he looked sharp. He had on brown slacks, polished leather loafers and a white turtleneck under a kiwi-lime shirt.

I looked pretty spiffy, too, all things considered. I wore a silk sweat suit of the sister's with matching tenny runners, a trifle big but wearable. The outfit was in a shade of huckleberry blue. Together, Patrewski and I were a fruit medley of color. Nicole's poultice also had worked. At least the bruise wasn't worse. With makeup and an artful arrangement of bangs, I was presentable.

The table was set with woven place mats, napkins and silverware. Patrewski pointed to an insulated carafe with glasses near it. "Fresh made orange juice. Help yourself. Coffee and cereal's on the counter."

I fixed myself a bowl of muesli with milk, poured a mug of coffee and carried them to the table. Rain pecked at the window by the sink, probably wanting to come in out of the blustery weather.

"I'm sure it's too early, but any word on Lily?" I asked sitting down.

"A plain clothes cop is watching for her at the hospital."

"Did you talk to Sammy there?"

"Morales did later. He knows nothing except that his gang didn't do in the Lys. No profit to it. He says that Lily's dad was in debt up to his eyeballs. He even sold his daughter's gold necklaces and bracelets to get money."

"Did Sammy say where Lily might be staying?"

"At first, he couldn't remember her girl friends' names or where they lived. Morales convinced him that cooperation was a good idea. He coughed up a few addresses."

"Are you following-up with Ly's former sister-in-law?"

"Jeez, O'Hern. You only told me about the sister-in-law last night."

I said, "Sorry. I've lost track of time."

"Morales is going over to her house with an interpreter this afternoon." Patrewski sounded peeved at having to explain.

"Both of you working on Saturday. Isn't that above and beyond the call of duty?"

Patrewski said, "It works that way when we're pushing for breaks in an investigation." He added, "I have to hand it to Morales, she hasn't bellyached once."

"It seems longer than one week since Sovath asked me to meet you. I sure want this to be all over."

"Me, too," Patrewski said. "Time's working against us. We've thrown out a lot of lines and haven't hauled in anything worthwhile."

As if anticipating my next question, he said, "The Richmond thing you mentioned. I've got our computer guy running it as a name, place, anything that might connect to the case. He stayed late working. I'll check my voice mail at the station for a message after I've eaten."

I pointed to the pad in front of Patrewski. Sovath and Chhun's names were on it with handwritten notes.

"I started a list like that at home."

"A suspect list?"

"Kind of. I did it as a creative problem-solving matrix. That's something I use in training groups."

Patrewski shrugged. "I guess it's not that different from what we do on a white board at the station. What'd you come up with?"

"Who, not what. I've made up a scorecard. I assigned points--one to ten--in categories under motive, opportunity, and method. Whoever has the highest total is the most likely suspect."

Patrewski studied me, apparently interested, or he was giving me the benefit of the doubt. "Were your crooks of choice, Chhun and Sang?"

"Chhun was. I didn't list Sang."

"Anything on there I can use?" Patrewski asked.

"I don't know. The list is at home, but I could fax it to you, for what it's worth."

"It will have a profile on your 'suspects' that might be useful."

Was Patrewski buttering me up or did he mean it? "I didn't list the kids. They should be on a suspect list. Now that we know about the gun."

"They have been all along, one way or another."

"Lily adored her father and Dak loved his mother. If one of the kids was responsible, why shoot the other parent?"

182

"Maybe each one took out the parent they didn't like."

I shivered and Patrewski's face settled into grim lines. Pushing back his chair, he said, "I gotta make some phone calls." He picked up his dishes and placed them on the counter.

Before he left, I asked, "Is it okay to use the phone in my room to check my messages at home? I'll use my phone card."

"Sure. I'll be on a different line in the den."

Patrewski turned in the kitchen doorway and said, "You heard of good cop, bad cop?"

"Yes."

"You're going to play good cop when you pick up Dak. I'll tell you what I want you to say on the way to the hotel."

"I thought you wanted me out of town?"

He nodded. "As far away from Seabell and the Cambodian community as you can get. No one knows right now where Dak is. For twenty-five minutes, while you drive him to school, I'll be leading you, and you'll be softening him up. After he finishes his test, he and I will have a heart-to-heart."

In my room, I brushed my teeth and freshened my makeup, feeling like a Judas goat leading Dak into a set-up. For all my talk about Patrewski's emotional involvement, I wasn't any better. I didn't want to be the one to trick Dak; I liked him. If he did talk--maybe confess--I didn't want to hear the details of a teenage murder plot. Let Patrewski do the dirty work. Thinking that made me feel disloyal. I would be leaving him to clean up a mess neither one of us had created.

After tidying the bathroom, I went into the bedroom, sat on the bed and called home. There were three messages from yesterday, the first one from Mary Rose. "Mother, I hope you won't be disappointed, but we won't need you to baby-sit. Tom has to work late. Sorry. Call me."

I had lucked out! By the time Mary Rose saw me again, my face would be back to normal and no explanations needed.

The second message was from C.J. but it was too early to call him.

The answering machine's digital voice told me the last message was recorded last night at seven forty-five p.m. After a pause, a man's muffled voice spoke first in Khmer then English. "Do not help police anymore or you die very bad."

I tapped in the replay number and held the receiver away from my ear. The words were as frightening the second time. I hung up without erasing the call.

Nicole peeked around the open bedroom door and I motioned her in.

She stopped when she saw my face. "Are you all right?"

I nodded. I didn't want to talk about the phone call while still collecting my thoughts. Not yet. Glancing down, I said, "Do you want the sheets stripped or should I make the bed?"

"Don't worry about it. How did you rest?" Nicole appraised me in a way that reminded me of C. J.

"Good. Just one dream, pleasant actually, and surprising." Talking about it let me tiptoe around the reality of the threatening call.

"Why, surprising?"

"It had my grandmother in it, and a homeless man I saw briefly at the hospital. She was trying to lead me to a special place. I never got there, though."

Nicole sat by me. "Some would say it's just indigestion from your late night sandwich."

Blowing out a breath, I thought about the dream. "No... No, it has something to do about why the Lys died." My emotions churned, but I ignored them. "The reasons for the Lys' deaths have something to do with their lives in Cambodia, the Pol Pot times. I think the elder monk was pointing us to that way. The killings can't be separated from that past. The trouble is, I've harped so much on the cultural angle that Jack doesn't want to hear about it."

Nicole pressed her hands together and studied the floor. "Don't underestimate John. We often reject what we believe and are afraid to admit. Follow your instincts. I think he's counting on you to do just that."

"I'm torn, Nicole. Deciding whether to stay or run. After being hurt in the alley, I'm afraid ... and a threat was left on my answering machine."

Nicole gripped my wrist. "Does John know?"

I patted her hand. "I'll tell him in a minute. I just found out. You know, he wants me to talk with Dak. I want to see justice done. But if the kids murdered their parents... what justice can there be, even if they're arrested and jailed?"

Nicole said, "In the Cambodian tradition, people would say all is inevitable because of their karma, the cause and effect of their actions in prior lives"

"In my tradition, we would simply say it's a rotten deal. Whatever happened to free choice?"

Nicole left, and I put on my raincoat that she had washed and repaired and waited in the kitchen for Patrewski. He walked in with a scowl.

"Morales called. The preliminary reports in on the grandmother. She was probably poisoned but the actual cause of death was her ticker. It gave out first. Morales went back to the apartment and found jars of dried mushrooms and Chinese herbs. She got a mycology expert out of bed to go check out her find. One of the jars contained mushrooms called Amanita Smith-something, very toxic... Think I'll stick to button mushrooms on my steak."

I stared at Patrewski.

"Uh, huh," he said. "The kids. If they'd been smart, they would have gotten rid of the mushrooms. Maybe there were too many people at the apartment before the service. Maybe they intended to throw them out when they returned later."

"We know Dak couldn't because he was with me. If Lily put mushrooms in the soup, why didn't she slip back to the apartment when she ran away from the funeral home?"

Patrewski said, "She disappeared before the grandmother keeled over. Maybe the kid thought she would have more time, that the grandmother would just get sick, not die right away. We need to pull in both kids."

"Lily may call you or me. I gave her our numbers at the hospital."

"Sure, and the tooth fairy will visit me tonight?"

His sarcasm stung. I still clung to the faint hope that Lily was innocent and would call for help.

Patrewski had put on his jacket, adjusting the collar while we talked. He glanced over, and said, "We got a bingo on the Richmond connection. Turns out Rick's real name is Richmond Howard Moorehead. Our computer guy ran Rick's social security number, transposing the middle two numerals. Wouldn't you know, out rolled Rick's record? The number switch is a good way to lose a background check. You give the wrong number to the bank and your employer. If a question comes up, you say the number switch was a mistake. Turns out Rick was arrested for involuntary manslaughter. Seems he and his fellow protestors were chaining themselves in front of the gate at the Bangor Nuclear Sub Base. A shoving match broke out with M.P.s, and Rick accidentally killed another protestor. Rick served time at McNeil."

So that was the secret Rick wanted kept from Sovath and the board. The news seemed to dash any chance of Sovath and Rick becoming an item. Perhaps it had been unrealistic to think it was possible.

"I hope Rick's not the Lys' killer," I murmured.

"Did he score up there with Chhun on your list?"

"Close, but it doesn't mean I want him to be *the* one."

Patrewski rolled his eyes.

"Am I still meeting Dak or is that off?" I asked.

"It's on. Morales is picking up Rick to answer more questions. I'll meet them at the station. But first, I'll follow you and Dak to his school. We'll let him take his test. If the kid's innocent, we don't want to ruin his future. I'll ask my buddy to cover for me while I sit in on the interview at the station. He'll stay at school till I get back. SPD's short on manpower."

And probably doesn't know half of what you're doing, I thought.

In the ten minutes or so that Patrewski had taken to fill me in, I'd waited for a break to tell about the phone call. Learning about Rick and the poisoned mushrooms had kept the memory of the frightening phone call at arms' length. But when Patrewski started to leave, I held my hand up. "One thing. My messages. One was a threat."

Patrewski searched my expression. "Did you erase it?"

"No. I didn't recognize the voice. It was recorded about the time you and I were talking out in the hall at the hotel."

"Was it the kid's voice?"

"I don't think so. Besides, if Dak called from the room, the long distance charge will show up on my bill."

We went into the bedroom, and Patrewski replayed the tape several times. Afterwards, he said, "What d'ya want to do?"

"Go ahead and pick up Dak, I guess. Then..." I shrugged.

"Let's talk on the way to the hotel. Whatever you decide, you still need your car. You up to driving?"

I nodded.

When we were ready to leave, Nicole hugged Patrewski then embraced me. She whispered, "Go where your dream leads you."

In the car, Patrewski jammed an unlit cigar in his mouth and said, "Here's what I want you to find out from Dak."

Gently rubbing my forehead, I congratulated myself that I had taken Tylenol and not the pain medication that fuzzed my brain. If ever I needed my wits about me, it was now.

186

Different Perspectives
Chapter 27

The atrocity stories told by Patrewski had left an oppressive presence in the car, causing my imagination to go into overdrive, and I squeezed my hands together to settle myself down. Even so, the hairs on the back of my neck stood up. The threat left on my voice mail had started a chain reaction of panic. I had tried to play down the call's impact in front of Patrewski. But now ... Sang must be behind the ominous warning. Would I ever be free of him?

I looked at Patrewski, wanting to tell him how scared I was.

"You still want to pick up Dak?" he asked.

I wanted to yell, "No!" Instead, I waited to answer. For one thing, my throat was too dry. For another, the running debate with myself had started again. To stay or go. If I didn't control my fears, I would never be my own person. After a moment, I said, "What exactly do you want me to find out from Dak?"

We had come to a stop at a red light and Patrewski turned to face me. "Forget seeing him. We'll get your car and take you somewhere safe until we get a handle on who's threatening you. I called the police and sheriff's office down your way. Trouble is there isn't much they can do about the threat, maybe keep an eye on your house when they have a car out in that sector and be on the watch for Asian strangers hanging around. That's about all." He added, "You could stay with Nicole and me."

"No. I'm doing this for me."

Patrewski shook his head.

I said, "Logically, everything should work out okay. You said so yourself. No one knows where Dak is or that I'm meeting him. Let's just hope the conversation's worthwhile."

The light turned green, and Patrewski accelerated through the intersection. He had been checking his mirrors periodically since we left his house. He studied his side mirror again and said, "We're not being followed. I've done four right-hand turns in a row. I would have spotted someone. When we leave the hotel's parking garage, we'll do the same kind of routine. Be sure you stick to my backside on the way to Buddy's house."

"Buddy as in name, not just friend?"

Patrewski's smile briefly lifted the worry lines in his face. "Yeah. His name makes him sound like a kid, but he's older than I am."

"Dak must have made it through the night okay."

"Yeah. I called Buddy this morning. He looked in on the boy several times during the night. According to him, the kid couldn't have faked that kind of snoring."

"Good."

The wind outside had picked up and was throwing rain with gusty enthusiasm at the windshield. The wipers thumped hard clearing a path. I stared at the rivulets of raindrops that the wiper caught at the top of each arc and whisked away. I thought about what I would do after I'd taken Dak to school and updated Patrewski.

Out loud, I said, "I'll go directly to St. Mary's after we finish. The person who called me probably got my number from my business card. My personal home phone number is unlisted. It's hard to find my house out in the country. If Sang was behind that threatening call, then if you tell him that I'm not involved anymore, say I've gone to Oregon on business, he'll stop looking for me."

Patrewski had been steering with one hand, his palm on the top of the wheel, his cigar jammed between two fingers. He stuck it back into his mouth, chewed reflectively and said, "He should."

He could have been heartier about it.

Resigned, I said, "Okay. What should I say to Dak?"

"The kids' stories need to be shaken up so we can sort out the truth. Explain that Lily told you about the gun. If Dak admits to having it, see if he'll tell you what he did with it. Ask him why he and Lily kept the information from the police that night."

"What if he turns sulky or defensive?"

"You're the friendly. Don't directly ask him why he lied. Talk about his parents, how he felt about them. See what you can find out about his relationship with the grandmother. We're looking for a motive."

"That all you want?"

"Patrewski nodded toward the glove compartment. A tape recorder's in there."

Folding my arms across my chest, I said, "No. Don't even think of it."

Patrewski snuck a look. "You'd have to tell him you had it, anyway, and he's underage."

I didn't reply.

He said, "Once Dak's inside the school, Buddy will watch to make sure the kid doesn't make a run for it out another exit. I'll meet you outside, and you can fill me in like you've been doing ... all along."

I had planned to fill him in with editing ... as I'd done ... all along. I still resisted the idea that Dak could have killed his parents. The shootings seemed so calculated, the way the couple was shot, almost mechanical, a single bullet to the middle of the forehead. I couldn't picture either Dak or Lily carrying out such an act. Sang or Chhun, I could see.

"Isn't there any evidence--any way--to connect Sang or Chhun to the murders?" I asked.

"Morales and I went back and talked to all the residents in the Lys' building. It was see no evil, hear no evil, and sure as hell, speak no evil from them. Morales towed Sang along one afternoon to interpret. That was a mistake. She said that when people saw Sang, they bowed and smiled, and their eyes glazed over like ice on pond water. They were scared to talk."

"I told you so."

Patrewski conceded the point with a shrug.

I said, "If you could charge Chhun or Sang for one of their crooked schemes and put them in jail, some Cambodian might feel brave enough to come forward with information about the Lys' murders. It's a long shot, I know. But..."

"What?"

I told Patrewski about seeing Phourim and Rick in Nordstrom's and what I had found out about Chhun selling stolen goods out of the temple's thrift store. "If you compare the State's Dept. of Revenue records to the IRS's 990 reports that the temple has to file for the store's unrelated business income, you might come up with some discrepancies. Particularly, if you could look at the temple's actual books. It'd be interesting to see where the store gets their used merchandise and who shops at the store. I'll bet you anything that Sang and/or Chhun are personally involved in running the thrift store or on its board."

Patrewski said, "The Dept. of Revenue records we can get. What about these 990s?"

"The 990 is like a person's 1040 income tax return. A nonprofit organization has to file a 990 if the organization takes in more than twenty-five thousand a year. The IRS makes the filed 990s public information on the Internet. I'll e-mail the website to you if you'll give me your e-address."

"I hate this computer stuff." Patrewski grumbled. "I'll get the department's for you before you leave town. Think the monks are involved in fencing hot goods?"

"Not the Venerable One. Who knows about some of the other monks, the novices? Men can come and go in the temple, apprenticing in the monk business so to speak. Nuns, too, for that matter."

189

"It's a good link, O'Hern. The store business ties into something Morales is working on."

We were in downtown Seattle and almost at the hotel before Patrewski informed me that he had arranged to have my room charges switched to his credit card. He added that there was no long distance charges. He sounded relieved. Me, too. I thanked Patrewski, and he asked if I needed to get anything from the room. I shook my head.

We circled the block twice, Patrewski scanning his mirrors to see if we were being followed, then drove into the hotel's underground garage. He parked near my car, asked for my keys and told me to stay put. As he got out, he asked, "Do you keep a spare set of keys anywhere on your car?"

I shook my head again.

He scoped out the parked cars around us, then went to the T-Bird and crouched down. He looked at the undercarriage from all sides. Then he unlocked the door on the driver's side, sat sideways on the seat and started the motor. He got out and beckoned me over. We exchanged cars. I plugged my cell phone into the automobile's jack and followed Patrewski into the morning traffic.

Buddy lived in Burien, a small urban community with no distinguishing features to set it apart from the half dozen small towns scattered south of Seattle and close to the I-5 corridor. His house was a 70's-era split level that had been cloned up and down both sides of the street.

Buddy had buzz-cut gray hair and blue eyes that sparkled with enthusiasm and seemed years younger than the worn face they were set in. He wore a short-sleeved polo shirt, buttoned at the neck and tan chinos. The two men greeted each other without a lot of fanfare, but with an unspoken affection that probably came from having been partners.

He led us into the living room where two young kids sprawled in front of a TV watching cartoons. They could have been Buddy's grandkids, but Patrewski had told me on the way over that his friend had remarried in his forties. The kids were the harvest of his mid-life sowing. Dak had been sitting on the couch with his jacket on, but he jumped up when we walked in. He came over and stood next to me.

Patrewski tapped Dak on the shoulder. "How 'ya doing, kid?"

"Okay." Dak smiled, but it only lasted for a couple of heartbeats.

Considering that the boy was on the suspect short list, I thought Patrewski's greeting and manner with Dak were as cordial as before. Maybe his bad cop act couldn't begin until I'd done the good cop routine.

Dak searched my face and said, "You got hurt."

"It's not much. I'm all right," I reassured him.

"Give me a minute here, then we can leave." Patrewski motioned to Buddy, and the two disappeared down a hallway.

"Aren't you taking me to school?" Dak asked.

"Yes," I said, and noted Dak's look of relief. "Detective Patrewski will drive his car and follow us. Until he finds the people who shot your parents, he's not going to take any chances that you or Lily might be hurt."

"I can take care of myself." Dak said, though he checked out my face again with a worried look.

Dak was favoring his injured arm. He had gotten rid of the sling, but he held the arm close to his body, his hand resting on his side.

"Have you had breakfast?"

He nodded. "Jean said I needed to load up on carbs so my blood sugar stayed up. She's a dietician."

"Buddy's wife?"

Dak nodded. "She's doing laundry downstairs. She says Saturdays are more work than being at the hospital."

"How'd it go with Buddy?"

"I heard him come in my room last night."

"Your talking about suicide scared us. He probably wanted to make sure you were all right."

"Well, I was just asking you questions. I didn't mean anything by it."

"Someone told me there's no such thing as an idle question."

Dak's face closed down.

I said, "You look more rested. Are you feeling ready for this test?"

Dak answered eagerly, as if I'd latched onto something safe to talk about. "I've been working to be ready for a long time. Other guys cram the night before. I guess it's good I didn't wait to study because--you know--because of what's happened."

"The school might have given you an extension"

Dak said, "I told you, I've got to do it now. If I do well, then next semester I'll be in advance placement classes, and the credits will count toward my freshman year in college."

"What do you plan on studying?"

"Criminal law. One day I will become a judge, and when I am successful, then I will go to Cambodia because they need judges."

"That's an ambitious goal," I said, taking in how pale he looked and the purple shadows under his eyes. Dak had little going for him, I thought, except brains and determination. I hoped against hope that he had not used them foolishly. "You would make your parents very proud," I added.

"I will make my grandmother proud. I will bring honor and remove the shame on my family's name."

"You're taking a lot on yourself, Dak. Your parents' deaths aren't anything you could have prevented. Isn't that right?"

Dak's chin trembled and he turned away. "My father brought shame on our house. He was not good."

"I know you said that he hurt your mother sometimes, until you stopped him."

"I don't want to talk about him."

"But you inherited qualities from both your father and mother. You can use what came from your father for good, even if he didn't."

Dak raised his voice. "I don't want to talk about him." The children looked at us, but when nothing more was said, the kids lost interest and turned back to the TV.

I wished I had some idea as to how soon Patrewski and Buddy would come back. I didn't want to start Dak talking only to have him dry up when the men walked into the room. I took a chance, though, and mentioned Lily. "I saw your sister yesterday."

"Where? Was that Sammy with her?"

"No. He was in the hospital, and Lily was going to see him. He'd been shot in a drive by. But he'll be okay."

Dak scowled, his face suddenly old. I wondered if I was staring at an expression used by his father. "Lily disappoints all the time. I have to work twice as hard to uphold the family when she does such bad things."

"She's only fourteen. What kind of bad things could she be doing?" I teased, "To me that seems so young."

Dak bit his lip. "I can't think about this. Please! Don't you see? I must do well on this test. Everything is depending on me. Lily's a girl, and she's fallen away from our tradition. My grandmother was very ashamed of her. Grandmother told me, '*Chmaa*, my reward for what I did right will be what you become as a man. Remember the old ways and bring honor.'"

"That's why you want to be a lawyer? To have a position in the community?"

"After I become a lawyer, I will practice and make money. I will go to Cambodia. All is corruption now, but one day it will not be that way.

"Did your father support your dreams?"

"I never tell him anything." Dak's anger flared but weariness replaced it, the kind that breeds desperation.

He said, "My mother was sick all the time, and he always yell at her. He said he wished she were dead."

192

My grandmother told the story of a wise man in Cambodia from long, long ago. He could tell of the future and said that the Khmer people would have a terrible thing happen to them. The ignorant would kill the educated and the good. The wise man said that only by being *kor*, mute like the kapok tree, would the Khmer people survive the very bad time. My mother and grandmother never talked back or speak happy because my father had been *Angkar*. That is why with this man who was my father. I was *kor*. I do not tell him what I plan."

Dak finished and thrust out his chin. No pity wanted and none given, I thought.

"Your poor grandmother. Was she up when you walked in and found your parents that night."

Dak tensed. "I told the police. She was in bed in my sister's room. I found my parents."

"It's unfortunate your grandmother didn't hear anything, surely the shots woke her up or Lily?"

"My grandmother took a strong medicine to sleep.

"But Lily?"

"She had on head phones listening to her music while she was in bed."

"So everything was left for you to handle."

"Yes. That is my responsibility."

* * *

When we left for Dak's school, Patrewski took the lead with Buddy behind my car in his Chevy one-ton. I felt like a dignitary with a security escort. I might have enjoyed the feeling more if my headache hadn't begun to throb again, knowing that I still had to ask Dak, "Did you ...?"

Dak rubbed his hand over the car's leather seat, and said, "Wow, this is cool. It smells good."

"I had the seats recovered in glove leather. Have you seen the ad on TV that says, you're not just eating steak; you're getting the sizzle, too? Well, I'm not just riding in a car, I'm sitting in *lux-ur-y*."

Dak laughed, a little puzzled, a little in envy.

"I've been thinking about what you said earlier, Dak. So much is expected of you. It's hard for Lily to accept that fact. She only sees the praise and attention you get. I can remember being mad at my older brother because everyone liked him better."

"I have tried to help Lily, but she won't listen."

"Now, you sound like a parent."

"Well, it's true." Dak swept a sidelong glance in my direction, and then stared ahead. "Did she say anything else about me?"

I kept my eyes on the road and mentally crossed my fingers. "She said you had a gun the night your parents were shot. She said you took it outside."

"Where does she get off saying that!" he blustered.

I cocked my head to one side. "Was it the truth?"

"She's just mad at me because I won't join the AZ's and make her important with her boyfriend."

"She said Sammy considers you a member because you're Lily's brother."

Dak sneered. "She is a stupid girl." He lifted his arm. "That's how I got this. They tried to jump me into the gang, but I escaped."

"You said you didn't know who beat you up. Now I learn that wasn't the truth." I paused. "You say you didn't have a gun the night your parents died. Can I believe that?"

Dak never answered my question, and we drove in silence the rest of the way. When we arrived, I parked in the school bus zone behind Patrewski's car. Buddy drove around to the side of the building.

I put my hand on Dak's arm as he unbuckled his seat belt. "You don't have to tell me, but Detective Patrewski knows what Lily said about the gun. If it's true, the best thing is to tell him everything. The police won't stop until they get the truth. You know that, don't you?"

"I know the law," he said. "It is her word against mine."

The Forms of Control
Chapter 28

Patrewski accompanied Dak into the school then trotted out to my car a few minutes later. He hopped in and brushed raindrops off his hair. "Well?" he asked.

"The bottom line is that Dak won't admit to having a gun that night. He really closed down when I mentioned how odd it was that Lily and the grandmother hadn't heard the shots." I twisted the steering wheel back and forth, debating whether to go on. "You've got a problem."

"Just one?"

"Apparently Dak's been looking up his legal rights. When I explained that Lily told me he had a gun that night, he said, 'It's her word against mine. He acted like 'you can't catch me'. To give him the benefit of doubt, his boning up on the law may be because he wants to become a lawyer. A judge in Cambodia, yet! He's a very focused kid."

"That's all I need. A 16-year-old street lawyer." Patrewski muttered. He asked me to start from the beginning, and I replayed Dak's comments-- without editing. At this point, Patrewski needed his information straight.

I finished by adding my own gut-level assessment. "It's apparent that the boy's feeling driven to succeed in order to bring honor back to the family name. His grandmother drummed that message into him. The father's Khmer Rouge past, his gambling and womanizing reputation here in the States, all brought shame on the family name. The way the parents died and now Lily's behavior have exposed the family to even more gossip. Losing face is a powerful force to controlling behavior in the Cambodian culture."

In all cultures, I thought. The Khmer community had no lock on the shame franchise. The Irish did a pretty good job of using disapproval to maintain social order. How many times had I heard my mother say, "What will others think!"

I added grimly, "Poor Dak. If Cambodia had a bird like an albatross, it would be hanging around his neck."

Patrewski absorbed the last with a quick, inquisitive look. He kept his voice level when he asked, "Do you think he was the shooter?"

I dropped my rationally thought-out answer into the mix of intuition and impressions always ready to color my thinking. When I hauled out the answer, it hadn't changed. "No. Dak hated what his father had done, but the boy is a protector. He would never harm his mother."

195

"The insurance money would help the kid go to a good university."

"Yes, but Ly was his wife's beneficiary. Were the kids named as alternates beneficiaries?" Have you found a will, yet?"

Patrewski shook his head. "No will, and Ly was the only beneficiary. Ly bought the policy on his wife's life. He probably didn't care whether anyone collected if he kicked the bucket. Maybe Dak knows his probate law, too, and figures that he and Lily are next in line with the grandmother gone. The aunt's not a blood relative."

We both watched the rain for a moment. Patrewski sighed and said, "A scenario that fits is that the father killed the mother for the insurance, and Dak walked in on the scene and shot him. Which means Dak had a gun, too," he added, obviously turning the idea over.

"But there wasn't any struggle."

"Maybe the kid surprised his old man, and afterwards, pressures the grandmother and sister to go along with his story. Then he thought his grandmother would talk because she was getting senile and did her in. That leaves Lily roaming around, and he'll have to shut her up, too."

Patrewski's face and voice hardened as he talked of Dak as the killer. He had deep-sixed his personal feelings about the boy.

"Lily only saw Dak hiding one gun."

Patrewski shrugged. "Doesn't mean that there weren't two."

Patrewski got out and then brought his car around. I followed him to the freeway exchange where we had agreed to go our separate ways. He wanted to be sure I was safely on my way home. He was hurrying to get to the station to sit in on Morale's interview with Rick. I had promised to go to St. Mary's and stay with C. J. or at least get out of town for a few days.

About a mile before the freeway entrance, Patrewski pulled into a Texaco Star Mart Station and parked. I pulled up next to him, and we talked through our opened windows.

He said, "Call as soon as you get home. My cell phone has a pager, too. You have the number, right?"

I nodded and looked at my cell phone's orange light to make sure it was on. "There's still a chance Lily might call. If she does I'll contact you."

"Arrange to meet her. But no matter what, you stay put. And don't tell her where you are. Got it?"

Patrewski put the car in gear, and I said hurriedly, "Will you let me how the case is going, or if you make an arrest?"

"Yeah, sure." He added, "Don't take any detours. Anything happens, anything, you feel like you're being watched, call the sheriff ... and me, too. You got Morales's cell number?"

"No."

He gave it to me, and I wrote it down on the back of a business card.

"If you can't reach me, call her."

He sped off and the adrenaline that had propped me up the last twenty-four hours drained away. Disappointment set in, despite the fear that hung around the edges. Maybe I'd become an excitement junkie. It was as if I'd been at a party and the action had moved on elsewhere leaving me trailing home alone.

The traffic bottlenecked at the Des Moines exit helped me to make up my mind and also change my direction. I turned north to Seattle. I needed to see Sarah Vignec face-to-face. Phoning her wouldn't do.

Sarah's nightwatch ministry was located in the heart of Pioneer Square, home to nostalgia, shoppers and street people. I parked in a lot near First Avenue and walked the few blocks to the ministry's office. The early 1900s building had been renovated, but years of use by tenants and poor heating systems had left a permanent musty odor in the rooms.

I walked in and said, "I've come for help."

Sarah Vignec was as wide as she was tall, her stone-gray hair stuck out in disarray. She wore a clerical collar above her shapeless brown sweater, and all in all, she reminded me of a female Friar Tuck. Like him, Sarah was a fighter; only she used her sharp tongue to slash stonewalling bureaucrats not the Sheriff's men of Nottingham.

While the Pioneer Square merchants and Seattle police had cracked down on the area's free-flowing vagrants, street kids continued to wander up from First Avenue to Sarah's three-room office that doubled as a mission.

She looked up without surprise at seeing me. "Sorry, all out of help today. Now you can give some..." She gestured to the yellow flyers she was folding and stapling.

I sat down. The flyers announced the Pioneer Square Ministry's Annual "Let the Good Times Roll" Fundraiser. "Good people, good food, and ... no preaching."

"How are you going to expand your flock, if you don't sermonize?" I asked, taking the pile ready for stapling.

"Not here to make flocks, packs or herds for that matter."

"No helpers?"

"You're it for now."

Two years ago, I'd conducted strategic planning workshops for the board of Sara's fledgling ministry. After my contract was over, I stayed in touch.

"I need answers about hurting kids and families," I said, and gave her a run down on my involvement in the Lys' homicides, and the latest developments with Lily and Dak.

"So what do you want to know?" she asked.

"Tell me how you get rid of shame. Is suicide an out?"

"Are you asking for the usual 'I have this friend ...' or for yourself?" She looked up, perhaps to check that my answer matched the one in my eyes.

"It's for Dak. His family is Buddhist. Which may make a difference."

"Well, since you're asking a priest, I'll tell you what function we do to get rid of shame. We officiate to get rid of feelings of unworthiness, of shame, so that society's members can get on with living. Priests, monks, shamans--whoever the culture designates to handle the spiritual side of things--serve as the go-between for individuals and their guilt or shame. We perform the rituals or magic to cleanse the unclean, restore the person to wholeness. If this boy has no way to get to the other side of his shame, no helper or friend, then suicide might seem the only out."

"Would being Buddhist make a difference, though? About committing suicide?"

Sarah folded a flyer and tossed it on my pile. "If you're feeling hopeless enough, it doesn't matter what label is stamped on your forehead. Then again suicide can be an act of protest--the ultimate sacrifice--if the cause seems right. Remember the Buddhist monks who immolated themselves in Vietnam during the war?"

I started to ask another question but turned because the door had opened. A dusky-faced teen with bleached hair plaited in rows walked in. He had a ring pierced in the corner of each eyebrow and a scowl that spread when he saw me. He brought in dampness like a dog at his heels. The scowl lifted long enough for him to send a surprisingly sweet smile in Sarah's direction.

"Get a cup of hot chocolate, T-Man," she said, jerking her head toward a Mr. Coffee glass pot filled with water. "My friend, here, has a problem. You're smart. See if you can help her out. Go ahead, Bridget, tell your story. T-Man may have a better answer."

I made the explanation short while the teen fixed himself a cup and sat across from me. He looked up when I stopped talking, then ducked his head down again.

He mumbled, "Does he got homies?"

"I think so. He's kind of a gang leader, he has a clique at school."

"He okay in school?"

"Yes. Good student. He wants to go to college," I said, aware that despite the cloud over Dak, he appeared to have more going for him than this kid.

"How old is he?"

"Sixteen."

"And he smart?" T-Man checked my reaction for verification.

"Yes."

"You helping him?"

"Me and others. Even the detective on the case, though that may be changing."

Sarah and I watched the young man tap strong fingers on his knees, apparently considering Dak's situation. Finally, T-Man, said, "Nah. He won't kill his self."

"Why not?"

"'Cause. He got options."

I left Sarah and T-Man folding, stapling and stamping--and feeling I'd tied up one loose end of a messy ball of string. My stomach growled reminding me that I needed to eat, so I walked down the block to the Elliot Bay Book Store.

Inside the store, I stashed myself between the Northwest gardens section and a table with remainder books and watched the front door. Satisfied after a few minutes that Sang and group weren't around, I bought a pop psychology book on shame, a grilled cheese sandwich and Irish Breakfast tea. Then I hid out at a corner table.

Before eating, I called C. J. so he wouldn't worry. He wasn't at his home or the café, so I left word that I'd be back in St. Mary's by dinnertime and would pick up Narvik. While I ate, I skimmed through the book looking for new insights and thought about grandmothers. Dak's and mine.

Both grandmothers had more influence on our lives than our mothers. I don't think either Dak or I had identified closely with our mothers--though the normal obligation to them was there. My grandmother had fought to free my spirit, not cage it like my mother. I could only guess at the hardships Dak's grandmother endured to get her daughter out of Cambodia and to America.

My dream about grandmother being with Booster had been odd, though. I could easily picture her picking up and helping a decrepit soul like him. I had the sense that if I had been able to follow the two, I'd be closer to finding out who killed the Lys. Booster's final words echoed in my mind, "Of course, I come back here. They know me."

While Booster's brain cells may have been pickled, he had been tracking enough to know that the hospital staff would catch him pulling his old tricks to get drugs. Still, he came back to the same place, the same people, repeating the same old history. We all fall back into ways conditioned over time, I thought, painfully aware of my own repeating patterns.

I could almost sense grandmother nudging me, saying, "Now, doesn't that make the sense of it all?"

My grasp on the idea slid away with the sudden jarring ring of my cell phone. I looked around wildly before taking it out of my purse.

When I held the phone to my ear, I heard sobbing on the other end. "Lily? Is that you? What's wrong?"

"C-can you come get me?" she stammered

"Where are you? What's happened?"

"Those people you told me about are hunting for me."

"Where are you?"

"I'm hiding."

"But where? Is your friend with you?"

"She went to find Dak at school and bring him. But they aren't here, yet."

"Where are you?" I asked again.

"At the center. We came to the Cambodian New Year party, but the creepy man with the evil eye told me that I had to go away with him. He said I was going to belong to an old man. My friend and I ran away."

"Are you in a phone booth?"

"I am in the room behind the big kitchen where they keep bags of rice and stuff. There's a phone on the wall."

She was in the storeroom behind the kitchen. I had been in it a couple of times helping out at the center's community Thanksgiving dinners. The only way to get out was either through the kitchen into the center's gym that doubled as a dining room for big events or by a delivery door that opened onto a small loading dock at the side of the building. How long would Lily be safe there?

I urged her, "Hang up and call 9-1-1."

"No." She wailed. "If the police come, everybody will hate me because the party will stop. If the police take me, I will never see Sammy. Never. You have to come, please, please." She broke out crying again.

My stomach tightened at the thought of getting anywhere near the "man with the evil eye." I looked at my watch. It was 1:45. The New Year celebration had probably started before noon. By now several hundred people would be at the center, excited and ready for the all day, all night party.

"Lily, find a grown up that you know, and tell--"

The girl broke in, whispering. "I hear voices. I will hide behind the bags. Come for me," she said, and the line went dead.

I called Patrewski's number and then Morale's. Neither answered, so I left detailed messages about Lily and gave my cell phone number. Then I started to dial 9-1-1 but stopped. Would I make things worse for Lily by calling and getting police there who might blunder around and leave without finding her? Would the dispatcher even consider Lily's situation a priority for immediate attention since I was giving a second hand account?

How could I turn my back on Lily and live with myself? I decided to start for the center. At least I wouldn't be ignoring her plea to come. If I didn't hear from Patrewski or Morales by the time I arrived, I would phone 9-1-1.

The Consequences
Chapter 29

The community center's parking lot was full, and every available space on the nearby streets had been taken. The rain had kept the activities and celebrants inside the building. Normally the grassy areas would be filled with kids and young adults playing games. Some would actually be playful versions of courting rituals. The teens would act them out under the watchful eyes of parents and elders.

Gold, silver and red plastic and Mylar decorations in intricate designs hung from the center's entryway. Laminated paper lanterns swung on ribbons stretched between poles. Scratchy Khmer music played over speakers and greeted people arriving for the annual event.

I tried Patrewski and Morales again on my phone. They didn't answer. I left messages, more urgent this time. I hadn't planned to go inside the center because of the possibility of running into Sang. I explored an alternative. The dock by the kitchen had a Loading Only sign by it and was probably the one place where, with luck, I could park for a few minutes and check the back door. If it wasn't unlocked, I'd rap on the door and hope Lily answered. If she didn't, I'd call 9-1-1.

I parked and ran up the steps and tried the door. It was locked. I knocked lightly and pressed my ear against the door, listening for sounds. "Lily. It's Bridg." Nothing. Then I thought I heard a cry cut short.

I tiptoed down the steps and around the corner and punched in 9-1-1 on my cell phone. When the dispatcher answered, I told her what Lily had said and gave Patrewski's and Morales's numbers. I said I'd wait behind the center for the police.

After 10 minutes, when the police hadn't arrived, I slipped round to watch the front entrance. When I saw several American couples arrive followed by a group of chattering Cambodian teens, I mingled with them and walked into the center.

People stood talking in clusters in the wide hallway leading from the entrance. Three large rooms used for meetings and craft activities lined both sides of the hallway. Parents and kids, and older men and women threaded their way through the groups, peering into the rooms' large windows.

The odor of hot frying oil and oyster sauce saturated the air. I kept an eye out for Sang as I moved toward the kitchen. Whenever I found anyone tall, I sidled over and behind the person to be less conspicuous.

203

When I reached the kitchen, I walked in and acted as if I were a staff person needing supplies from the storeroom. It was the best I could think of on the spur of the moment. When I asked, no one in the kitchen seemed to know if anyone was in the storeroom. Or maybe the volunteer cooks and dishwashers shook their heads because they didn't speak English. Or were afraid.

At the storeroom door, I listened, then rapped on it and waited. I turned the doorknob slowly. The door was unlocked. "Lily?" I said softly.

The room was deep, narrow, and without windows was very dark. I felt for the light switch on the inside wall, and found instead a cold, dry hand closing over my fingers. "Let me help," said the voice I had come to dread.

A hand yanked me into the room and the door slammed shut behind me. When the overhead light came on, I blinked and stared into Sang's mocking eyes. The stuffy room smelled of dust, grain and my own fear.

Two men about Sang's age stood casually pointing short-barreled weapons at Dak and Lily. Both kids sat on the floor, their backs against big bags of rice, their knees drawn up and hands behind them. Lily had her head down, sniffling loudly. She didn't look up, but I could see where her tears had mingled with mascara, leaving smudged trails down her cheek. Dak stared at Sang, his eyes black with fury and defiance.

Sang held a gun, too, and traced the tip of the barrel slowly down my arm. He smirked and bowed, "*Or kun churon.* Thank you for coming."

He turned and spoke in Khmer. The shorter of the two men shoved me toward the kids. Pushing me down, he jabbed with his gun, rattling off something in Khmer. Dak interpreted. "He wants you to sit on your hands. They have not tied us because we are moving soon from here. They want us to walk out as if there is no problem."

Sang smirked again. "Oh, my karma is good. I have a young girl for my very old friend, I have the boy to make example of to my people, and I have the woman to teach lesson with. I have good karma," he repeated.

I wanted to reassure the kids, especially Lily, that the police were on their way. But I stayed silent, afraid Sang might kill us right away if he knew.

"Let the kids go," I said to Sang. "They haven't hurt you. They will keep quiet like all the rest of the Cambodian people in Seabell. They will be too scared not to."

Ignoring me, Sang spoke to one of the men in Khmer. The man nodded and went out the door leading to the loading dock.

204

Sang turned back, and said, "I will keep the three of you until I have what I want."

When his henchman returned, he had replaced his weapon with a small pistol. He yanked Lily to her feet and pulled her close, wrapping his arm around her shoulders. She struggled until he shoved the pistol into her side. An angry exchange took place between Dak and Sang. Then in English, Dak said, "We are to walk outside, Bridget, to a van and get in. We must act happy so no one will be suspicious if we are seen. If we do not obey or if we call for help that one ..." Dak jerked his head angrily at the man holding his sister. "He will shoot Lily."

We climbed into a black Voyager van with dark-tinted windows. Lily and her guard sat behind the driver, Dak and I behind them. Sang sat next to me, his gun pressed to my side. With his other hand, he stroked my thigh and smiled when I tensed.

Until we actually drove off, I had held out hope that the police would arrive in time. When they didn't, I knew our last chance was that someone would see us leave and would tell the police when they arrived and asked questions. It was a slender thread of hope to hang onto.

I wasn't surprised when we pulled up to the thrift store across from the Buddhist temple. We were taken inside and locked in the basement. Used stereos, TVs and electronic equipment were stacked everywhere and on metal racks three tiers high. Either the store had done well on securing donations, or it was doing a booming business in stolen merchandise. The windows were small, soaped over so no one could see in, and covered with wrought iron grills. The fact that Sang had let us see where we were going and what he had stored in the basement was not a good sign. He didn't plan on us telling anyone.

The men had tied us up, but we were not blindfolded or gagged. Sang seemed to take particular pleasure in saying, "Please talk and think how you will find escape. Maybe you think someone will hear you. But I disappoint you. No one comes to the store. It is closed for the New Year. In the end, you will have bigger pain because you held a little hope in your hand now. But no one will come for you. When it is night, you will be taken away and see each other no more."

Sang said something to the men and the three left by way of a stairway leading up to the store's main level. At the top of the landing, they went through a door, locking it behind them.

Lily started crying again, leaning against her brother. Dak looked over her head at me, despair in his eyes. I also saw in them the bleak end Sang had planned for us.

Dak said, "They will let Lily live. She is more valuable alive." He wore the face of an ancient. He said with no emotion, "You and I have seen too much. They will need to get rid of us."

The men had tied our ankles and wrists behind us and propped us against a metal rack holding TV sets. Lily sagged against her brother, and said, "I knew you would come, but I am sad that you did."

Dak said, "You are little *chmaa*, my sister. I could not leave you. We will get out somehow."

Lily shook her head. "It is not to be."

I spoke softly to Dak, in case Sang had left a guard behind the door who could hear us. "How did you get away from Buddy? Do you think he followed you?"

Dak sighed. "He does not have young legs. Ratanah and I ran from him. She let me have her car. I drove to her house first and left her there. I told her to forget that she had seen Lily and me."

Sang was right about dashed hopes; they were the cruelest kind.

Lily's eyes had been closed as if she'd dozed off. Suddenly, she opened them and said to her brother, "I said bad things about you to her." Lily glanced at me then back to Dak. "I wanted you to get in trouble. But I always know in my heart, you did not shoot our parents."

The two touched their foreheads together.

"I know, too, Dak," I said quietly. "It was not you, and it wasn't Lily. And not Sang, though I thought he might be the killer because he is such a wicked person."

Dak pulled away from Lily and looked at me. "What do you know?"

"I'm pretty certain, but I think only you know for sure."

Now Lily switched around to look at me, curiosity momentarily taking her fear away.

I said, "Before I went to the center for Lily, I had been thinking about a dream and about grandmothers, yours and mine. We both loved our grandmothers and wanted to protect them. They both were willing to sacrifice for us so we could have better lives. That's what your grandmother did for you. Didn't she?"

Puzzled, Lily turned back to search her brother's face that was stubbornly closed.

"Tell me, Lily, did you and your brother often pick mushrooms with your grandmother?"

The girl shook her head. "Dak and I stayed home. It was our mother who went with her."

I spoke to the two in a soothing voice, only glancing at them once in a while. "You see, when I thought about the tragedy of the deaths, I could understand a little bit how it could happen to your parents, but not your grandmother. Why would someone be so unkind--kill--an elderly woman? Then the police said it appeared that she had been poisoned with bad mushrooms that she ate after the funeral. The police went to your apartment and found some stored away. I thought about who would know the most about the different kinds of mushrooms and their uses. Your grandmother would have known. Your mother was already dead. I realized that your grandmother--more than any other person--would have had the opportunity to put mushrooms in her own soup bowl."

When I looked at him, tears were sliding down Dak's face, his shoulders shaking.

I went on, "Your grandmother's love for her family, her desire for honor were so important to her. What if she had done something that she did not want the world to know. What if she knew her body and mind were failing and was afraid she would talk. When I considered all these things, an answer came to me.

I said gently, "Dak, we have so little time. I think you can tell the rest of the story. Maybe for your own sake, you need to."

Even though we sat trussed, waiting for death--or worse--in the gloom of an old store basement, a kind of liberating light seemed to come from Dak as he told his grandmother's story.

He said, "That night when I walked in, grandmother was sitting on the floor by my mother, the gun next to her. I rushed over and held grandmother. She shook so hard I thought she would break apart like a house in the wind. Grandmother wouldn't talk. I kept saying, 'what happened, what happened.' Then I listened for my mother's heartbeat." Scornfully, Dak added, "I did not care about my father. Grandmother cried, 'I did it. I did it. Like before.'

"I shook her. 'Grandmother, you shot our mother!'

"She pulled at my clothes. 'No. The *Angkar* did it,' and she pointed at my father."

Dak's voice had turned hoarse, his body rigid. He was no longer with us but back in the apartment smelling the blood, the acrid gunpowder and hearing his grandmother cries.

He said, "Grandmother was afraid that night. My father had drunk too much and was talking about the gambling money he owed. He said that his wife was worth much dead, but nothing alive. He got his gun and gloves.

He made my grandmother get up from her sleeping mat, then he told my mother to stand still, or he would shoot grandmother and then kill Lily."

Dak began crying, but he continued talking, his anger pushing words out in a harsh stream. "Grandmother said, 'let him shoot me, daughter,' but my mother said, 'no.' Grandmother had to watch while my father put on gloves and got a gun. Then he stretched out his arm and shot my mother while she waited like an animal in the field.

"My father told grandmother, 'You are crazy old woman. You have killed your daughter. Look at what you have done. You deserve to die like her. Shoot yourself, so no shame will come on this family.'"

Dak rocked backwards and said, "My father's words twisted like a serpent around my grandmother's mind. Grandmother said she could see the checkered *kramar* headscarf of the Khmer Rouge on him. A cloud filled her head.

"She told me, 'I did not think I had shot my daughter, but I could not remember. The *Angkar* put his gun in my hand and wrapped my finger around the part that fires. He took off his gloves and said, 'You must do as you saw. Remember how your husband and sons died. You are ordered to do the same.'"

Overcome, Dak stopped, and then rested his forehead on Lily's shoulder.

He raised his head, and said, "Grandmother answered my father, thinking he was the *Angkar*. 'Of course, I see it many times.'

"Grandmother took the gun, and my father pushed her hand up, so that the gun pointed at her own head. She said that when she looked at him the cloud in her head became a lake of water. In it, she saw the face of the soldier standing in front of her husband. The soldier told him that if he moved, he would be shot in the arm, and if her husband moved again, then he would be shot first in one leg and then the other. So if he did not want to die painful, he must stand still. Her husband did not move, and the soldier shot him in the head and then shot each of her sons. She said her heart died like a bird crushed in a tiger's jaws. When she remembered all that a burning came back to her dead heart. She turned the gun and aimed it at my father. He threw his head back and laughed at her. 'Old woman, you could not shoot me. This house will have shame forever. You are nothing unless I give you the right. Shoot yourself, and be done with it.'

"When he said that, she pulled the trigger and the bullet went into his forehead." Dak straightened, pulling away from Lily. "That is the shameful thing my grandmother did."

He asked, "Is grandmother in hell because of what she did?"

My voice sounded small in the heavy silence, but I said firmly, "No, Dak. I believe she's finally found peace."

After a moment, I said, "That's why you told Lily to keep quiet and interpreted for your grandmother with the police. What did you do with the gun?"

"I put it and my father's gloves in a plastic bag and buried it under a stone in the walkway. It will have my grandmother's fingerprints on it, but not mine. I thought one day I might need to prove that I had not fired the gun."

Even now, Dak was thinking of a "one day" being out there somewhere in the future. I hoped there would be. The prospect seemed faint.

He said, "I washed my grandmother and gave her Chinese herbs so she would sleep, and I got Lily up and told her our mother and father were dead. I made Lily stay away from grandmother because her mind broke that night. Just before the funeral grandmother said the good things I would do as a man would bring her good credit and help her in the next life."

Dak looked at Lily. "I lied to you because I did not want you hurt."

The brother and sister murmured to each other in Khmer as if they had so much to say, to make up for. I thought about Mary Rose and Danny, the grandchildren, and how I'd miss them. Sang had been right, I could see no way to escape. But I knew I would not go quietly to whatever ugliness he had in mind for me.

Worn out, we dozed until I awakened with Lily calling my name. "What is it?" I whispered.

"I have to go to a bathroom," she said.

Dak stirred and spoke to her in Khmer and she answered. He said, "She cannot tell me, it is a woman thing."

Lily leaned across her brother and said, "You know, what I said in the hospital. I was wrong. Something is happening."

My thoughts, as stiff as my muscles, scrambled to figure out what she meant. Then, whether the information could help us. "Dak," I said, If you call the guard in Khmer, he'd probably let Lily go to the bathroom. She really has to go or have an accident. He wouldn't want her to be a mess for Sang's friend." I turned to Lily. "This may be your one chance to get away. When you go upstairs, act as if your legs are numb, walk slowly, and stumble a bit. Make the guard untie your hands, but act weak so he'll feel you're no threat. Look for a phone or for doors to the outside. If there's a window in the bathroom, see if you can get it open and crawl out. Run water in the sink to cover the noise."

Lily whimpered and Dak reassured her.

"Call the guard, Dak. Tell him that I need to go, too."

Dak shouted for the guard who opened the door above us and poked his head in. He replied in Khmer and slowly came down the steps, his gun pointed at us. Lily pleaded, crying while she talked. Her brother angrily taunted the guard, probably sneering that he was afraid of a girl.

I said, "I have to go, too. Take me." Dak interpreted, but the guard shook his head and hauled Lily to her feet. He took out a knife and cut the rope around her ankles so that she could walk. He left her hands tied.

When the two had gone, I said to Dak, "If Lily can't get away when she's upstairs, then when they return, I'm going to throw a fit. I'll roll around and scream and babble. Maybe the guard will come over and Lily can break away. Tell her in English that once I start the act, she's to run up the stairs and shut the door, lock it if she can."

"The guard will beat you or shoot you," Dak whispered.

For the boy's sake, as much as mine, I shrugged. "I will not go willingly with Sang."

Dak started to reply but stopped at the sound of gunshots, and loud shouts. Our heads jerked around like puppets on a string, our eyes focused on the landing door.

We heard yelling and crashing noises, as if doors or furniture were being broken. Suddenly, the door to the landing door flung open, and a figure, face blackened and wearing camouflaged khakis burst through, dropped to one knee beside the open doorway, and swiveled gun back and forth over the room. Three other figures rushed through the opening and down the stairs.

The first one down knelt by Dak and pulled off a balaclava. Morales's long braided hair tumbled out, and she looked anxiously at Dak then me. "Are you guys all right?" She patted Dak's shoulder. "Don't worry, we have Lily. She's safe."

"Why didn't you call me back?" I demanded.

Jack and I sat across from each other in his living room. After I'd completed my statement at the station, he had once again dragged me home. Nicole had gone on to bed but not before making sure I was warm, fed and the spare room ready.

"Why?" I repeated.

Jack tipped a bottle of Bud to his lips and swallowed. He said, "I call, your phone rings, the bad guy answers or get nervous and knocks you off. That's not a good plan."

"You took so long to get us." The memory was still too sharp to dwell on without churning my stomach.

Jack waggled his beer bottle at me. "You should have been a hundred miles away, sitting in front of your fireplace. You were lucky Morales had the thrift store staked out. Otherwise we wouldn't have known you were there. It takes time to ready a SWAT team, regardless of its name. We had to find someone to tell us the layout of the building."

I nodded and breathed deep. "I'm so glad to be alive."

"You were lucky."

"I know. Thanks."

"We were both right."

I raised my eyebrows. "How's that?"

"About the motive for the homicides. I said money, you talked culture."

Shaking my head, I said, "Funny, how that worked out. They both played a part. The killing fields revisited in Seabell."

Jack sat forward. "I want to ask you something. I already ran it by Nicole."

"What?"

"The kid. I want Dak to come live with us. He's okay with his aunt for a while, but we could help him in school, make sure he gets into a good college." Jack tipped his beer bottle again, and seemed to think about the situation.

I waited, knowing his reason would come out. Maybe more story with it.

Finally, Jack said, "You've probably figured some of this out. Nicole had. Guess she was waiting for me to realize it, too." He propped his forearms on his legs, the bottle dangling loosely in his hand. "I was eighteen in Nam. I met a Vietnamese girl and she had a baby, ours, a boy. I could have tried to marry her, get her and the kid out of the country, but I didn't. When I came down with a bad case of malaria, they shipped me out... I should've taken my pills. When I went back, she was gone. Disappeared. I didn't try that hard to find them."

"Is that why you went back to Vietnam? To see if you could trace them?"

Jack said, "Who told you I went back?"

"Morales. She said that's when you quit the Seattle police force, after you came back."

Jack acknowledged that with a disgruntled look.

"Why Dak," I asked, still puzzled that the boy who wasn't Vietnamese, had struck a chord with Patrewski. No one would call the cop a soft touch.

"You know it doesn't matter. There's something about him... the kid's got guts. Guess I feel we screwed up things in his country, too." Jack smiled reflectively. "Maybe we were related in a different life."

"Nicole's feeling all right about this?" I laughed and answered myself. "I bet she thinks it's a good idea because you'll be happy and she can fatten Dak."

Jack laughed. "You think it's okay, then?"

I nodded. "Now you only have to convince Dak and his aunt."

* * *

In the jargon of human services workers, Sovath and I were bringing closure to my obligations to her agency and my commitment to help after the murders.

She had just told me that she was leaving the agency.

I asked, "Are you being forced out?"

"No. I am going to graduate school at Seattle U. I will work there part time as a career counselor. As an employee, I will get a special tuition discount."

"Is Rick in your future anywhere?"

Sovath blushed but her eyes crinkled with humor.

"Rick is going to be the acting executive director while the board searches for a permanent replacement. Who knows, maybe he will stay on in the position." Sovath added, "As for me... he is a wounded person. I don't think he is a survivor like I had to be."

"But he was loyal to you," I said. "He didn't try to edge you out when he was being pressured by Chhun. Rick could be a comfort to you in your old age."

"I think he needs me more than I need him."

"Perhaps now but that's not necessarily bad."

"Oh, Bridget, I think you believe in romantic fairy tales of love where everyone is happy at the end." Sovath shook her head and looked wistful for a moment.

I smiled but felt wistful, too.

* * *

A week later, Narvik still hadn't quite forgiven me for being gone so long. When C. J. dropped by the house, she sat close to him, not me. The three of us were outside in the back yard, catching a few rays of spring sunshine. I had filled C. J. in on the details of Chhun and Sang's arrests.

C. J. said, "A puzzle piece is still missing."

"What do you mean?"

"Why did Sang want you out of the investigation bad enough to kill you?"

Even hearing Sang's name caused an involuntary shudder, and the feeling that I needed to look around to make sure I was safe.

I answered, "Shame. I caused him to lose face. He couldn't stand that. Later, he was after Lily because she had no one to really care whether she was sold like a piece of beef. Dak and I happened to get in his way."

"It doesn't explain why he repeated his threats to stop your involvement in the murder investigation. After all, he knew he hadn't killed the Lys."

I leaned over and stroked Narvik's head. "Maybe Sang was afraid that I'd learn about his illegal dealings with Ly and tell the police."

"That's a big *maybe*," C.J. said, giving me a searching look.

C. J. wasn't going to let me off the hook. He wanted a better answer, or one that I could live with.

I mused, "Why did Sang hate me so much? It was so irrational. Do you know what Sovath said?"

C. J. shook his head

"She said the logic of evil is that it acts to exist and exists to act." I sighed. "But I think there was another reason. Sang wanted control over me. And for once, I wasn't giving it up to anybody. Sang couldn't stand my defiance."

213

C. J. turned in his chair. The approval in his eyes was as close to an emotional "atta girl" as I would get. He made a motion, pretending to turn a page.

I laughed. "Yes, I guess I have. Maybe I'm a step further down the road toward my bliss."

* * *

The Patrewski's and I went to Phourim's wedding reception at the King's Table Restaurant in Federal Way. Phourim had called several times to make sure we would come. I took it that more ritual politeness was involved. We made sure to show up. When we did, we found ourselves part of a crowd of two hundred or so gathered in the noisy banquet room.

The reception celebrated Phourim's marriage to Malati. The festivities also were an occasion for him to announce that he and his bride were expecting a baby in November.

When I congratulated the couple, Phourim said, "I am happy, so happy." His smile split his face and happiness spilled over. He grabbed my hand and pumped it. "You are a good friend. Thank you. If we have a girl baby, she will be called Elizabeth Bridget."

I laughed and hugged Phourim. "Don't wish such a long name on a tiny baby."

Jack and Nicole seemed to enjoy themselves--I caught them holding hands at the table where we were seated. They had brought Dak, who was living with them now. The aunt had agreed that Dak would have more opportunities with them.

Looking at the boy across the room, Jack said, "The Prosecuting Attorney's Office decided not to charge Dak as an accessory after-the-fact. He got a break. It's a good thing the gun had the grandmother's prints on it. Anyhow, with the cultural angle and his age, the case wasn't strong." Jack added, "It would have been bleeding heart stuff for the press."

"We can be thankful for that news," I said, thinking that it was also good news that Lily wasn't pregnant. Unfortunately, her prospects didn't look as bright as Dak's.

Jack said, "Lily's off the hook as an accessory because she didn't see the shootings, and Dak kept her out of the loop about the grandmother's role. The aunt tells us she's worried because Lily's taken up with Sammy again."

"The aunt will have her hands full," I said, making a mental note to call Lily. At least, I could take her to a movie or shopping for clunky heels.

Later, when the ritual wedding blessing dance began and guests joined in, Nicole pulled Jack out of his chair. He followed her protesting into the line of swaying dancers.

When the dance ended, the young couple started their rounds, carrying silver trays and an ornate bowl to the tables where guests laid gift envelopes of money into the bowl. Sticking several bills into an envelope, Jack leaned over. "I think this is where we came in, O'Hern." He smiled--perhaps a touch cynically.

I made a face and put money into an envelope, too.

When Phourim and Malati came to our table, they stopped in front of Jack as the elder. According to Cambodian custom, Jack could ask the couple to perform or do something in exchange for the envelopes.

Instead, Jack toasted the couple, wishing them a beautiful life and beautiful children. He added, "It's an American custom."

Phourim's irrepressible smile surfaced at those words. Putting his arm around his tiny bride's waist, he said proudly, "I took citizenship test last week and passed."

"That's great news," we said.

His eyes sparkled. "Do not call me Phourim. I am now legally Peter Nath. You can call me Pete."

Nicole clasped his hand, and said for all of us. "Welcome, new American, Pete Nath."

-End-